JAMES DUFFY

SIMON & SCHUSTER
New York London Toronto Sydney Singapore

DOG
BITES
MAN

A NOVEL

CITY
SHOCKED!

SIMON & SCHUSTER
Rockefeller Center
1230 Avenue of the Americas
New York, NY 10020

SIMON & SCHUSTER and colophon are registered trademarks
of Simon & Schuster, Inc.

Designed by Jeanette Olender
Manufactured in the United States of America

10   9   8   7   6   5   4   3   2   1

Library of Congress Cataloging-in-Publication Data
Duffy, James.
    Dog bites man, city shocked! : a novel / James Duffy.
        p. cm.
    1. Mayors—Fiction. 2. New York (N.Y.)—Fiction. I. Title.
PS3554.U319194 D6 2001
813'.6—dc21   00-049282
ISBN 0-7432-1082-4

FOR SOPHIA

DOG
BITES
MAN

CITY
SHOCKED!

ONE

In less than a week, on New Year's Day, Eldon Hoagland would be sworn in as the new mayor of the City of New York. He still could hardly believe it, but the stacked shipping cartons crowding the desk in his modest faculty office and the two city policemen guarding the door confirmed his changing status.

Incredible, he thought. Unreal. The David Grey Professor of Political Science leaving Columbia University for politics. A Swedish-American originally from Fosston, Minnesota, population 1,500, becoming the leader of over seven million New Yorkers.

As winter darkness settled outside, he reflected on the tectonic shift in his circumstances, a shift that had occurred in less than ten months' time.

．　．　．

It had all started over dinner at Wendy Halstead's Park Avenue apartment. Wendy was a woman who fancied herself a combination of Dolley Madison, Eleanor Roosevelt and Pamela Harriman. She was not entirely wrong, as she had Dolley's amplitude, Mrs. Roosevelt's plain looks and Mrs. Harriman's rapacity. Plus unlimited funds put at her disposal by her husband, Ralph, a minor-league conglomerateur whose acquisition and resuscitation of moribund rust-belt industries had proved enormously successful.

Wendy had ambitions to become an ambassador's wife. She would have preferred an ambassadorship in her own right but realized that Ralph would never be a willing consort. So she had built up his credits by supporting Democratic politicians (with his money and in their joint names) at all levels. Aside from a noisily flapping checkbook, she sought further advertisement for herself and her husband by giving frequent dinner parties for local and visiting politicians, journalists and assorted intellectuals with an interest in public affairs.

Invitees did not refuse her summonses. Presence at her table not only confirmed their status as members (or at least acolytes) of the power establishment but offered a chance to dine on the extraordinary preparations of her very own prodigy-protégé chef, Marc Murffay, whom she had co-opted when he graduated from the Culinary Institute. And Ralph, while a *premier cru* wine bore, did serve—if one could ignore his didactic descriptions of hillsides, rainfall, soil conditions and storage techniques—rare and exquisite wines not usually quaffed by the guests. Especially the academics, used to the latest bargains from Chile or South Africa.

Eldon had long been on Wendy's guest list. His dispassionate, professorial views, seeded with dry humor, often kept her soirees from degenerating into shouting matches or, conversely, being stultifyingly dull. Not that he was merely a donnish, pipe-puffing scholar. Far from it. His more acid observations were eminently quotable—to the point where they occasionally landed him in trouble. His comment, for example, that if a certain local congressman "spent as much time and energy on public matters as he did with the bottle, he would be the greatest legislator since Henry Clay," had made its way back to the frequently lubricated subject and the two men had not spoken since.

At the dinner, Eldon recalled, Wendy, as was her custom, made her well-fed guests sing for their supper by responding to the question she posed at the beginning of the meal. That night it was: who is going to be—and who should be—the next mayor? This was an issue of some immediacy, as the city's term limits law (enacted through the efforts and expenditures of a wealthy "civic reformer" who mistakenly thought that shorter terms for incumbents would eventually give him a chance for elective office) was about to bring the current administration to a close.

Giggles and guffaws greeted the names of the two announced Republican candidates—a law-and-order black minister named Otis Townsend, who favored the death penalty and increasing the already draconian sentences for narcotics offenses, and a successful Wall Street trader who had convinced himself (if few others) that shaving basis points on bond trades was really the equivalent of political expertise.

Everyone surmised that the Republican governor, Randilynn Foote, would not intervene in the expected primary. A tough-minded politician, she had become the state's first woman governor in a very tight race by verbally bullying an able but ineffectual Democrat. Since her election she had made no new friends in office to broaden her power base. The two GOP mayoral candidates being generally seen as clowns, it seemed unlikely that she would squander her limited prestige by making an endorsement.

If the two Republicans were ridiculed, the names of Democratic possibilities thrown out across Wendy's table, party hacks and petty officeholders, elicited groans.

"I doubt that a one of them could walk and use a cell phone at the same time," Ralph Halstead observed.

"Those three fellows who want the nomination have a combined IQ less than Professor Hoagland's," observed Justin Boyd, editor of Manhattan's new and irreverent weekly newspaper, *The Surveyor.*

The dozen assembled guests laughed at Boyd's crack. Then

something strange happened. Everyone turned to Eldon, sitting at his hostess's right, as if seeing a divine manifestation. Wendy, suddenly aflame, shouted, "Of course! That's it! Eldon Hoagland for mayor! Perfect! Don't you all agree?"

They did. The Hoagland bandwagon had started rolling.

"It will take a lot of messaging and a mountain of cash," Boyd said.

"Don't worry about the money," Wendy cut in. "Ralph will do the fund-raising. There's no one better at it." Her husband looked pleased at the recognition.

Within minutes the others, all good New York liberals, eagerly chimed in. Eldon tried to brake the exuberance.

"That's the silliest idea I've ever heard. The only time I ran for office—for president of my high school class—I lost. Please, let's change the subject."

The putative mayor's protest did not stop the groundswell as the group worked its way through dinner. By dessert (and after a generous quantity of Ralph's wine), there was no longer a facetious edge to the conversation.

Boyd, seeing the possibility of an enlivened political season that would give a boost to his fledgling paper, led the charge.

"What the devil's wrong with having a mayor playing with a full deck?" he asked. Wasn't Eldon the leading academic expert on big-city problems? Hadn't he already had a fair amount of exposure on TV? And didn't he have other bona fides—as a participant in the civil rights marches of the sixties, a proponent of (sensible) affirmative action policies at Columbia, a family man with his wife, Edna, actually living with him?

Edna, a medical doctor, tried to come to her husband's aid. "Look, friends, my husband is brilliant. I know that and you know that. But there's no way he could run this city." She didn't add then (but made her views clear to Eldon on the way home) that he had been less than a success as chairman of his department, unable to reconcile the older traditionalists with the younger, politically correct gang.

"Why, with his delicate stomach he'd be vomiting like George Bush if he had to eat knishes and tacos out campaigning. He gets sick on McDonald's hamburgers for heaven's sake."

The others laughed good-naturedly and continued their strategizing. Only the Hoaglands' departure after a final nightcap brought the rally to a close.

Wendy and Boyd floated the idea of a Hoagland candidacy far and wide; within weeks there was pressure from many quarters for him to run. When Eldon talked the matter over with Edna, she was still cautious, warning him of the pitfalls and the uncertainty that would be brought into their secure, steady academic existence. But in the end he decided to run, and from that moment forward his wife was totally supportive. Whatever reservations she had, she kept to herself, including her realistic assessment that, as the city's first lady, she would have to curtail or perhaps even give up her busy practice as a dermatologist.

Eldon reflected on why he had made such a rash decision. A sense of duty? Yes, that was it. Princeton in the Nation's Service: Woodrow Wilson '79, Adlai Stevenson '22, Eldon Hoagland '54. A chance to practice what he had preached as an urban affairs specialist at Columbia. A chance to break out from giving an outsider's advice on city matters to his students and that part of the general public who watched earnest Sunday morning PBS talk programs.

Once he was in the race, *The Surveyor* came to resemble a campaign handbill with its lavish praise of the dream candidate. George McTavish, New York's senior senator, to whom Eldon had been a backstage adviser on several tricky urban issues, endorsed him vigorously; he was delighted to have a candidate who would not embarrass him or the party, as the throwbacks eager for the nomination surely would have done. And he not only endorsed Eldon but convinced the president to buy off the three stooges—a federal judgeship for one, the Vatican ambassadorship for another, a promise of more serious attention to patronage and project requests to the third.

Eldon emerged as the unopposed Democratic nominee. The Republicans, meanwhile, committed fratricide, ending up with Otis Townsend, the law-and-order black, as their candidate, after a primary campaign so putrid and moronic that Randilynn Foote continued to withhold her endorsement straight through the general election. (There never was any question that she would endorse Eldon, both because he was a Democrat and, he was sure, for personal reasons going back into the distant past.)

Prodded by Ralph Halstead, the city's CEOs and Wall Street sachems contributed heavily to the Hoagland campaign, enabling his handlers to buy expensive television time and to hire the noted image maker and all-round fixer, Jack Gullighy, to turn the David Grey Professor into a viable candidate.

The city's black and Hispanic leaders, unable to stomach Townsend, nonetheless could not agree on an alternative Democratic candidate; even though blacks and Hispanics now formed a majority of the city's electorate, they eyed each other with mutual suspicion. Ultimately they settled on Eldon as the least of white evils available. The Hispanic press referred to him rapturously as "El

Don," and those emerging from Sunday services at black churches just prior to the election were flooded with leaflets containing a photograph—which a clever Gullighy had been able to unearth— of Eldon, then a young assistant professor at the University of Minnesota, standing with the Selma marchers in 1965.

Hoagland did his part, too, by endorsing Artemis Payne, a black city councilman, for the post of public advocate, which, under the city's Charter, was the second-ranking job in municipal government.

Boyd continued his weekly drumbeats in *The Surveyor*, much to the chagrin of the members of the editorial board of *The Times*, who did not want any suggestion that their ultimate decision to endorse Eldon had in any way been influenced by Boyd's propagandizing.

Only *The Post-News* refused to board the bandwagon. The paper was the product of a recent merger of the city's two tabloids, a marriage of convenience designed to save each from bankruptcy. The result was an eccentric publication, to say the least, its new title giving rise to precious jokes about "postnews" as a subset of postmodernism. It was edited almost exclusively by expatriates, veterans of yellow journalism in London and Australia, who had deeply conservative views as to how New York City should be run, even though they were newcomers and mostly lived in the suburbs.

The paper's editorial board also had it in for Eldon. In an appearance on one of the Sunday morning shows at the time of the merger, he had been asked for his opinion and had replied that "two wrongs don't make a right." *The Post-News's* choleric owners neither forgot nor forgave his remark. They probably were emotionally incapable of supporting a Democrat anyway, so it was no surprise when the paper backed Townsend—a stance that disgusted some but merely amused others.

.   .   .

Glancing at his watch, Eldon realized that his woolgathering had to cease; he could savor his easy election day victory in all five boroughs some other time. He took out his pen and signed with a bold signature the letter of resignation from Columbia he had prepared and printed out earlier in the day. He had closed the door on academia and opened a new one into the public arena. Where he hoped he would be a gladiator and not food for the lions.

TWO

The new mayor's inauguration, scheduled for the steps of City Hall, was moved to the council chamber inside when a sudden and violent snowstorm hit the metropolitan area. The crowd was cheerful despite the weather and warmly applauded Eldon's succinct acceptance speech, which echoed the "Great City" theme Jack Gullighy had devised for the campaign.

At the reception that followed, several spectators, for want of anything else to say, fatuously told Edna Hoagland that her husband "looked like a mayor." She good-naturedly agreed, as she thought the observation correct: Eldon was tall and thin and, despite a receding silver-to-white hairline and some small lines in his face, looked younger than his 67 years.

That night the Halsteads were hosts at a celebration at their apartment. Several of the guests from the original groundswell dinner were present, along with a sprinkling of the more significant contributors Ralph had tapped.

Chef Murffay outdid himself that night, dressing up New Jersey foie gras with pomegranates and mangoes. As the goose innards disappeared, there was much triumphalist banter.

"Edna, Edna, did Eldon ever barf on the campaign trail? All that dim sum, and fried calamari, and huevos rancheros? And junk stuff we've never even heard of?" one asked, giggling.

"No, he never did," the new municipal first lady replied, with a small smile. "But I was busy writing Prilosec prescriptions."

Boyd, the most exultant of the group, proposed a toast to "El Don" as the man who had "courageously" visited an IRA gunrunner in detention; boycotted a reception for the aging Yasser Arafat; supported the canonization of Pope John XXIII (a cause dubiously requiring the endorsement of a Swedish-American Lutheran); applauded a proposal for a statue of Golda Meir in Central Park; sung "Santa Lucia" in Italian at a Queens rally (he'd learned the words in Italy on a trip as a graduate student); and come out foursquare for Taiwanese independence. The editor, of course, neglected to say that none of these courageous stances had anything to do with the governance of New York City.

In fairness, Eldon had proposed in his campaign sensible, innovative, incremental programs for enriching education, creating jobs and jump-starting the city's economy. Recently converted to the wonders of the computer and the Internet, his pride and joy was a proposal to create a development zone in the city to attract the increasing number of companies striving to profit from the Internet revolution. He envisioned a zone, backed with tax incentives, that would rival California's Silicon Valley and be the 21st-century version of New York's Radio City of an earlier day. It would have not only space for corporate offices and plants but a school and a City College branch to educate the workforce needed by the participating businesses.

Jack Gullighy, who was present, was also toasted, for his discovery of the Selma photograph and for cobbling together statistics that demonstrated that Otis Townsend's law-and-order program would have led to the detention of one in five New Yorkers.

Eldon responded modestly and soberly, thanking his backers for their support, assuring them he would do his best and that his energies would be directed to improving the city's economic prospects and making it a place where educating a child was possible, where tax dollars would be wisely spent and where those present, and all New Yorkers for that matter, would be happy to live.

"Mr. President! Mr. President!" one tiddly reveler shouted out.

"Please, please. That's crazy talk. All I want is a very, very tranquil and peaceful four years in office. Trying to make this a better city . . ." His voice trailed off as he resisted repeating the Great City speech, his mind awash with the ethnic variations—*grande, magnifica, maravilhosa, città, cidade, ciudad, Stadt, ville,* though he had on one occasion excised Gullighy's citation of St. Matthew's "city on a hill." (And he shuddered as he thought of an appearance at a Queens mosque, where he had stood in his stocking feet and choked on the phonetic *aazeem madeena* written on his cue card.)

. . .

Now, a year and a half later, he had weathered a threatened New Year's transit strike; a police slowdown after his attempt (thwarted by the City Council) to name an Asian-American police commissioner ("'No Irish need apply' was discredited fifty years ago," the police union president had thundered); Italo-American outcries after he had attended the opening of *Padrone,* the latest Mafia movie (produced by one of his larger financial backers); a gay/Planned Parenthood rebellion after he had taken an "under study" stance to a proposal for condom machines in subway stations; a picket line of militant Catholics at City Hall protesting that same "under study" cop-out; and hundreds of messages, ranging from the chiding to the psychotic and only occasionally positive, on the Web site he had instituted at Gullighy's urging, www.hoaglandmayor.com.

There had been some triumphs. The State Legislature, in Albany, had been remarkably passive when picking at appropriations benefiting the city, in part because Governor Foote's description of that august body as "hack heaven" had leaked to the press and canceled any effectiveness she might have had in leading an anti-city assault. And the metropolitan press (with the exception of *The Post-News*), led by Boyd and *The Surveyor*, gave the new mayor a free pass. Discreetly manipulated by Gullighy, they bought the line that the new mayor was a class act and that the city was the beneficiary of a sort of meritocratic noblesse oblige, with one of its most prominent intellectuals unselfishly serving them in public office.

.   .   .

The world, or at least the metropolis, assumed that all Eldon's problems and cares involved matters of high policy. They did not know about Amber Sweetwater, a political groupie who had offered her services as a scullery maid in exchange for a meager salary and a bed in the tiny serving pantry alongside the kitchen at Gracie Mansion, the mayor's residence. She performed valuable services as a dishwasher, recycling sorter and vegetable dicer for the marginally competent *chef de cuisine* (a semi-hysterical Hispanic gay—two points on the affirmative action scale) the mayor's staff had located.

The chef, Julio, had barely kept his job after preparing something he called "puerco festivo" for a mansion dinner for a group of rabbis from Brooklyn whom Eldon hoped to mollify in their noisy crusade to get public school funding for their yeshiva. That evening had been saved by Amber, who, once Edna discovered pork on Julio's menu, hastily chopped up and assembled a vegetable plate of broccoli rabe, boiled cabbage, canned corn and beet salad. The rabbis were puzzled at the fare but nonetheless expressed satisfaction at having been invited to dine at the mayor's house (while not giving one inch on their money demands).

Ms. Sweetwater had written Eldon soon after he was elected, seeking the job she had thought up herself. He was intrigued by her initiative and after an interview hired her, thus giving himself an anecdotal example of the kind of thrift he hoped to impose on local government. He had not consulted Edna before making his decision. A mistake. Her husband, coming from the university, was not bothered by Amber's small silver nose ring or the astrological tattoo on her left arm; Edna was. She was also suspicious: surely the girl's motive was to gather material for a book or perhaps to make a pass at her husband. And even though the new kitchen helper had averted the crisis with the rabbis, Edna had a complaint about her almost every day, which had the effect of turning Eldon into her defender. Having cut back on her medical practice, as planned, Dr. Hoagland was often in close quarters with Amber at the mansion, and the result was not salutary.

This particular June morning Edna had groused at breakfast that Amber, enjoying the summer rays of sunshine the day before, had stretched out topless on the mansion lawn, "where everybody going by on the East River Drive could see her."

"So what?" Eldon had replied, telling his wife that she really ought not to waste his time with such petty matters. He left the breakfast table in a foul mood, soon exacerbated by what he felt to be unusually inane and irrelevant questions at his weekly press conference.

"What is your policy on serving hormone-treated beef in school cafeterias?" a petite journalism intern from one of the honor high schools asked.

"That's a fine question, young lady"—be gentle with the young—
"but I'll leave that one to the health commissioner and the schools
chancellor to work out."

"Do you agree that the *Art of the Phallus* show at the Guggen-
heim is pornographic?" This from a wire service hack often observed in the City Hall pressroom, feet up, perusing *Hustler* and its
sister publications.

"Haven't seen it."

"Are you going to?"

"Probably not."

Gullighy, although standing behind the mayor in the Blue
Room, nonetheless could tell that his boss's tolerance level was
rapidly approaching, and declared the session finished.

"I said when I took over that I'd have a weekly press conference,"
Hoagland grumbled to his aide as they parted at his office door.
"In the interest of promoting openness. Not as a work opportunity
for the feebleminded."

. . .

Once alone, Eldon called his old Princeton roommate Milford
Swansea on his private line, to confirm their plan for dinner together that night.

Swansea was known to one and all as Leaky, the result of an unfortunate bladder accident in the excitement of a spelling bee at St.
Paul's School when he was nine years old. He had hoped desperately to shed the moniker when he entered Princeton, but it followed him then and had ever since, not least because "Milford"
was a given name one could not do much with in the nickname department. (His mishap had occurred when he was asked to spell

"farinaceous" and only he and one other student remained in contention.)

Leaky and Eldon had been freshman roommates: Leaky the worldly Easterner in the lower berth of a bunk bed, which he had claimed after arriving early, and Eldon in the upper. They were an unlikely pair, the only obvious common bond being their tall, gangly physiques. The preppy Leaky came from old New York money, a trading and shipping fortune going back several generations; Eldon was a hick from Minnesota, son of the assistant foreman at the local Fosston grain elevator, and a scholarship student.

To the great surprise of both, they hit it off and began a lifelong friendship, in contrast to many if not most of their classmates, who spent their upperclass years avoiding and disassociating themselves from the freshman roommates they had been arbitrarily assigned by the campus housing office.

Both boys were intelligent and curious, and intellectually brave (or perhaps arrogant) enough to argue about and discuss the prime academic interests of the other—politics and history in Eldon's case, classics in Leaky's. They were also strangely compatible politically, Eldon the Midwestern populist and Leaky a liberal with a patrician WASP's social conscience. Together they closely followed the burgeoning civil rights movement, including the Supreme Court's monumental desegregation decision, handed down the year they graduated. They did so abstractly, since in the Princeton of their day there was nary a black to talk to and argue with about the subject; the only concrete arguments came from the good ole boys too much in evidence among their contemporaries, who assured them of the invincible truths that "nigrahs" were inherently inferior and, unless wrongly egged on by Red agitators, perfectly content with their lot. Eldon and Leaky's shared interest led them to spend a year together in the South after graduation, demonstrating, marching and persuading blacks to register and vote.

Intellectual and political compatibilities to one side, their other shared interest was mild carousing. Not at the expense of their studies, but as a self-giving reward for hard academic work. Eldon, no stranger to robust drinking (mostly beer) back in Minnesota, had his taste refined by Leaky, who introduced him to the glories of a properly prepared martini.

In their routine, Thursday night was for relaxing, sometimes in their room, more often at whatever local bar was willing to wink at the 21-year-old minimum drinking age; they anticipated by almost half a century the urban careerist yuppies' routine of blasting off on Thursday night, then coasting and resting through Friday in anticipation of the weekend. By the time they were juniors, they had learned to arrange their schedules so that they did not have Friday classes.

Leaky and Eldon went their separate ways after Princeton and their year in the South, Eldon to his academic career, Leaky to a life as a "private investor," husbanding the family money and reading and rereading the classics. But they stayed in contact, with a wet evening here and there in Cambridge when Eldon was studying for his Ph.D at Harvard, or later in the Twin Cities, and then in New York.

Eldon had earlier determined that Leaky was free that night. His wife, Carol, was in the Hamptons to confer with her gardener so they had agreed to meet at Leaky's apartment.

The day's bombardment of pettiness was getting to the mayor and he looked forward to meeting his old roommate. By the time of his last appointment for the day, receiving a delegation of Bangladesh nuns in town to learn about the newest vaccination techniques, his tongue was figuratively if not literally hanging out as he anticipated his first double shot of Dewar's. It was going to be a good evening.

THREE

E ldon Hoagland emerged from 818 Fifth Avenue, the apartment house where Leaky Swansea lived, at 11:45 p.m. Their get-together had been a rambunctious success and the mayor, not to put too fine a point on it, was plastered. His principal bodyguard, Gene Fasco, a head shorter than Eldon, did his best to hold his charge on a steady course.

Fortunately the late-night doorman was not to be seen. Just as well, as the tall figure being helped through the lobby toward the door would not have inspired civic pride or reinforced faith in the democratic selection process.

Eugenio Fasco had been part of the Hoagland security detail during the campaign. Eldon had liked the policeman and, after the election, had requested that he and his partner, Thomas Nolan Braddock, be permanently assigned. A career officer ending his years in the department as a plainclothesman, Sergeant Fasco was happy with his new post and the not infrequent brushes with glamour that it entailed. Had he not shaken hands with, and been impulsively kissed by, Cameron Diaz? (He had not been quite certain of her identity, but his teenage son certainly was, adding that his aspirations were much more licentious than a mere buss by Ms. Diaz.) Or shaken hands, and even exchanged a few words in the mother tongue, with the president of Italy?

Fasco had a reputation as a dutiful but nonetheless scrappy officer. It was true that if positions in the Police Department were allocated on the basis of brains, Fasco might have been on limited duty. But the mayor's protectors did not have to be rocket scientists, merely wide awake and always suspicious.

The higher-ups in the NYPD Intelligence Division had been confident enough in Fasco's ability that they thought he could even handle a "full Arafat," departmental slang for a counterdefense against a terrorist threat (every three weeks), a credible terrorist threat (once a year), or an actual terrorist attack (none yet, leaving aside the messy 1993 attempt to blow up the World Trade Center). Or the panic that occurred when a young Pakistani, detained by two foot patrolmen in City Hall Park on God knows what suspicion—sheer racism comes to mind—was found to have in his possession an architectural diagram of the building, complete with red-penciled arrows at crucial points. It turned out that the poor fellow, completely unarmed, was an Oxford-educated architectural scholar with a passion for studying spaces influenced by the Place de la Concorde in Paris. City Hall qualified, as the work of Joseph François Mangin, a collaborator on the design of the Concorde. The red marks were never explained, though closer police analysis showed that they all pointed to the location of the exceedingly rare rest rooms in City Hall. The wronged scholar brought a false arrest suit against the city that was settled for an undisclosed sum, so no attorney ever had a chance to determine what the bathroom red marks meant.

Fasco's partner, Braddock, was an imposing black man. Tommy overshadowed both the mayor and Fasco when they walked together; Fasco insisted that if there ever should be a shooting on their shift it would be up to Braddock to throw himself in front of the mayor.

While Eldon was inside Leaky's apartment, Fasco and Braddock had spent the waiting time seated in the mayor's unmarked black Chevrolet (the modesty and anonymity of the vehicle were security measures), discussing food, one of their few shared interests. Fasco had been convinced that all African-American fare was made with greasy pork, while Braddock believed that Italians ate only watery, tomato-laden pastas. Their nocturnal conversations had broken down, to some extent, their stereotypes. This night Fasco had been rhapsodizing to his skeptical colleague on the joys of preparing, and then eating, scaloppine alla capricciosa: "the veal sautéed, mushroom sauce with oregano, then cheese and ham on top—can't beat it." As his description reached a crescendo his cell phone rang, and Fasco heard a semicoherent pronouncement from the mayor himself, announcing that it was time to go home.

The mayor had forbidden his herders to accompany him inside presumably safe New York apartment buildings. Having guards standing about with visible earphones and heavy-laden suits struck him as ostentatious and undemocratic. "This is not the Former Yugoslavia," he had declared.

So now Fasco had to enter the building and take the handoff of his charge, who had been supported by Swansea to the foyer outside his apartment. The two inebriated Tigers were loudly bellowing a chorus of "Going Back to Nassau Hall" (the recessional for most drinking evenings they had together). Leaky asked Fasco if he would give him a receipt for his delivery.

"It's all right, sir," the detective said gravely, ignoring the idiotic request. "Leave him to me."

"I want a receipt," Leaky demanded again, but staggered back into the apartment without arguing further about it.

As the pair approached the front door of 818 Fifth, Hoagland squared his shoulders and affected a drunk's notion of dignified, steady walking. This lasted for three steps, as Fasco prevented him from lurching forward, straight onto the marble floor of the lobby.

Fasco had maintained telephone contact with his partner during his downward journey and now alerted him that Egghead—the mayor's code name—was about to burst onto the street.

Braddock turned on the engine of the mayor's sedan and then jumped out to help Fasco, struggling to maneuver Eldon toward the car. But there was not a clear path from the entrance. Between was a shiny-coated, broad-shouldered black dog taking a luxurious, large-stream pee at the curb alongside the back door of the sedan. Fasco did not need this obstruction, so he barked at the tall youth holding the dog's leash to "move aside, buddy."

The young man perhaps did not understand or, more likely, given the circumstances, was unable to move the dog. Fasco tried to maneuver his boss around the vigorously peeing canine, but despite his iron-firm grip, the mayor lost his balance and stepped on the dog's hind leg.

The reaction was immediate. The dog yelped in pain, reared up, turned, sprayed urine on the mayor and bit his right calf, tenaciously locking his jaws on the First Citizen's pants and flesh.

Eldon, brought to alertness by the incisors gripping him, shouted, "Son of a bitch! Off! Off!" as he struggled to get free of the enraged animal. It was unclear who was more deranged, biter or bitee.

The dog's walker, meanwhile, tried to restrain the dog and to pull him away from the mayor.

"Shouesh! Shouesh! Pusho! Pusho!" the young man shouted, to no avail.

Fasco was equal to the task. He pulled his Glock automatic from its ankle holster and fired two shots in rapid succession at the salivating animal. It collapsed, then writhed, emitting fiendish howls, on the pavement. Fasco fired again and Braddock, getting into action, delivered the coup de grâce with a fourth bullet.

Amid the hail of gunshots, the dog's walker took his leave, dashing across Fifth Avenue and scaling the low-level wall into Central Park.

Fasco and Braddock were so intent on exterminating the dog that the youth's departure was of secondary interest. He was too fleet for them anyway, lost now in the dark recesses of the park.

They shoved Eldon into the backseat of the sedan. Then, silently and simultaneously, they both pointed to the dead animal. Without speaking they quickly wrapped its bloody remains and leash in a blanket and put the bundle in the trunk. And for good measure retrieved the four spent shells lying in the street.

They took off into the night, eager to dispose of the two carcasses in their custody.

FOUR

After a stealth trip back to Gracie Mansion—no sirens, no flashing lights—Fasco and Braddock dragged Hoagland inside and upstairs to his bedroom. Called a "mansion," Gracie had actually been a modest Dutch burgher's residence and the interior rooms and stairways were small and narrow; manipulating the mayor's lanky frame up the stairs was not easy.

By now Eldon was quiescent. Fasco had applied a tourniquet to his leg in the car, and while his pants leg was a torn, gory and soggy mess, the bleeding seemed to have stopped. Edna, sleeping apart in her own room (as she did on her husband's nights out with Leaky), had been awakened by the bumping and scraping and appeared in her doorway.

"What happened this time?" she asked resignedly, spotting the blood.

Fasco explained the encounter with the dog and that "we thought we'd better bring him home instead of to a hospital."

"Good thinking," Edna said. "Don't need a picture of him looking like this on the front pages." She shuddered, thinking of her husband in the middle of the stab-wound victims, battered women, OD'd junkies and puking children that came to the city's emergency rooms at night. "Put him on the bed and let's have a look."

Eldon started, apparently under the impression that he was being robbed. He offered noisy resistance as the two detectives and his wife tried to depant him.

When they had done so, it was plain from Edna's professional

31

examination that the mayor's bite was serious and the tooth marks were deep. She ordered Braddock to fetch the emergency kit she said was kept downstairs in the kitchen. Then she quizzed Fasco about the exact details of the attack, satisfying herself that the dog's actions were provoked by Eldon's clumsiness and not by a case of rabies; sending out the policemen on a mission to locate rabies vaccine could be avoided.

Braddock was uncertain where the first aid materials were located. As he searched about, Amber Sweetwater heard him and came out from her improvised bedroom next door.

"What's going on?" she asked.

"Nothing. Mayor got a little cut on his leg."

"Drunk?"

"No comment."

Amber pointed the officer to a large emergency kit. Braddock picked it up, along with a supply of towels from a pile nearby.

"Can I help?" Amber asked.

"Nope. Go back to bed."

She started to follow Braddock, but he turned with a look that made it clear she was not wanted.

Back upstairs, Edna dressed the wound, after some more wrestling with the patient. The task completed, the policemen said good night to her.

"Thanks, boys," she said quietly.

. . .

Braddock and Fasco, relieved to be rid of one body, went to the kitchen for a needed cup of coffee. Braddock cautioned his partner to keep his voice down, as Amber was undoubtedly still awake next door. They discussed in low tones their other problem—the bloody remains outside in the trunk of the mayor's car.

"I dunno, Gene, you think we had to shoot that dog?" Braddock asked.

"Hell, yes. He would have wounded us all. And besides, Egghead told us to off it, right?"

"I guess so."

"You think the dog belonged to that kid?" Fasco asked.

"No. No. He was walking it for somebody. If it'd been his, he would have put up more of a fight."

"What the hell kind of language was he speaking? Sounded something like *shouesh, shouesh, pusho, pusho.* Not English."

"Dunno. My guess he's an illegal. That's why he ran. Afraid we'd turn him in to Immigration."

"Hey, that animal had tags," Fasco said, in a burst of insight. "Let me go look." He went out and returned minutes later, a collar with an ID attached in hand.

"Owner's named Sue Nation Brandberg, Twenty-nine East Sixty-second Street, 212-744-2163. Mean anything to you?"

"Think I've heard the name. Sue Nation. Sue Nation Brandberg. Can't place it, though. What's the dog called?"

"Wambli."

"Jesus."

"And what are we going to do with Wambli?" Fasco asked.

Stumped, the two men drank their coffee without speaking.

"Well, we could go call on this Brandberg broad and give her the bad news," Braddock said. "'Your little Wambli is dead, ma'am. We're *most* regretful!'"

"Yeah. 'We shot your dog. We're very sorry!'"

"Great."

"Nobody saw us, right? Or heard us?"

"We were lucky. Nobody except that *shouesh, shouesh* kid. And I don't think he's a problem, Gene. As I said, I'm sure he's an illegal."

"You got a better nose for that than I have," Fasco said, referring obliquely to Braddock's Jamaican ancestry.

"Brotherhood time, partner," Braddock replied, using their agreed code expression for acknowledging ethnic digs at each other. Fasco's remark was not meant as a slur, but it came (in Braddock's view) close.

"I think we better deep-six the body," Fasco said.

"Ah, the Mafia."

"Shut up. Brotherhood time yourself. No corpus delicti, no crime, no questions."

Braddock seemed dubious but had no alternative to propose.

"Put Wambli in a garbage bag with a couple of rocks, take a spin down the Drive and dump him in the East River somewhere in midtown."

"No, uptown. That was an uptown-type dog."

"What you mean?"

"Stupid, don't you realize Wambli was a pit bull? Never seen a pit bull?"

"Guess I haven't."

"Well, I sure as hell have. Every lowlife in Harlem's got one. Saw one bite off the head of a cat once."

"Jeezus, Egghead may have been lucky to get away alive."

"You said it, Gene. Now let's get going."

Braddock searched around the kitchen, opening cabinet doors, searching for a garbage bag. Exasperated, he called out to his partner, "Where the hell do you suppose the garbage bags are?"

"Ssh. You'll wake the Wiccan," Fasco cautioned, pointing to Amber's doorway.

"Never mind, here they are," Braddock said. "Nice big plastic trash bag for Fido. He'll fit in that real good. Then a few rocks, we tie it up and off we go to dump him in the East River. Just like you eye-ties would do it."

"Brotherhood, brotherhood, Tommy. Oh, and may Wambli— what the hell kind of name is that?—rest in peace."

FIVE

S

huj! Shuj! (pronounced *shouesh*) and *Pusho! Pusho!* were Albanian, and the strapping young man who shouted those words was Genc Serreqi. Now, in the dark recesses of Central Park, he caught his breath and tried to calm himself, rubbing the front of his sweaty T-shirt to help untie the knot in his stomach. The knot that always came when there seemed to be a chance that his status in the United States might be challenged.

Officer Braddock had been right. Serreqi was an illegal, here on a tourist visa that had expired a year earlier. Prior to his travels, he had earned a degree in electrical engineering at the University of Tirana. Confronted with high, double-digit unemployment in his impoverished country, he had worked at a series of menial jobs, bricklayer the most dignified, until he had saved enough to leave.

Here in the States, he had hooked up with an acquaintance from home who worked as a doorman at a fancy Park Avenue apartment building. He was able to get Genc a job as the substitute handyman there and in another one nearby. The newcomer's skill as an electrical engineer had proved useful and he was in constant demand in both places. Within nine months he was able to rent a one-room apartment of his own in the East Village.

Serreqi worked on his English and diligently tried to read the throwaway newspapers available in the boxes on his corner, including the newly free (given away, that is) *Village Voice*. It was in the classifieds in *The Voice* that he saw the ad for a houseboy for a "middle-aged widow." This sounded more appealing to him than his handyman job; the widow was likely to be a better boss than the rather disagreeable and demanding supers he reported to. And he knew that his good looks had not hindered his popularity with the housewives, if they could be called that, in the buildings where he worked; perhaps he would be popular with the widow, too. The job offered would certainly beat most of the other jobs available to him as an illegal: busing slots in marginal restaurants (those willing to flout the immigration laws) or drug dealing (not appealing, and dangerous besides).

The prospective employer turned out to be Sue Nation Brandberg, widow of Harry Brandberg. She hired Genc after the briefest of interviews, expressing indifference to his illegal status. "I myself am a Native American," she explained, "without much use for the United States government."

The new position turned out to be a comfortable one. He had his own room—the biggest he had ever occupied—and ate well at the hands of the motherly Jennie, Sue's cook. His duties originally were quite light, walking Wambli three times a day, doing some shopping and errands, fixing things up around the capacious brownstone on East 62nd Street.

After about two months, Genc and Mrs. Brandberg, on Jennie's night off, found themselves alone in the house. Normally Sue would have gone out with her cook away, but her dinner date that evening had canceled. Genc offered to make supper and the two ate together in the kitchen, washing down his veal goulash with a superior bottle of Chardonnay.

At the end of the meal, Sue thanked him for preparing it. Then, before he knew it, she was kissing him full-front and fondling his crotch. He responded, and nightly service in his employer's bed was added to his job description. Genc, at 26, was half Sue Brandberg's age but she was in excellent shape, with a sexy figure. Now, leaving aside her affection for Wambli, she seemed to direct her passion and feelings toward the Albanian hunk who shared her bed.

Gradually Genc's stomach calmed down and he reviewed in his mind the horrid scene he had just fled. Who the hell were the three men in black suits, one of them noticeably drunk? Gangsters, most likely, though their appearance would have seemed more natural on Tirana's streets than New York's. The fact that they were armed did not surprise him; he came, after all, from a country where at least half the population was said to have weapons. Nor, as an abstract proposition, did murdering Wambli disturb him. Like most Albanians, he did not have any particular use for dogs; they were an extraneous expense in a poverty-ridden country. But as a very concrete matter, he now pondered how he would break the news to Sue about her beloved pet.

Making sure he was not being followed, he made his way home as he planned a strategy. By the time he had come to the steps of the town house he had decided to join Sue in bed (she would be waiting), have a more than usually passionate romp and tell her about Wambli's demise in the morning.

.   .   .

The night's adventure had taken a greater emotional toll than Genc had realized. Once he slid under the Porthault sheets in Sue's bed, and was toyed with and embraced by his half-awake mistress, he realized that he simply was not up for the sexual frolic that was part of his plan. She petulantly turned away after muttering crossly that perhaps he needed a dose of Viagra.

Genc quickly went to sleep. Sue, on the other hand, now fully awake and angry, pitched about for most of the night. By dawn she had reviewed the whole course of her life, which had not always involved a king-size bed in an elegant Manhattan home, with a de Kooning *Woman* on the opposite wall to stare at. ("I'll never sleep alone again," her husband had boasted after he had successfully bid for it at a Christie's auction.)

Sue had been born as Marie Bravearrow on the Pine Ridge Sioux Indian reservation in southwestern South Dakota, beginning her life in an honest-to-goodness tepee, later upgraded to a secondhand house trailer when her father landed a construction job in Rapid City.

Sue had gone to the reservation school, where she was both admired and envied for her good looks and made fun of for her insistence that she would someday break loose from the reservation. To that end, she had entered and won the annual beauty pageant to select Miss Sioux Nation (long enough ago that it was "Miss" and not "Ms."), and then had been chosen as Miss Native America in the contest in Santa Fe. With long, deep-black hair and mysterious, almost Asian features, she was a striking beauty.

After a year of appearances at Indian-run casinos around the country, avoiding the crude propositions and furtive gropings made to or at her, she chose to use the prize scholarship money that went with her title to attend the Fashion Institute of Technology in New York ("as far from the Platte River as I can get," she explained at the time). And by now she had a new name: no longer Marie Bravearrow, she was Sue Nation. The play on words amused her, though there was almost no one to whom she had explained it.

By then the dirt-poor days were over. (Drinking in Genc's half-covered body, she realized that he, too, had escaped deprivation; maybe her affection for him was more than just physical.)

FIT had been only the beginning of the escape. She had shown real talent, especially for fabric design. By the time she graduated, she was being sought by the city's garment and textile manufacturers, her striking looks not hindering her job search. Brandberg Industries had made the best offer and she went to work for its Amy Reed division.

At first she had been little noticed as the junior member of the design staff, responsible for dreaming up fabrics for Amy Reed's midline clothes for career women—outfits that made their wearers look businesslike without resembling transgendered replicas of their male colleagues.

As the clothes became more and more popular, Sue Nation was featured in flattering stories in the fashion press and later in mainstream journals that were increasingly feeding their readers trendy pap about styles and clothes in lieu of hard news.

In the hands of Amy Reed's publicity department, she became a beguiling Native American princess, a direct descendant of Chief Red Cloud. (Her father, long since dead from the effects of firewater, and her mother, more recently deceased from natural causes, were not around to correct the record.) She even went back to the environs of the Platte, to be inducted as a member of the South Dakota Hall of Fame.

Public notice brought private attention to Sue as well, most notably from Harry Brandberg, the chairman of the board of Brandberg Industries (or BI, as everyone called it) and the assembler of the odd cluster of businesses that it owned (from charcoal grills to burial caskets to the Amy Reed division). A *W* piece on Sue had caught his eye and he invited her to lunch at La Grenouille. The chemistry was good and Harry was proposing the next date by the time the cerises jubilee were served.

No fool, Sue had seen a possible opportunity to increase even further her distance from tepee life. She considered several relevant statistics about Harry: his net worth (in excess of $1 billion), his age (72), his girth (46 inches and climbing), his chins (two and a half) and his complexion (ruddy, ruddy red). From her handicapping she concluded that he would not be racing too much longer, so she was enthusiastically receptive to his advances.

There was only one problem: the reclusive little brown wren named Paula Brandberg, sitting quietly in the family nest in Chappaqua. Quietly, that is, until she learned of Sue's insinuation into her husband's life and even less quietly when Harry proposed a divorce.

Fortunately Paula eventually saw the light of day, or more precisely the bottom-line figure of the proposed marital settlement, and quietly flew away from the nest a sadder but much richer chick (her husband's anachronistic term for all women).

Once married, by a Native American federal judge in Florida (a nice touch), Harry proudly showed off his new trophy at every opportunity—charity benefits in New York and Palm Beach, movie premieres (BI owned a studio) and house parties at their new, highly decorated mansion (fabrics by Sue) in Salisbury, Connecticut.

Harry himself had gone through an interesting cycle after the marriage. Energized by his new partner, with sex of a frequency and variety that were not at all wrenlike, he basked in the reflected glamour radiated by his sexy acquisition. Then his excesses began to catch up with him—first a warning siege of gout, then a tricky heartbeat.

Having always been of the *if*-I-die, devil-may-care school, he came to realize that *when* I die, and the question of his posthumous reputation, were more realistic considerations. He retired from BI, the better to enjoy his sybaritic life while he could and to devote greater attention to philanthropy.

Sue had cheerfully supported Harry's eleemosynary undertakings and had left her own job at Amy Reed to help dispense the largesse; she was well provided for and there would be plenty of money left over for her once Harry's heart stopped pulsing. And she could not deny that she enjoyed being accepted, albeit often with condescension, in what passed for New York high society.

She did have reservations about the medical-scientific focus of Harry's gifts. Why not the arts? she pleaded. Music, dance, the theater, the Fashion Institute. Finally one night, as they frisked in bed, he made her a proposition: for each "Clinton" (his cute expression for oral sex) she performed, he would donate $100,000 to any arts charity she chose. The result was impressive: the Harry and Sue Brandberg Print Room at the Metropolitan Museum, the Harry and Sue Brandberg Production Fund at the Metropolitan Opera and even the Harry and Sue Brandberg Poetry Fund. Fortunately the couple's private bargain was their secret; had it been known, the lewd nicknames attached to their benefactions would probably have been legion.

In fact, Harry's demise, at age 77, had come as Sue performed another of her dollars-for-the-arts fellations on him, though newspaper accounts noted only that he had died "peacefully at home" of a heart attack.

Sue came into her own after Harry's death. With a fortune— her own fortune now—to supervise, she commanded a small regiment of lawyers and accountants and investment advisers. Not to mention the persistent grant proposers, development officers and smooth leaders of not-for-profits, all now more smarmy than ever.

The widow Brandberg enjoyed the attention; it suited the temperament and instincts of a former (if minor) beauty pageant queen. Being lady bountiful to her favorite charities pleased her immensely. Most aspects of her existence were a constant reminder that she really had left the reservation.

But there was a hollow center. She had no really close friends, at least friends who did not want something from her. Thus it was that she had bought a dog from a small community of monks in upper Westchester who raised purebred Staffordshire bull terriers. They were not considered city dogs, but she liked their looks, and none had been more appealing than the puppy she called Wambli, with a "cute" white stripe running down his chest. In private amusement she had chosen the name, the Lakota Sioux word for "eagle," though she only shrugged and smiled when others asked her what "Wambli" meant.

After the dog equivalent of a Harvard education—obedience school for learning "appropriate behaviors," pet-facilitated therapy for herself (she had never owned an animal) and several sessions of canine psychology for Wambli—she had set him up, intact, in the 62nd Street town house.

Wambli had partially filled the void. But there was one other notable blank spot. Sex. She had always physically enjoyed it and, with her exotic looks, never had trouble finding it. But after her years of obligatory ruttings with dirty-minded Harry, she desired something more exuberant and vigorous, preferably with a lover who was young and handsome. And insatiable.

The adventurers looking to be kept turned her off; they tried too hard at pleasing her. Then, of course, there was the stable of "walkers" she maintained—trustworthy, loyal, helpful, friendly, courteous, kind and irreverent. And not the least interested in heterosexual sex.

Then Genc had providentially come along. Tall and angular, and now beefed up after the sessions at the gym Sue had insisted on, he was a thing of beauty. Life was now much improved. Wambli and Genc brought her fulfillment, the only shadow over the happy picture being Genc's vulnerable illegal status, though she was sure her cadre of lawyers was taking care of that. At least she had made it clear to them that her continued patronage depended on their success in procuring a green card for her lover.

She looked over at her muscled captive now, peacefully at rest. Soon contentment gave way to more restless stirrings and she wished he would wake, erect as he always was in the morning, and excitedly scream, OOOH! SHPIRT! as he invariably did as he came to orgasm. (She had never dared ask him what this Albanian phrase meant, fearful that it might refer to his mother or a past lover, or mean "whore" or something equally disconcerting. Not knowing, it only served to excite her in ways that Harry's squeals had never done.)

Yes, why doesn't he wake up? (She had put out of her mind his temporary impotence.) They could have sex and then a satisfying breakfast with Wambli at their feet.

The mayor of the city of New York woke up confronting the cumulative pain of a massive headache and a painful leg. The pounding in his head he understood, but what was the throbbing below? He looked down and saw the bandage his wife had applied and gingerly felt it, sending sharp pains up through his body.

Edna entered and saw that her husband was awake. "Well, you did it again," she greeted him.

"What's this all about?" he said, pointing to the bandage.

"You were bitten by a dog."

"What?"

"Bitten by a dog when you staggered out of Leaky Swansea's apartment house."

Eldon tried hard to restart his memory cells. Without success. "How's the dog?" he asked after this attempt, managing a weak smile.

"Very funny. I haven't the faintest idea. You'll have to ask Gene and Tommy."

"See if they're still around," he said, as he started to get out of bed.

Fasco and Braddock had both gone home. Once he was dressed and sitting in the dining room waiting for breakfast, he called the security gate and asked the guard to locate his rescuers from the night before. They reached Fasco and transferred the call to the mayor.

"How you feeling, Mr. Mayor?" the officer asked.

"Fine, fine. Gene, what happened last night?"

"You stepped on a dog who was taking a pee."

"Oh?"

"And he bit you."

"Yes, I know that. What happened then?"

"Tommy and I shot him, sir."

"You *shot* him?"

"Yessir."

"Was that necessary?"

"It was your orders, sir."

"My orders?"

"Yessir. You told us to *off* him."

Could he have given such a command, Eldon wondered. He could hardly believe it, but such were the evils of drink. So the boys had an Eichmann defense: only carrying out orders.

"So there's a dead dog full of bullets putrefying over on Fifth Avenue?" Eldon queried.

"No, no, Mr. Mayor. Tommy and me got rid of the body. Dumped it in the East River."

"Oh my God. What are you going to tell the owner?"

"I think that's up to you, Mr. Mayor."

"Who was the owner by the way? Do you know?"

"Yeah. Woman named Sue Brandberg. Sue Nation Brandberg."

"Holy God. Are you sure?"

"It's what the tag said. Know her?"

"Know her? She's one of the biggest lady bountifuls in the city. Don't you ever read the papers?"

"Don't recall the name, sir."

"Look, Gene, I think you better get hold of Tommy Braddock and come over here. Right away."

Eldon hung up the phone and turned to Edna, who, though

having heard only one side of the conversation, realized there was trouble. He recapped the conversation.

"Excessive drinking can be dangerous to your health," Edna said.

"Please, dear. Skip the medical advice. We need Gullighy."

.   .   .

Eldon Hoagland, in his years in New York before becoming mayor, had moved comfortably in a wide maze of concentric circles that together encompassed the city's power centers. The first circle was, of course, academia, which overlapped with publishing and the media, banking and finance, politics (principally through his association and friendship with Senator McTavish), the vast network of foundations and not-for-profits and, glancingly, entertainment and the arts.

If intelligence was defined as the ability to connect things up, he did a good job, sensing the political ambitions of certain actors, for example, or the secret dreams of artistic hegemony of at least one foundation head, or a real estate mogul's deep-seated desire to be considered an intellectual.

If Eldon was good at this sort of connecting up, Jack Gullighy was a genius. He knew absolutely everyone, and everything about them. His father, an old-line Democrat from Brooklyn, had revered Jim Farley, Franklin Roosevelt's political right-hand man, and had passed on to his son the importance of knowing and remembering everyone's name, as the legendary Farley had done.

Gullighy went further. Names were not enough. He had to know the vital statistics, the personality quirks and the buried secrets as well: the true age of the many-times-made-over charity queen, the closeted (homosexual) sex life of a married Wall Street banker, the usurious organized crime loans that had enabled a prominent and now upright developer to get his start.

He brought to the task the discipline of a Jesuit education, from Regis High and Fordham, and the natural inquisitiveness of a diligent newspaper reporter, which he had been before setting up shop as a political consultant.

Hypocrisy did not bother him, as long as he understood the real truth being obscured. Attempts at larceny, in small doses, didn't either, though he was of the general view that they were usually unrewarding, as well as foolhardy.

Jack Gullighy was a familiar name to readers of the gossip columns—he was adept at promoting himself as well as his clients—and his public image was that of the jolly Irishman, red haired, bearded, of medium height and heavyset. He was also skillful at adapting that persona as circumstances required. With the cardinal or the clergy he was the former altar boy, deferential and dutiful. In a meeting of tough-talking pols he was the toughest of all, with a longshoreman's vocabulary. He could even hold his own with a group of New Agers, his beard giving him a gurulike appearance as he spoke of "closure" and "issues" and "self-esteem."

In his personal life, Gullighy had taken seriously the Ten Commandments, so carefully inculcated by the Jesuits—seriously, that is, as a guide for disobedience. Married and divorced twice—the Gaelic charm apparently stopped at the domestic threshold—his personal relationships with women were as awkward as his professional maneuvers were deft. If he ever spoke bitterly, it was about how his two greedy ex-wives had left him impoverished.

Impoverishment was a gross exaggeration, as Jack had become a highly successful political operative. His freelance fees were high, but those paying them were more often than not rewarded with success. Eldon had been so grateful for his help in navigating the dangerous shoals of city politics that he had invited him to be his press secretary. Gullighy did not want to take the hit to his income, but he finally gave in to Eldon's relentless pressure, promising only to stay in the job for two years.

Now he wondered what disaster had occurred, for surely it was not good news for which he was being summoned to Gracie Mansion at eight o'clock in the morning (he usually began the day at City Hall at nine). Edna, who had called him at home, had simply said that there was a "serious problem" and, in passing, that drinking with Leaky Swansea was involved.

Gullighy knew that Eldon's drinking evenings with Swansea were a potential time bomb. Before he had signed on to Hoagland's campaign he had conducted the two-tier private interrogation that he always made a prerequisite to accepting any political assignment. First there was an interview with the candidate, looking him straight in the eye and asking if there was anything—*anything*—in his past life that could prove embarrassing in the campaign. Eldon had said there was nothing, but after prodding acknowledged that as a young instructor at the University of Minnesota he had fallen behind on his car payments and been threatened with repossession. Not a problem.

Phase two was an interview with the candidate and his wife. Same question. Eldon repeated that there was nothing, but Edna quietly prompted him. "Your outings with Leaky Swansea, dear." Whereupon Eldon acknowledged his "occasional" nights out with his old roommate but pointed out, rightly, that they had never resulted in scandal or trouble, drunkenly boisterous as they sometimes had become. And that they were not, at least in his view, all that frequent.

Gullighy was a master of what he chose to call "Preemptive Pro-phylaxis," and had spread the word among his reporter cronies that Eldon "was not adverse to having a good time"—and was himself relieved that there were no furtive abortions, adorable illegitimate offspring, talkative mistresses, seduced and abandoned graduate students, secret S&M practices or other delectable truffles for the press to root out and feed on.

. . .

Gullighy found the First Couple a portrait in dejection when he joined them in the dining room at Gracie, Eldon with his leg awk-wardly propped up on a chair, Edna finishing a cigarette and cof-fee. (Aside from actively practicing pedophilia, being a smoker in Manhattan was the surest way to social ostracism. So she smoked only in private, resenting mightily the fact that the self-appointed tobacco police demanded that she not smoke elsewhere or, for that matter, at public functions at the mansion. It was, after all, her home, she argued, and as a physician she was fully aware of the foolish risks she was taking, but she had been overruled by her hus-band's staff.)

"Whassup?" Gullighy asked.

"My memory's a little hazy, but apparently I was bitten by a dog last night," Eldon explained.

"Apparently."

"Outside Leaky Swansea's building," Edna added.

"And what am I supposed to do about it? Send you a get-well card?"

"There's more to it than that. My bodyguards, Gene Fasco and Tommy Braddock, shot the dog."

"Oh."

"The monster attacked me. It was a pit bull, they tell me."

"Pit bull, that's good. Better than a lovable collie or, God forbid, a Pekinese. Clearly self-defense, right?"

"I guess so."

Braddock, out of breath, joined the trio and colored in the details.

"Why the hell did you have to shoot the damn creature?" Gullighy asked.

Braddock hesitated, looked at Eldon, and finally said, "The mayor told us to."

"You sure?" Gullighy asked sharply. "What did he say?"

"He told us to off the son of a bitch."

Gullighy turned red and stroked his beard. Edna lit another cigarette.

"You *sure* he told you that?" Jack asked.

"Pretty sure, yes."

Eldon himself offered no elucidation; he simply could not remember what he may have said.

"But the mayor was in danger, right? From an unprovoked and vicious attack by a pit bull," Gullighy persisted.

"Well, the mayor did step on his leg," Braddock said reluctantly. Eldon winced and stroked his wound.

"The dog was, ah, urinating, sir."

Silence. Then Edna turned to Gullighy. "I'm afraid, Jack, we haven't reached the beauty part yet."

"I can't wait. Make my day."

"The dog's owner was Sue Nation Brandberg," Eldon told him.

Gullighy swallowed hard, then said hoarsely, "Well, I guess that's better than a quadriplegic blind man. Seeing Eye dog, you know. Or Yoko Ono . . . Jesus God in heaven, Eldon!"

"Dog's name was Wambli," Braddock interjected, trying to be helpful.

"Wambli, Schwambli. Poor dead little Schwambli. Where's the body, by the way? Gonna lie in state at City Hall?"

"We dumped it. In the East River."

"Whose brilliant idea was that?" Gullighy asked.

"Gene's, actually."

"Damn. Just what you'd expect from a guinea bastard. Sorry, Tommy. Didn't mean that."

Fasco arrived, expecting to be congratulated on his clever waste-disposal scheme. Then Gullighy, all business, ran the two officers through their story again and completed his grasp of the incident, including the flight of the mysterious dog walker.

"Aside from this guy, did anybody see or hear you?"

Both officers agreed that they had not been seen or heard, as far as they could tell.

"Leaky wasn't waving bye-bye out the window? A bus didn't go down Fifth? Kitty Genovese's neighbors weren't peeking through their curtains?"

"Don't think so, Jack," Fasco said.

"You tell anybody about this? Make a report? You notify the be-reaved widow—I mean the owner, Mrs. Brandberg?"

The officers said that they had not.

"What about the bullets?"

"We picked up all four shells. I've got 'em."

"Four! You guys are real sharpshooters."

"That dog was real wild, Jack," Braddock said.

"Yeah, I'm sure. Now, boys, let me talk to Edna and Eldon alone for a few minutes. But stick around."

. . .

The portrait in dejection now had three subjects. Gullighy, fortified by a cup of coffee that Amber brought (and some silent reflection until she had left the room), began speaking. Lecturing, really,
to an untutored but eager student body of two. His mind had been
racing. He did not want to see his boss and friend in trouble.

"When your Keystones first started talking, I thought the answer was self-defense, or at least the tale of two cops doing their
best to protect their mayor. Everybody understands what a menace
pit bulls are. But then they turned it into the St. Valentine's Day
massacre. So, I dunno.

"But that's the first option. Disclose what happened, have the
facts—with a little lip gloss—explained to Ms. Powwow about
what happened to Wambli. What the hell does that name mean,
anyway?"

The Hoaglands shrugged.

"Only one problem there. If I know Sue Nation Brandberg,
she'll be one angry squaw after your scalp—no, change that. After
your Swedish behind. She'll do a goddam rain dance and stir up
every animal rights crazy around the world."

"There can't be that many," Eldon protested.

"Dear, have you been reading your *Princeton Alumni Weekly*
lately?" Edna asked.

"Yes, yes," Eldon said impatiently. "They have that ethics—
ethics—professor down there who says that animals are really people, in funny furry disguises."

"You'd be surprised, Eldon," Gullighy went on. "They're all over.
Most of them would sell their mothers to ransom a stray cat."

"We've got one downstairs, I think," Edna said. "Amber. I

caught her making a vomiting face when she served Eldon a steak the other night."

"Exactly. They're everywhere. So let's go on to option two. But a question first. How much do you trust Fasco and Braddock? Will they keep quiet, or sell out to *The Enquirer* or even *The Surveyor?*"

"Hell, don't forget Justin Boyd's my biggest fan."

"Today."

"As for Gene and Tommy, I trust them. I've felt no pain with Leaky before this, but I'm sure they haven't breathed a word about my drinking. Right, Edna?"

"I think so."

"Okay, option two is to bury this whole mess. To use a very dirty word, a cover-up. I don't need to tell you this is very risky and very dangerous. You've got at least three possible traps:

"*A.* A major scandal if it ever comes out that your two heavy suits didn't report this incident and no Firearms Discharge Report was filed and investigated. Police misfeasance, and right on your doorstep.

"*B.* That kid may not be the wetback Braddock thinks he is. He may have recognized you and he may talk.

"*C.* Somebody may have been looking out on the street, or come to the window when they heard shots.

"But there it is. Option two—*omertà,* and if anything comes out, we do a world-class stonewall."

"Is there an option three?" Edna asked.

"Yeah. Jump. From the top of the ASPCA headquarters."

"Then it's option two," Edna said. "Eldon?"

Eldon rubbed his still-throbbing head. "Yes, option two," he said quietly.

"All right. Let me talk nice to Fasco and Braddock. I'll do it. We want to preserve your deniability, Mr. Mayor."

Deniability, Eldon thought. A word he'd seen used only in exposés of Central Intelligence Agency hijinks. And now it was being applied to him.

. . .

"Okay, boys, let me make something perfectly clear," Gullighy said to Fasco and Braddock, in the adjoining anteroom, realizing too late he was using one of Richard Nixon's favorite phrases. "First off, I think—and the mayor agrees, despite what we said earlier— that you were absolutely right to deep-six Wambli. This was a stupid, silly, pissant incident and nobody has to be any the wiser about it. Silence is the order of the day.

"Now, of course, if anything ever comes to light and you're asked about it, you *must* tell the truth—that you were trying to protect your mayor, our mayor, from a lethal attack by that dog. Right?"

"Yes, Jack," Braddock replied, as Fasco nodded.

"Whatever else you say is up to you and your consciences, thinking of your duty to your families, your city and the man you have so loyally worked for. I personally would not think it necessary to add that the mayor may have been a bit tipsy, that he may have used some language that might be interpreted as threatening or that he accidentally mashed poor Wambli's leg. But as I say, that's entirely up to you. And your consciences. Okay?"

Two respectful nods this time.

"Case closed. Go home and get some sleep."

SEVEN

Genc, who had been sleeping soundly, suddenly interrupted Sue's reveries by tossing violently and screaming, *"Shouesh! Shouesh! Pusho! Pusho!"* over and over.

Poor, sweet boy, Sue thought. What dream was tormenting him? The secret police in Albania? The threat of deportation? She took him in her arms and stroked his back.

"Genc! Genc! What's the matter?"

"They kill him! They kill him!" he responded in a choked voice.

"Now, now, sweetie. That's all in the past. The long, long ago past," Sue cooed in hypnotic tones. "This is America. No one is killed here. You're with Miszu. Everything's all right. Miszu will take care of you." She squeezed him harder and kissed his cheek as she invoked the nickname Miszu—his corruption of "Miss Sue"—that he called her.

"They kill Wambli!" he blurted out.

"Oh Genc, dearest, you're having a horrible dream. Just be calm and come to Miszu." She gently stroked his belly and blew in his ear. The small zephyr she created brought him fully awake; he rose up on his elbows and looked straight at her.

"No, no, Miszu, they kill Wambli. Last night."

"Oh, darling, how silly. Who killed Wambli?"

"The three men. Gangsters. Made many shots. Killed him."

"Sweetie, everything's all right. Be calm. I'll show you." She got up, put on her shiny crimson dressing gown and went out to Wambli's quarters behind the kitchen. The baby gate that penned in the animal was open. No Wambli. In a panic she returned to her bed, where Genc was stroking his hair and prodding himself fully awake.

"Where is he?" she shrieked. "Where is my eagle, my Wambli?"

"I told you, Miszu, he is killed. The men in black suits."

"What men? Where? What happened?" She was hysterical.

"Miszu, I was walking Wambli last night. On Fifth Avenue. And three men shoot him."

"Oh my God. Wambli! Wambli!" She was screaming still, and shook Genc by the shoulders. Sobbing, she collapsed on the bed. It was now the boy's turn to do the calming and he stroked Sue's shoulders and bent over and kissed her breasts. Such techniques had worked marvels in the past, but now she brushed his face away.

"How could you let that happen?" she shouted amid sobs. "Oh, Wambli! Wambli!"

"Let me tell you the story, Miszu," Genc said sternly. He held her down on the bed by her shoulders as he described the massacre, speaking loudly over the woman's moans: Wambli urinating, the two men appearing, one telling him to move on, the other drunk and smashing into the dog's leg. Then the volley of shots, joined in by the third black suit.

"I ran, Miszu. I was in much fear they would shoot me," he concluded.

"You coward! You coward! You lily-livered coward!"

"Lily liv-er-ed?"

"Genc, it's no time for an English lesson. You failed me, you failed Wambli."

"It was not my fault, Miszu. Not my fault."

"Who *were* these men?"

"Gangsters."

"Gangsters! Ridiculous. We don't have gangsters in New York that go around shooting dogs in the middle of the night!"

"I'm sure of it. Black suits. Guns. Black car. I know, Miszu. I know." He did not say that he had seen a drunken band of his countrymen—gangsters—shoot a dog, and its owner as well, outside a Tirana bar for the sport of it.

"I want the police. Right now. Call them." She pointed to the phone beside the bed. "Nine-one-one. Dial it."

Genc hesitated.

"I said dial it. Right now! NINE-ONE-ONE!"

He did not do so, but instead leaned back on the pillows, his body now unsheathed after his wrestling with Sue.

"No, Miszu. I cannot do it."

"What! What are you saying?"

"We cannot call police. They will make questions and take me away. Send me back to Albania. I cannot."

Genc brought the situation into perspective: "You call police, they take me off. You not call, I stay with you. It is simple, Miszu— my deek or your dog. And the dog is dead and I am alive." To emphasize the point, he shook his penis vigorously.

Mrs. Brandberg calmed down and considered her options. Her beloved Wambli was dead and she wanted to find his killers, to avenge his murder. Yet she also realized that Genc was probably right. If the police became involved she might lose him. She closed her eyes and breathed deeply, OOOH! SHPIRT! reverberating inside her head.

"I'll call the mayor. What kind of a city is he running?"

she said. The mayor had recently been eager to channel Brandberg Foundation resources into cultural programs for the city's
schools.

"Same problem, Miszu. I'm the only one who can tell anybody
the facts, and I must be the nonseeable man."

"Oh, God. Oh, God. I need to think. Have Jennie bring coffee
to the den."

Sue became calmer and asked Genc, as they drank coffee, to repeat over and over the details of the previous night's incident. By
the third repetition, she realized there was nothing Genc could
have done and ceased blaming him. Though she was utterly mystified as to why three strange men would kill her dog.

"Wambli was so perfect, Genc. A gentle Staffordshire terrier
bred by monks. You know that."

"Yes. Good dog."

"He was the head of his class in obedience school. First on the
American Kennel behavior test. Everyone loved him. Never hurt
anyone. Did he, Genc?"

"No, Miszu," Genc said dutifully, though remembering episodes
in Central Park where it had taken all his considerable strength to
keep Wambli from fighting and biting other dogs.

"My poor, dear Staffy. My poor Wambli."

Sue sighed and then stared off in the distance, focusing on the
Jasper Johns on the wall. Except that now she could barely make
out the hazy numerals in the painting; it was like failing an eye examination. Then she spoke again to Genc.

"You're right, my dearest. I don't want to endanger you. I don't
want to lose you. But I'm going to find those monsters who killed
my dog. I don't know how, but I will."

Then she had an inspiration. On the top of a pile of newspapers on the coffee table was a copy of the latest *Surveyor.*

"That's it!" she exclaimed, pinching Genc's thigh. "Justin Boyd can get to the bottom of this. And you'll be strictly off the record."

"Off the record?"

"Never mind. Justin will get me the answers I want."

EIGHT

Everyone agreed that Justin Boyd was an interesting specimen. He had made his reputation as the swashbuckling editor of one of London's steamy tabloids, credited with bringing down three cabinet ministers, both Labour and Conservative. In no case did the downfall have anything to do with the competence of the official involved—bigamy, buggery and wife bashing had been the fatal charges, all detailed and proclaimed in screaming headlines in his crudely irresponsible daily.

A short man, he perspired a lot, but even through the softening sweat one could see a hard face. He usually wore a brown suit (despite Lord Chesterfield's admonition that no gentleman wore a garment of that color) of a mysterious shiny fabric, with cuffless trousers, which had been modish in London a generation earlier. Despite the Oxbridge overlay to his cockney accent, he was, deep inside, a bounder.

Appearances were deceiving; Justin had a razor-sharp mind, the razor honed to slit the throats of any who challenged him. And his stubby but spidery hands at least figuratively had a clawlike quality, with which they calculatedly ratcheted their owner upward in the business and social circles that mattered to him.

Finding friends in his new home had not been difficult; there were plenty of other strivers who understood and protected him (in exchange for approving stories or mentions planted by him in *The Surveyor*).

Justin had been lured to the colonies by an obscure New Jersey millionaire (or probably, billionaire) named Ethan Meyner. The latter had made a fortune selling replacement automobile mufflers throughout America (and later much of the world) and in his dotage—he was 82—decided that he wanted to own a newspaper, and a muckraking, scandalmongering one at that.

Most people who followed the rise of *The Surveyor* were mystified by the muffler king's motive. He copiously bankrolled the paper, a weekly, set it up in lavish uptown quarters and permitted the payment of salaries and freelance fees at the very least competitive with those at the most established publications. He had done this not, as some thought, as a sounding board for his political views (he really had none). Nor was it a matter of inflating his ego. It was, at bottom, a bridge-and-tunneler's revenge.

Meyner and his wife, Lola, had both been born in New Jersey and had lived there all their lives, most recently in a stupendous penthouse in Jersey City overlooking the Hudson River and Manhattan. Their experience of New York had been as infrequent visitors until Lola, deciding that she was becoming bored as a senior citizen, persuaded her husband to support a variety of New York City institutions, with an eye to becoming part of the New York cultural scene.

They had not received a warm welcome. While they had money, they did not have the youth, the good looks (Ethan, unfortunately, resembled a desiccated cross between John D. Rockefeller and John Paul Getty) or the witty small talk that appealed to Gotham's beautiful people. Despite large donations to the New York City Opera—thought to be more receptive than the more established Metropolitan—no invitations to join its board, or even the committees for its benefits, were forthcoming. Nor did the Whitney Museum of American Art prove any more accessible, though

Ethan and Lola were significant, and intelligent, collectors of modern and contemporary work.

After enduring jokes about the bridge-and-tunnel crowd from Manhattanites who did not realize where the Meyners came from, and overhearing a prominent socialite remark that a particular benefit seemed to be "overrun with dentists from New Jersey," they retreated back to the Garden State, deciding to spend their charity dollars on the new Newark Arts Center and to bequeath their art collection to the Newark Museum.

The unhappy attempt to break into the New York whirl had left Ethan embittered. It was out of these negative feelings that the idea for *The Surveyor* grew. It was to be a journal exposing the pretensions and corruptions of New York's movers and shakers.

Ethan himself had no journalistic experience and had no desire either to direct the editorial process or even to influence it. His only directive to Justin Boyd, whom he had recruited after being assured by London friends of the editor's scrappy bona fides, was to expose mercilessly scandal and perfidy wherever he found it, preferably in the precincts of Manhattan that had shunned him. Causing as much embarrassment and discomfort as possible were Boyd's marching orders.

Justin was delighted for the chance to leave London; unhorsing the prime minister's cabinet had become something of a bore. The timing was right. Boyd had recently gone through a bitter divorce with his wife, a powerful and successful literary agent. And the personal salary and budget Meyner offered, plus the free editorial hand, were too tempting to refuse.

In the two years he had edited *The Surveyor,* Boyd had engaged in a delicate balancing act. On the one hand he needed to print enough scandal and dirt to keep his publisher-owner happy. On the other, there was his desire to be loved and accepted by the very people he was supposed to be trashing. So far, he had served up enough red meat to satisfy Meyner's appetite, without slaughtering too many sacred cows in the process. His specialty was weekly lists, always catnip for the prurient and curious: the 50 most charming dinner guests, the 50 most boring dinner guests, the 50 richest widows and widowers, the 50 largest personal bankruptcies in the Southern District of New York and so on. (The publication's lawyers had stopped "the 50 most prominent closeted gays" and "New York's 50 most prominent bastards"—as in illegitimate—but inexplicably allowed "the 50 most famous couples living in sin.")

Although his tenure had been brief, *The Columbia Journalism Review* had already been on his case, accusing him of paying cash to sources, using pieces about composite characters and including both fact and fancy in his editorial mix, in what *The Review* called "faction." These accusations the editor blithely ignored. The reader was the ultimate judge, he argued, not a bunch of jealous failed journalists up on Morningside Heights. And so far, despite the scabrous copy he printed, *The Surveyor* had not been faced with a libel suit.

Boyd had been at his barber when his cell phone rang and his secretary told him that Sue Nation Brandberg wanted to see him urgently. Thinking that she must have a scandal to reveal, he left without his customary blow-dry, omitted his normal paltry (5 percent) tip and arrived at 62nd Street with still-wet hair, sweating as usual.

Sue answered the door herself. Judging from her appearance, Justin was sure there must have been a death in the family; her eyes were puffy and red, her tight-fitting pants-and-blouse outfit jet-black (though that, of course, could merely have reflected contemporary chic). And he noticed traces of runny mascara as he stretched up on tiptoes to air-kiss her. This was a woman in deep grief (deeper, if truth be known, than she had either felt or displayed when her beloved Harry died).

"Sue, what's wrong?" he asked as they headed to the sitting room upstairs.

"It's too terrible," she said. "My dog, Wambli, was *shot* last night."

"Migawd, Sue, how perfectly awful," Boyd responded, in his plummiest accent.

"I was supposed to have a play date with him this morning," she said, after which Hoover Dam broke and the flood of tears was fearsome.

Boyd tried to console her and then asked what had happened. It might or might not be a story; the gunshot angle was intriguing, but a mere dead dog was less so. He listened attentively as Sue recounted the sorry epic she had been told, identifying Genc as her houseboy.

"What do the police say?" Boyd asked.

"I haven't talked to them," she said.

"Good Lord, woman, why not?"

She explained Genc's illegal status and how she did not want to risk exposing him.

"I see," Justin said, though he really didn't. If she was so wrought up about her dog, as she obviously was, why would she care what happened to a household servant? That Genc had a more special role did not at that moment occur to the editor.

"I need you, Justin. You're clever and you have the resources to pursue this. Find out who those three bastards were."

"I admit it's pleasantly puzzling. And for you, dear, I'll try to help." She had been one of Justin's numerous smart-set dates, but no lasting relationship had developed. (One too-short lover in a lifetime was enough, Sue had concluded.)

She reached over and patted his knee, cooing, "Oh, Justin, I knew you would."

"I've got a young reporter who came to work for me not long ago. Worked so hard on the newspaper at Harvard he flunked out. He's smart, and God, is he eager. I'll put him on the case."

"Just one thing," Sue said. "Genc must be totally, totally off the record."

"Even if it should mean the difference between getting to the bottom of this mystery or not?"

Once again, there were echoes of OOOH! SHPIRT! in her head. "Yes," she replied. "Yes. Genc must not be compromised."

"Okay, I'll figure how to play this and I'll tell my man. His name is Frederick Rice, by the way, though he's usually known as Scoop."

NINE

Some people called Freddie "Scoop" Rice brilliant, while others thought him only glib. Some thought his ever so slightly chubby boyish features sexy, others that he resembled an overgrown choirboy who had eaten too many Hershey bars. But the words that almost always occurred in any conversational description of Freddie were "brash" and "dogged." (Whether "dogged" had flashed through Justin Boyd's mind before assigning him to the Wambli affair is uncertain.)

Freddie, at 22, was too young to remember Watergate, but as a teenager back in Columbus, Ohio, he had seen a video of *All the President's Men* and decided, then and there, as some youngsters make the career choice to become firemen when they see the flashing hook and ladder go by, that he would be an investigative journalist.

His practical father, an architect, pointed out that outlets for reporters were shrinking in number and that hundreds of young folk had already followed Bob Woodward and Carl Bernstein into a crowded field. Freddie was undeterred and finally a bargain was struck: he would go to college and then could do whatever he wanted.

He was accepted at Harvard and his parents paid the not inconsiderable tuition without complaint. In Cambridge he immediately became immersed in the affairs of *The Crimson,* the campus daily. As a general rule, freshman candidates on the *Crime* were meant to be seen but not heard; Freddie was both, although he never really blew the lid off a major scandal. He was best remembered for an exposé of blurbs, those quotes designed to sell books, for works by members of the faculty. He discovered, for example, that the warmest encomium for a certain law professor's tome was from the woman he was living with and about to marry (as soon as his divorce was final), while praise for a volume of history came from the author's college roommate, and so on. It was all good fun (except for those he had fingered), the faculty loved it and Rice became a minor campus legend.

Unfortunately what befitted a legend most did not include serious attention to studies—reporting really had become an obsession with him—and at the end of his sophomore year, he flunked out.

Unlike at least 85 percent of his classmates, Freddie did not have a desire to go to Los Angeles and write screenplays, so he headed instead for New York. His father, feeling that the bargain he had made had been broken, cut off his allowance, so it was imperative that he find work. Most of the alternatives seemed distasteful: an apprenticeship at *The Times* seemed daunting, the rewards uncertain and in any event a long stretch away. He studied the newsmagazines intently and decided that they were not really any longer purveying news. Reporting on a starlet's struggle at the Betty Ford Clinic or the man in the street's reaction to the latest serial killing; covering for one journal what other publications were doing; writing about the least debilitating laxative—these were not the sort of assignments he had in mind. And the thought of working at *The Post-News* was just too laughable to contemplate.

On pure spec, he wrote a letter to Justin Boyd. Called in for an interview, the Harvard reject impressed Boyd with his brashness, and the baby Bernstein was hired.

Boyd counseled him to "hang out," to make friends at police headquarters and City Hall and the journalists' watering holes around town. "I'm new here myself, I'm feeling my way," the editor explained. "So are you, so I suggest you do the same. Keep your eyes and ears open and your mouth pretty much shut and the stories will come."

At once Freddie started going to Elaine's, the uptown saloon where journalists and writers of all sorts nested. He made friends there fast, even though the old-timers laughed at his high-energy eagerness and, behind his back, started calling him "Scoop."

One of Elaine's regulars, a well-known criminal defense lawyer, gave Scoop his first break. He leaked to him sordid details of early incestuous child abuse to build sympathy for a client, a brutal murderer of his actress-fiancée. Rice was not much taken with the headline Boyd put on his story, "Aunts in His Pants," but the bold front-page byline—"By FREDERICK P. RICE"—he thought looked quite nice.

Then Rice came up with an idea for an article that pleased both Boyd and Ethan Meyner greatly. To the great surprise of Wall Street, Meredith, Mead & Co., one of the country's most distinguished investment banking houses, merged with Canby, Schnell & Co., a wire house with a wide network of retail customers and a déclassé reputation. Rice, like every other phone user living in Manhattan's more affluent zip codes, received frequent cold calls from stockbrokers promising untold riches to those wise enough to open accounts with them. None were more ubiquitous or persistent than the phone jockeys for Canby, Schnell (which had continued to use its household-word name after the merger). Rice, who had roomed at Harvard with a son of a Meredith, Mead partner, could not believe that that old-line, not to say stuffy, firm had anything to do with the churning, hard-sell tactics of its newly acquired Canby, Schnell division.

With the cooperation of Meyner, he put his suspicion to the test. Meyner found a friend who was a long-standing investment client of Meredith, Mead and persuaded him to furnish a list of his holdings. The publisher turned these over to Rice, who posed as a new customer to Canby, Schnell and submitted the list of Meredith, Mead–approved investments for evaluation. Needless to say, the Canby, Schnell assessment was that the customer had not been served well; allocations between debt and equity and among industry sectors were wrongheaded; decisions to buy and sell were ill timed. In other words, Canby, Schnell could do better by this customer than his sleepy existing broker, whosoever that might be.

Faces in the affected shops were crimson when Freddie's story appeared. Meyner and Boyd were jubilant. That jubilation increased a week later when the head of the Canby, Schnell division resigned "to pursue other interests" and the establishment dailies covering the story had to make begrudging reference to Rice's *Surveyor* piece when speculating on the reasons for the resignation.

Scoop was roundly congratulated by his new friends at Elaine's on the Meredith story. To them it was a perfect job—an original idea, a devastating conclusion arrived at by clever legwork, a tweak (actually a purpling, hard pinch) to an iconic institution.

As the weeks went by, the irregulars at the restaurant kept asking Scoop (they now called him that to his face) what he was going to do for an encore. He tried to act appropriately mysterious, but the truth was he had not come close to sniffing out a new opportunity.

It was while he was in the doldrums that Boyd called him in. "You know who Sue Nation Brandberg is?" he asked.

"Yeah," Freddie replied. He had done his homework on the local celebrities, and besides, as an aficionado of the ballet, he had noticed in the programs a reference to the Harry and Sue Brandberg Toe Shoe Fund (little realizing that its genesis was a *real* story of the sort Justin Boyd would relish).

"Good. Her dog is dead. There may be a story in it."

Scoop's heart sank. He had heard his new friends at Elaine's scoffing at journalism "out there," where one might be relegated to covering the story of a cat stranded up a tree.

Boyd saw the look of disappointment on his young reporter's face and quickly added that "the dog was shot."

More like it, Rice thought. But as his editor recounted the details, "about Wombat, or Woo-woo or some such name," he found himself wondering how on earth he could track down the three black-suited killers. Again, his doubt showed in his expression.

"It's a tricky business, too. I promised Sue we wouldn't blow the cover of her alien houseboy. I've been mulling that over and I think the best approach is for you to interview the fellow, let him tell you what he knows. We'll peg him as an anonymous source who came to you out of the blue. I'll get Sue to give you a big 'No comment' and we'll go with the mysterious-anonymous-source story. His name is Gink, or some such, but we'll just call him 'G.'"

Scoop still looked dubious. It seemed to him that his boss was being a trifle manipulative. Was this what hardheaded editors did?

"I'll call Sue and set you up with the immigrant."

.   .   .

It was arranged that Scoop would call at 62nd Street the next afternoon. Sue would be conveniently out, but Genc would meet him there. When he rang the bell, a young man slightly older than he opened the door. They shook hands stiffly, and Genc led him to the drawing room upstairs.

Rice took in the scene: highly tasteful modern and contemporary art all around, except for a perfectly ghastly oil painting of a black dog over the mantel.

"That the deceased?" Scoop asked, pointing to the picture.

"Deceased?"

"The dead dog."

"Ya, that's him. There, too," Genc said, indicating two silver frames on a side table. Freddie picked up one and noted that "Wambli" was engraved in script across the top.

"Mrs. Brandberg thought he is beautiful," Genc offered. Scoop tried to detect whether he agreed, but could not. As far as he could tell, the dog had not been beautiful at all. The picture in the silver frame showed a medium-sized jet-black animal with an ugly pug face and a white streak down his chest. He had seen more attractive skunks.

"What kind is he?"

"She tell me, but I probably not have it right. I think maybe Staffordshire?"

"Got me."

"She buy from the monks."

"Monks?"

"Ya. Upstate somewhere."

"Can we go to the scene of the crime?" Freddie asked.

"Okay."

.   .   .

"Your name is Genc, right?"

Genc nodded.

"But I'm supposed to call you 'G.'"

"G?"

"To preserve your anonymity. You're an immigrant, right? Without a green card?"

Genc nodded again, this time warily.

"Where you from?"

"Albania."

"Albania! Not Kosovo?"

"I have cousins in Kosovo, or did have. But I lived in Tirana. In Albania."

"You in the army over there?"

"Sure. Eighteen months. Every guy is unless you buy your way out."

"Pretty tough over there, right?"

"Ya. Not good situation."

Genc stopped outside 818 Fifth. "Here we are. Wambli was pissing right here," Genc explained, pointing down at the curb. "Beside a black car parked there. Then this guy came out the door. There. 'Move! Move!' he said to me, or something like that. But I couldn't pull the dog away while he was pissing, you know?

"Then this other guy, who stagger, stagger, and step on Wambli's leg. So he turned around and bit the guy. I would do that, too. Then the first guy pulls gun and starts shooting. Bam! Bam! I get the hell out."

"I was told there was a third man."

"Ya. He was shooting, too. I turned around and saw him just before I jump the fence."

While they had been conversing at the curb, a doorman had been watching from inside the front door. Scoop approached him.

"We were just talking about the shooting that took place out here on Monday. What do you know about it?" Scoop said.

"I'm sorry, sir, I don't know what you're talking about," the doorman said icily.

Scoop persisted. "A shooting. It happened about midnight last Monday. A dog was killed."

"I know nothing about such a thing, sir."

"What about the night doorman? He must have known about it and talked it over with the rest of you."

"Sir, I'm sorry. We do not have shootings here."

It was clear no information, if the man had any, was going to be forthcoming. But before he left, Scoop foisted his *Surveyor* business card on the recalcitrant.

. . .

Scoop walked back to Sue's with Genc.

"What made you think it was gangsters who shot Wambli?" Scoop asked.

Genc took his hands out of his jeans pockets and shrugged.

"That's what gangsters do."

"Shoot dogs?"

"Sure. In my country. Shoot dogs, people, horses, anything."

"Maybe they were policemen. Policemen have guns," Scoop offered.

"Nah. No uniforms. No badges. No sign on their car."

They were stumped.

"Say, Mr. Rice—"

"Scoop."

"Scoop. Okay. So, Scoop, what means word 'squaw'?"

"Squaw? That's a lady Indian. Or female Native American."

"Native American?"

"That's the PC term for 'Indian.'"

"PC? Personal computer?" Genc asked brightly, trying to comprehend.

"No. Forget it. 'Native American' and 'Indian' mean the same thing. And 'squaw' is the female of the species. Why?"

"Oh, a deliveryman came yesterday and I guess Miszu"—then he corrected himself quickly—"I mean Mrs. Brandberg, gave him too small a tip. I heard him say, 'That damn squaw,' when he went out the door."

"She is that technically, I guess. A squaw. Indian. Native American."

"Indian. Means red-blooded, no?" Genc said with a grin.

"Yeah, that's what they say."

TEN

Jack Gullighy broke his 9 a.m. routine twice a week and had breakfast with the Hoaglands at the mansion. After Wambli's murder, the subject was raised gingerly each time.

"Anything new about the Incident?" Jack usually would ask. (The "Incident" had become their neutral shorthand for the shooting, though Edna had wanted to call it "Operation Blockhead.") For three weeks the answer came back "No," and finally one morning Gullighy cautiously told Eldon, "Looks like you're in the clear."

That same day, at City Hall, Gullighy, as was his usual practice, held a meeting with Betsy Twinsett, the mayor's principal scheduler. Betsy was what would have been called, in a less sensitive time, a sweet young thing. Pretty, pert and blonde, she had been recommended to Eldon by her father (a campaign contributor), and since she had asked for only a modest salary (which appealed to the mayor's sense of thrift), he had hired her.

Betsy had a small office at City Hall, just big enough for a desk and one file cabinet, and was charged with processing the invitations, requests for appearances by the mayor and other claims on his time that arrived by the score each day. Conscientious to a fault, she toiled through the mounds of correspondence and, as she worked, gently dislodged blonde hair from her face with a little blow that sounded as if she were exhaling cigarette smoke (a cute tick that was much admired). The only problem was that, only three years out of Smith, she was not as sophisticated as she might be; she was not suspicious or cynical by nature, and for her to smell a rat it had to be very dead and very pungent.

Eldon had asked Jack, the great connecter-upper, informally to oversee her performance. He did this in a friendly meeting each Wednesday morning. His supervision had paid off. Betsy, for example, had been thrilled when the manager for Vito Mombelli, the internationally renowned tenor, had proposed that his client receive the Handel Medallion, the city's highest award for cultural achievement. As a quid pro quo, Mombelli would be willing to give a recital at Gracie Mansion.

Gullighy had had to dampen his young charge's enthusiasm by pointing out that the rakish Mombelli had been pursued for years, in court and out, by a young woman calling herself Vera Mombelli who claimed that he was her father. (Met security had started years before to keep an eye out for her, as she was known to stand and scream "Papa!" during ovations for her putative father.) The paternity rap had never been pinned on the tenor, but Jack had visions of a blazing *Post-News* headline along the lines of "Opera Buffa at Gracie: Vito Sings, Vera Squawks." Receiving this information, Betsy had blown her hair back, and Mombelli's chances for a medallion along with it.

This morning, as Gullighy shuffled through the stack of invitations and proposals Betsy had assembled for him, one in particular caught his eye. A letter from something called the Coalition for Animal Welfare requested that Eldon host a celebration on the upcoming feast of St. Francis of Assisi, October 4, to focus attention on "the need for continuing vigilance in the battle for animal rights." The leaders of the organizations making up the coalition would attend the event, on the lawn of the mansion, each bringing along his or her own pet or an animal "temporarily adopted for the day."

While chances of the Incident ever being exposed had lessened,

Gullighy saw in this proposal a chance to employ his principle of Preemptive Prophylaxis, marking the mayor as a friend of animals, with photo ops of Eldon holding a cat or stroking a dog.

He asked Betsy what she thought, and she was enthusiastic. "Neat! Little kittens and puppies on that beautiful green lawn."

"We're talking October, kid. What if it rains?"

"A rain date?"

"Yeah, I suppose. Couldn't do it with a backup tent, I guess. Too smelly."

Then Betsy, a dutiful Episcopalian, remembered that the Cathedral of St. John the Divine had an annual St. Francis fete, at which an amazing menagerie of pets were blessed by the rector. She told Gullighy of this.

"That's all right, sweetie. I'll get the cardinal behind our shindig— he has first call on St. Francis, don't you agree?"

"I'm not a theologian," she replied, blowing back a blonde lock.

"I thought not. Leave it to me, honey."

Jack leaned back in his chair (as best he could in Betsy's tiny office) and focused seriously on the proposal, looking, as he always did, for hidden land mines and leaving aside for the moment the rector of St. John the Divine. Mentally he debated the pros and cons. The letter before him had been signed by a prominent board member of the Zoological Society. He did not know all the outfits listed on the letterhead, but there certainly were respectable ones, like the New York branch of the ASPCA and the Humane Society.

Would the cardinal go along with the idea? We'll have to find out. But why should he object? (Besides, if he approves, it would help heal the tiny scar left when Eldon had politely declined to intervene in a fight over landmarking a Bronx parish church that the cardinal wished to close—and sell.)

The Jews? Americans United for the Separation of Church and State? The Muslims? (Others had not yet detected Muslims on their political radar; Gullighy had.) Hell, we're talking St. Francis, for Chrissake, Jack thought, not Torquemada. The white male angle? Maybe have to include St. Clare as well.

The more he thought about it, the more CAW's proposal appealed. Caw? Caw? Isn't that what crows say? Oh, well. They had thought up the acronym, he hadn't.

And it suddenly occurred to him that the festival might be an occasion for softening up new campaign contributors. Pet shop owners? Professional dog breeders? Cat food makers? This could be brilliant.

"Betsy, let me take this one," he finally said, putting the CAW letter in his pocket. He could let the proposal go through channels, via Betsy, but she would be unable to explain the Preemptive Prophylaxis benefits to her boss. "I'll talk to Eldon about it."

The good-natured Twinsett was not offended by Jack's usurpation, and the two turned to consider the other proposals on the agenda.

.   .   .

Before the next breakfast meeting, Jack checked with the Chancery Office. His pal, Msgr. George McGinty, gave his approval (after a quick check with the cardinal). The only condition was that His Eminence would expect to be invited. He also pacified the annoyed rector of St. John's, who did not at all like moving the date of his own animal love-in to the Sunday before St. Francis's feast, as Gullighy proposed. But an ironclad commitment on the latter's part to produce an appearance by the mayor at whatever future event the rector designated persuaded him.

And Jack had another bright idea. Why shouldn't Eldon and Edna have a pet of their own? A lovable and irresistible bowser. The mutt could make its debut at the festival—more pictures, more publicity, more touchy-feely goodwill. No more "offing" a helpless dog.

By the time of the next breakfast meeting, Jack had not yet thought up a name for the mayor's prospective house pet, but his enthusiasm for his exercise in P.P. had not diminished. Unfortunately, he found the First Couple in an extremely grumpy mood that did not lift, so he asked what was bothering them.

"Amber," Edna snapped.

"Amber? You mean your hippie servant girl?"

"Yes! She brought us our coffee this morning *in her bare feet.*"

"Now, Edna," her husband temporized. "It's not as if she made the coffee with her feet. You know, ground the beans between her toes."

"Eldon, you just do not understand that she's impossible. If outsiders saw her in action, they'd say we were crazy."

"Do you think we're crazy, Jack?" the mayor asked.

Gullighy thought fast to avoid taking sides.

"Yes," he said. "Truly crazy. But for entirely different reasons than keeping Amber."

His jape broke the tension and he quickly started to present his "two-parter" for their consideration. He told them first that they needed to get a pet, probably a dog. And second, the mayor should host the St. Francis Festival.

Gullighy got so carried away with his enthusiasm that he did not notice—a real lapse for him—the lines hardening in Eldon's face, his lips pursed tight, his eyes narrowing.

"So there it is," Jack said, concluding his rhapsody. "What do you think?" He sipped his coffee with deep pleasure, waiting for the expected congratulations.

"No and no!" Eldon roared. "Never, never, never!"

"Why?" Jack asked, startled.

"Yes, why, dear? We have to do public events—that's why I trimmed my practice, remember? This sounds as harmless as you'll find."

"I'll say it again. Never, never, never. We've never had a goddam pet. Christ, we never even had a goddam child. But that's a different story."

"The subject never came up," Edna said. "The pet, I mean."

"Goddam right it didn't. You don't know it, Edna, but I'll tell you right now, and I'll tell you, Jack, I hate dogs. Hate, loathe and despise them!"

Neither Edna nor Jack spoke, waiting for the tirade to continue.

"You never peddled papers in Minnesota. I did. The *Minneapolis Star.* Forty below zero, ninety degrees in the shade. Didn't matter—I was out there every day. Eighty-six customers. And I swear, seventy of them had a dog. Now, I suppose, they'd all have guns, but back in my day it was dogs, dogs, dogs. Little yippie ones that just made you nervous. And big monsters that threatened your goddam life. Leap up on you and lick your face. Revolting! And every so often, bite. 'Oh, Skippy didn't mean it,' the idiots would say, when Skippy had just tried to take a substantial chunk out of my ass. They'd call up and complain when I left the paper on the sidewalk to avoid a confrontation. 'That Hoagland boy's not doing his job,' they'd tell the guy who bossed the paperboys.

'He leaves the paper anyplace but on the porch.' Then I'd catch hell, 'cause no one would believe their precious animal had endangered my life.

"And I don't like cats either. Stick their rear ends in your face when you hold them and try to be friendly—"

"I had no idea, dear," Edna said quietly. "You've certainly kept this a secret from me all these years. Maybe it explains the Incident."

"It may."

Jack seized on the mention of the Incident to explain how pet ownership and the festival were wise P.P. He expounded his thoughts on the festival again, albeit more quietly. And brought in the contributions angle, making nice with the cardinal and every other makeweight he could think of.

"As for the pet, Amber could take care of it," he added, he thought as a joke.

"That's not a good idea," Edna said flatly. Had Jack lost her support?

In the end, after Eldon had calmed down, he realized that Gullighy probably had one decent idea—the festival.

"All right, you win," he said. "We'll honor St. Francis and the animal nuts. But no beasts in this house. Not now, not ever. And don't expect me to pet a single creature at your lawn party."

"When you die, can we put a dead dog in your pyramid?" Gullighy asked.

"Not funny, Jack. Not funny at all."

ELEVEN

Scoop Rice lay on the bed in his fourth-floor studio apartment on 87th Street. It was a walk-up and a remarkably inexpensive one, subject to the city's tangled rent stabilization laws. He had come by it serendipitously, on the basis of a meeting with the one Harvard professor he had gotten to know well (not through classes, but as the result of an interview for *The Crimson*), Albert La Falce.

La Falce had fled Harvard at roughly the same time Scoop had, in almost as dishonorable circumstances. He had been threatened with a sexual harassment suit by an English Department coed and had felt it expedient to accept a teaching offer from New York University.

Scoop, brand-new to New York and lonely, had encountered his professor friend in an East Side singles bar called Squiggles. Both were presumably looking for the same thing, hoping to find a young woman looking for a sympathetic brother type (Scoop) or a daddy (La Falce). Spying each other amid the crush, each discreetly ignored the other's salacious quest and insisted that he was there simply to have a quiet nightcap (this yelled over Donna Summer projected at full volume). Shouting, Scoop related his difficulty in finding an affordable apartment; he had already confronted the reality that his budget would most likely support only a sordid pad in an ancient Lower East Side tenement largely occupied by Chinese illegals.

La Falce could not help bragging that he, by comparison, was comfortably set up in a penthouse apartment owned by NYU on Washington Square Park. But he had help to offer.

"I made a mistake," the professor said. "I rented this little studio on Eighty-seventh Street because I thought I needed a place to write. But with my wonderful new apartment and my office at NYU, I really don't need it. Would it suit you?"

It did, and the rent was affordable. So Scoop took it eagerly, though he couldn't help but wonder why his middle-aged friend thought that he needed a separate pad so inconveniently located from the university downtown. A love nest, perhaps? For a nestling who had decided not to roost? Scoop's suspicions were confirmed when his benefactor cautioned him that he was never to mention his "writing hideaway" if and when he should ever encounter Mrs. La Falce.

As he lay uncomfortably in the summer heat (no air-conditioning) he reflected on *l'affaire* Wambli, wondering how he would ever get to the bottom of the mystery. The Pulitzer Prize or any other award seemed remote. As a good child of the nineties, he decided to look to the Internet for help.

Clad in his underwear and sweating, he turned on his outdated notebook ("outdated" meaning it was six months old) and searched Sue Nation Brandberg's name on the Web. He found it on an impressive array of donors' lists and charity committees but unearthed nothing more personal or revealing. He was impressed with the causes she (and Harry before her) had supported; they seemed intelligent and worthwhile choices.

Scoop did notice that her name had begun to appear in connection with groups involved with animals, starting with the Humane Society. He correctly guessed that this new interest coincided with the acquisition of Wambli.

Giving up, he got dressed and visited once again the scene of the crime. He had been there several times already, hoping that some brilliant Holmesian insight would occur to him as he viewed the apartment building, the sidewalk and the curb. Why hadn't the killers left a bullet lying in the gutter or some other identifying clue?

Scoop had returned to 818 Fifth Avenue to try to break through the reserve of the doorman who had brushed him off so summarily the first time. With a $50 subvention from the modest slush fund Boyd had provided, the employee identified himself as Everson and his reticence became less pronounced. While still denying any knowledge of a shooting, he confirmed that there was a doorman/night watchman on duty at 818 Fifth every night, all night. Unfortunately the fellow on duty on the fateful evening had been fired for drinking on the job.

Everson said he would try to get the man's name and address, which he subsequently did and passed on to Scoop in a phone call. The miscreant was one Cornelius Barry and he lived in the Bronx.

It took Scoop a week to get in touch with Barry, who had been visiting relatives in Pennsylvania. But a meeting was arranged and Scoop, unfamiliar as he was with the Bronx, managed to find the shabby row house where Barry lived only with difficulty.

Barry was not taciturn but was beerily incoherent when Scoop tried to question him.

"Do you remember the night of August sixteenth?" Scoop asked. To aid the man's memory, he showed him the calendar in his engagement book.

"The nights were all pretty much the same to me. But I think that was a night when the mayor came to visit his friend Mr. Swansea. Yeah, a Monday."

"Do you know why? Was there a party?"

"No, no party. Mayor Hoagland came every so often to see Mr. Swansea. Somebody said they were friends from college.

"Nice guy, the mayor," Barry added, as he helped himself to another Budweiser. "Always very polite and with a smile for you. Unlike some of the others." ("The others" turned out to be a surly Mick Jagger and a cross, unknown mother whose three young children had trashed the lobby.)

"You know, there was supposed to be a shooting outside 818 Fifth that night."

"Shooting? First I've heard of it."

"Yeah, three guys shot a dog."

"Pfft. Someone's been pulling your leg, my boy."

"I don't think so. I've talked with a witness to the incident. You didn't hear gunshots? See three guys in black suits? Hear a dying dog? See his body?"

"Nah. I'd sure remember that."

Scoop had his doubts. He decided to quiz Barry on his own movements.

"Were you on duty there full-time?"

"Until the bloody bastards fired me."

"I know. I'm sorry."

"Was I on duty? What do you think? Of course! When Cornelius Barry has a job to do, he does it!"

"So you never left the front door that whole evening?"

"Oh, well, of course I did. Man has to spend a penny every so often, you know. And I occasionally, but very occasionally, mind you, took a break down in the basement for a cigarette. You want one, by the way?"

Scoop declined.

As Barry lit up and coughed a deep smoker's cough, Scoop pressed the matter of the man's absences.

"So, Mr. Barry, you might have been on a break when the dog killers came out of the building and the shooting took place?"

"No dog killing, boy. I tell you."

Scoop pressed for a direct answer, but Barry interrupted. "Mr. Rice, you're a newspaperman, you said?"

"Yessir."

"Looking for a dead dog."

"And the men who killed him."

"Well, I'm sorry I can't be more help to you. What newspaper did you say it was?"

"The Surveyor."

"Never heard of it."

"It's new. A weekly. In Manhattan."

Which won't be in business very long if all sources are like Cornelius Barry, Scoop thought as he took his leave. A dry hole, or more accurately perhaps, a keg filled with beer.

. . .

Scoop was depressed that Barry had been unable to answer his sharp investigative questions. His next tack was to get a list of the apartment owners at 818 Fifth from Everson. He knew that he would be prevented from roaming the building and knocking on doors, so he resorted to the phone.

More discouragement. In several cases servants with less than a full command of English answered and became totally confused when asked by a reporter about gunshots and a dead dog. Scoop gamely asked them to leave messages for their employers to call. None did.

Then there were those who banged down the receiver as soon as he said, "My name is Frederick Rice, from *The Surveyor.*" Like many of his generation he did not say this in a straightforward, declarative way; his voice rose at the end of the phrase, making it sound as if he were asking if he *was* indeed Rice of *The Surveyor.* He was mystified by the unpopularity of his publication, not realizing that his opening gambit resembled that of the unbidden phone solicitors who had sparked his Canby, Schnell stockbroking story.

One of the recipients of Scoop's calls was Leaky Swansea, who answered the phone himself, at 7:30 in the evening, somewhat the worse for wear (there had been two preprandial martinis). The conversation was not illuminating.

"Mr. Swansea? My name is Frederick Rice, from *The Surveyor*[?]"

"If you say so."

"Sir, I wonder if—"

"I'm already a subscriber, though I don't know why."

"No, no. I wanted to ask if you had heard any strange noises on the night of August sixteenth. Gunshots? A dog being shot? I'm a—"

Leaky slammed down the receiver, but not before Scoop heard him bellow the word "nutcase."

. . .

On a whim, Scoop turned back to the Internet. Why not try to find out more about Wambli, the Staffordshire terrier? As always, he was overwhelmed at the outset, the Alta Vista search engine informing him that there were 2,580,842 Web references to "dogs." "Refine your search," Alta Vista wisely advised, which he did, seeking entries for "Staffordshire terriers." The quest was agonizing as he spent hours downloading pages describing the lovable virtues of individual pets. These were usually accompanied by pictures, which came up on his screen extremely slowly, with each animal shown seeming more nasty-featured than the last.

There was also much confusion, since three dog breeds seemed to be related (and maybe, depending on how you looked at it, were actually the same). The American Kennel Club said one thing, the Union Kennel Club another. There was the American Staffordshire terrier, the Staffordshire bull terrier and the American pit bull terrier. All, Scoop thought, unspeakably ugly, just as he had thought when he'd seen Sue's pictures of Wambli. Stocky creatures with silly tiny ears and big feet.

But once he got to the term "pit bull" Scoop knew his hours before the tiny screen might have paid off. Hysterical owners screamed that many municipalities had banned them or were about to, giving rise to wails about unfair "breed-specific legislation" that not only was unfair to well-behaved pit bulls but, some of the more strident owners argued, was downright unconstitutional.

"You can't legislate against blacks, or women, or Jews or homos," an owner in Texas screamed from his site. "How can you legislate against a whole species of dog?"

Well, the owners could howl but the public certainly knew all about pit bulls, whether they were Staffies, Amstaffs or just plain APBTs (American pit bull terriers). And even the dogs' defenders on the Web implied by negative implication that these animals are creatures capable of doing great damage: they have "great strength for their size" and "strong jaws," and they are "muscular" and have "tenacity." They are "very territorial" when dealing with other dogs—and presumably strangers who interrupt their bodily functions.

Those less enthusiastic about pit bulls pointed out that they were the canine of choice of drug dealers and street gangs, that their jaws locked when they bit, and that they had "biting power" of "1,600 pounds per square inch" of size (though it was unclear how that statistic had been arrived at).

As usual, one could not tell which of these megabytes of information were true and which were false or made up. But one thing was certain, Scoop thought jubilantly: darling Wambli had had the capacity to sink his muscular, tenacious jaws into his hapless victim's flesh.

Sweet Wambli, my ass, Scoop crowed to himself. More like the Park Avenue Pit Bull!

Proud of his character research on Wambli, Scoop nonetheless realized he was far from a solution. Like a good, determined reporter, perhaps he should go back and go over old ground again. To that end, he decided to ask Genc out for an evening. Perhaps over a few drinks at Squiggles some new fact would come out.

Genc was hesitant when Scoop called but did agree to meet him at Squiggles at ten o'clock the next night, adding that he couldn't stay out too late. This seemed odd to Scoop, who could stay up until any hour and often did, but he let the remark pass.

Squiggles was booming when Scoop arrived, followed almost at once by Genc. It was a Thursday night, so the place was packed with young careerists eager to drink as much of the world's supply of tequila as possible, having only to face a Casual Friday at work the next day.

Genc—how did he know?—was dressed perfectly for the pretumescent crowd: tight T-shirt over his comfortably bulging physique (the shirt with DAYTONA BODY WORKS imprinted on the front), white Levi's (Scoop stole an envious peek at the telltale leather label in the back: 30" waist, 35" length) and Michael Jordan Airlift sneakers. Scoop, on the other hand, had learned long ago to wear what the GAP charitably called "loose-fitting" khakis, realizing that with his chubby frame tight jeans would make him look like a rifle-toting foot soldier in the American Nazi Party.

They managed to squeeze behind a small table at the rear of the dark saloon.

"What'll you have?" Scoop asked. "I'm having a margarita. All-margarita evening. Margarita drink, margherita pizza."

"Margarita? What is margarita?" Genc asked. From his time at Sue's he was familiar with whiskey and gin, but this was a new one. Whatever it was, however, it was bound to be better than the juniper-berry diesel fuel called raki he had been used to in Albania.

Scoop explained the concoction and ordered two from the waitress.

"Strawberry?" the waitress inquired.

"No. Just regular."

"But frosted, right?"

"Right."

"No problem."

He also explained, on the basis of his one summer trip to Europe, the invention of the pizza margherita in Sicily for a visit by the princess of Savoy. Genc looked politely perplexed at the disquisition.

Scoop wanted to bear in and inquire about Sue, but first he had to find out about DAYTONA BODY WORKS. "Have you been to Daytona?" he asked.

"Daytona?" Genc queried back. "Oh, Daytona. Florida, no?" He looked down and stroked his pecs. "No, no. I buy this cheap down in Soho."

The pec stroking (and the 30"/35" label) led to a second query. "You go to the gym?'

"Ya. Three times a week. Mrs. Brandberg wants me to. I go to the Equinox around the corner."

Preliminaries over, Scoop mentioned Sue, asking how she was taking her loss.

"She's not very good. But tonight she went out for a change. That's why I could meet you here. Went to dinner with Mr. Walker."

"Mr. Walker, who's he?"

"Not just he, many he's."

"All called Mr. Walker?"

"That's what she calls them. She say to me, 'Tonight I go out with Mr. Walker.'"

"Oh, Genc, get with it. She goes out with *walkers*."

"What I said, with Mr. Walker."

Scoop explained the concept of walkers. Charming and harmless gay men.

"So, there's no sex with Mr. Walker—the walkers?"

"Absolutely not. Against the rules. If not against the laws of nature."

Genc looked relieved, though Scoop missed the look by which he conveyed this.

"Mrs. Brandberg very moody," Genc went on. "She cry a lot. I try to tell her she must forget the dog, but this make her cry more."

"She going to get a new one?"

"She say not. Nobody can replace Wambli, she tell me. And she talk, talk, talk about finding the gangsters. I would not like to be them."

"How's she going to do that?"

"That's what make her moody. She don't know. I think she hopes you and your boss, Boyd, will find them."

"God knows I'm trying. But I haven't a clue, as they say. The only thought I had—see what you think of this—is that those men were drug dealers. I've done some research and it appears that dope sellers like Staffordshire terriers."

"I don't see that."

"Maybe it was a case of mistaken identity—they thought Wambli belonged to a rival pusher and killed him as a warning to the other guy."

"Like *Godfather,* you mean?"

"What?"

"You know, the horse's head. I saw Sue's tape of that movie."

"Yeah! Maybe they took the body and dumped it at the other pusher's house."

"No, Scoop, I don't see that, like I said. They shoot dog because it bit the guy. It was not, what you call it? Assassinating."

Genc shared Scoop's pizza as they continued to chew over the crime. No new wisdom emerged, in part because there were no new facts, in part because of the cumulative effects of the margaritas. (By now each had downed three.)

While they were talking, Scoop noticed two girls sitting together at the bar. One was a redhead in a peasant skirt and sandals, the other was clad in black from top to bottom. Both had been staring intently in their direction. Or, as Scoop realistically told himself, probably staring at the gym-conditioned Genc, one of the more striking males in the place with his Equinox body, copious black hair and angular, chiseled face. As an articulate and usually jolly Mr. Chubby, Scoop knew he had charms, but they did not telegraph themselves as strongly as Genc's to young women in singles bars.

Fortified by the margaritas, and seeing the girls' stares continuing, he suggested that they invite "the peasant and the poet" over to their tiny table.

"No, I think better not," Genc said.

"Oh, come on. Just for a drink," Scoop said. Without waiting for a reply, he went unsteadily to the bar and accosted the admiring ladies. They were coolly puffing at their cigarettes, Joan Crawford style, and needed little encouragement to accept his invitation.

Scoop expansively ordered a new round of drinks and introduced both himself and Genc. (Fortunately, given the first-name etiquette that prevailed at Squiggles, Genc did not have to use his last name, Serreqi, which could have led to a drunken spelling bee for the rest of the evening. "What do you mean, there's no 'u' after the 'q'?")

The black-clad lady (Gretchen by name) had long, tapering fingers, which, very soon, were playfully touching Genc's hard body. A joke would be told, and everyone laughed. Gretchen not only laughed louder than the rest, but simultaneously lightly stroked Genc's leg or pat-patted him on a bicep.

The peasant girl was the Gracie Mansion pantry person, Amber Sweetwater. Her Pre-Raphaelite reddish locks and not so discreetly revealed décolletage intrigued Scoop. He asked the time-honored New York question, "What do you do?" and Amber told him she worked at the mayor's house.

"Social secretary?"

"Not quite. I work for his chef."

"The mayor has a *chef?*"

"Of sorts."

"Cool."

Amber asked the reciprocal question and Scoop replied that he was an investigative reporter for *The Surveyor.*

"What's that?"

Jesus Christ, doesn't anybody read my paper? he thought, but explained its status as a hip, jazzy and crusading weekly.

"What do you investigate?"

"Oh, most anything. Corruption, crime. Right now I'm working on a murder case."

"Wow. Whose?"

"Can't say, I'm afraid. You'll see the headlines when I'm done."

"I've never met a reporter."

"You haven't lived, baby. We're the Fourth Estate, remember?"

Genc, who had been half listening, asked what the Fourth Estate was.

"Just a phrase, Genc. Doesn't mean anything." It was too late at night to explain the structure of Louis XIV's government.

By now Gretchen's rubbings and pit-pats had intensified. Genc, and the obbligato of the drumming music, which had been turned up louder, had excited her.

"Why don't we go to my place? It's only six blocks."

Amber was enthusiastic—to Scoop's surprise and delight—but Genc was not.

"Thank you. I must go."

"Why?" Scoop demanded.

"I will be expected. Mrs. Brandberg will be coming home." Then he quickly added, "She will probably want to tell me what I'm supposed to do tomorrow."

"You think about it," Gretchen said, pinching him. She got up to go to the loo, taking Amber with her.

"You jerk!" Scoop told his friend. "Can't you see these girls are asking for it?" He anticipated a sexual triumph, with a girl thrilled to be making it with an investigative journalist. (It was rumored that Woodward and Bernstein had had girls chasing them. Why shouldn't he?)

The prospective conquests returned, but Genc was still adamant.

"I'm very tired. I must leave," he said.

He had put a damper on the *après*-margarita fun, and the others reluctantly agreed to end it.

"Okay, let's go," Scoop said. "My treat, by the way." He would justify the payment out of the Boyd slush fund.

The group departed in different directions, but not before Scoop had learned that he could reach Amber by calling the number at Gracie she gave him.

Walking back to his apartment, Scoop was puzzled at Genc's behavior. Here was an attractive, sexy girl eager for him and he had resisted. Was he gay? No prior evidence of that. Albanian. A Muslim, maybe? But they didn't have anything against sex, did they? He was reasonably sure the contrary was true. A born-again Christian? Unlikely.

All the possibilities occurred to him except that it was bedtime at 62nd Street. King-size-bed time with Miszu.

TWELVE

Lingering concern over the Incident was not Eldon's only worry. There was another thorn in his side: Governor Randilynn Foote. The public assumed that the evident animosity between them was simply partisan Democratic-Republican sparring, but the roots of the ill feeling went back a number of years.

The fiftyish governor had grown up in Elkhart, Indiana, where her mother, long since deserted by her husband, had been the proprietress of a rough, working-class saloon, the Rat's Tail.

As a youngster, Randilynn had spent almost every night at the bar; there was not enough money to provide her with a sitter. Usually found doing her homework at a back table, she was subjected to much teasing from her mother's clientele.

The experience had two effects on the future politician: she developed a very tough skin and a rough, obscenity-laced vocabulary. Four-letter and even double-digit indecencies became a natural part of her word stock, much as "thee's" and "thou's" might have colored her speech had she been reared at a devout Quaker hearth. Small in stature (she was five feet five in heels), her outbursts were all the more surprising to others, coming as they did from such a diminutive source.

Randilynn was both smart and energetic and had been right at home at Oregon's Reed College, where she did honors work as a politics major. Graduate study at Columbia followed; she was going to save the world, and shrewdly realized that respectable credentials, of the sort conferred by Columbia, were necessary to achieve her goal.

She arrived at Columbia just in time to join the late-sixties protests that rocked that institution. She became an activist in the campus chapter of Students for a Democratic Society. Older than most of the undergraduate protesters, she was a sort of den mother to the budding anarchists.

It was at Columbia that she first met Eldon Hoagland, the new associate professor in the Political Science Department, freshly recruited from the University of Minnesota.

Randilynn had enrolled in Eldon's graduate seminar on government budgetary techniques, a dull subject he made come alive through his wit, intelligence and fresh-faced enthusiasm. But she was not listening, being more sensitive to the drumrolls of her fellow SDS agitators. She performed badly in the seminar—often absent and delinquent in meeting Professor Hoagland's requirements for papers.

Eldon, still feeling his way, had a traditional view of grading, based on his own experience at Princeton, Harvard (where he had earned his doctorate) and Minnesota. So he gave her a B minus, oblivious to the trend toward grade inflation that made such a graduate school grade the equivalent of failure. Randilynn protested loudly, but Eldon held his ground. She never forgave him and became quite bitter about the issue, even more so when she was turned down for a position as a program officer at the Ford Foundation. It never occurred to her that her Tugboat Annie persona might have had something to do with the rejection; in her mind the B minus blot Professor Hoagland had placed on her record had been the decisive factor.

The newly minted Ph.D. did land a job with the Agency for International Development and spent three productive years helping

to get a housing project started in Ankara, Turkey, bulldozing bu-
reaucrats and contractors as she went.

Returning from her foreign experience, Randilynn began her
New York career as a civil servant in the State Housing Authority.
She soon acquired a reputation for getting things done, and the
governor at the time, a Republican, lifted her out of the civil service and gave her a political appointment as the deputy chairman
of the Authority. He was intrigued by this small dynamo with a
garbage mouth and, when he stood for reelection, asked her to run
with him as lieutenant governor. (His first LG, a dim party hack
from Buffalo, had been such an embarrassment that he was
dropped after his first term.)

Randilynn was torn about accepting the offer. Her housing job
was engrossing. The lieutenant governorship, by contrast, was generally thought (correctly) to be one of the most useless jobs in politics. Running as a Republican didn't bother her—the SDS days
were ancient history by then and she was not without political am-
bition—so when the governor persisted, she agreed to accept the
nomination, and they won in a landslide.

The press corps took to Randilynn, with her tough attitude and
blue vocabulary. At her insistence, she was always called by her full
given name, though the reporters uniformly called her "Randy
Randy" behind her back. Receiving more attention than usual as
the lieutenant governor (to the annoyance of the man who had
brought her into politics), she was the logical candidate to run for
her boss's job when he retired at the end of his second term. She
did so, and by the narrowest of margins became the Empire State's
first woman governor.

The election that Eldon won was deeply frustrating to her. She wanted to see him beaten, but she simply could not bring herself to endorse his rabble-rousing opponent.

One day, while wandering around the second floor of City Hall prior to a hearing in the council chamber, she made an amazing discovery—the building contained an elaborate three-room suite that had originally been set aside for use of the governor when in New York City.

The very next morning she set her executive assistant, Pedro Raifeartaigh, to work finding out about the suite.

(Raifeartaigh was the governor's ever-patient sounding board as well as trusted adviser. Born Peter Rafferty, he had decided in midlife, at roughly the time he had given up drinking, to honor the heritage of his Hispanic mother and Irish father by changing his name. A political operative who had first worked for the governor when she was at the Housing Authority, he had moved with her as she successively became lieutenant governor and then governor, to the chagrin of copy editors at newspapers throughout the state.)

After a few hours of research and inquiries, he confirmed that the rooms had indeed been intended for the governor's use when City Hall was completed in 1811. The privilege had never been exercised and there did not appear to have been any agreement between the city and state concerning the space.

This did not deter Governor Foote, who hatched a plan that she told Raifeartaigh would drive Mayor Hoagland "apeshit." She would simply request that the suite now be put at her disposal for use as her personal city office.

How could Eldon refuse? she asked her assistant. The new mayor had promised economy in government, and what more visible example could there be than converting the Governor's Suite, now a museum that was seldom visited due to antiterrorist security precautions, to office use?

She asked Raifeartaigh to set up an appointment with Hoagland. She would come down to see him (the better to show him the hidden treasure upstairs from his own quarters).

Eldon was puzzled. Why was the mountain coming to Muhammad? He found out when the governor, looking like a miniature Michelin Man in her unfashionable alpaca parka, arrived at the scheduled time the next afternoon. She wasted no time on small talk but quoted Eldon's inaugural address on the subject of saving the people's money and then made her bid for the Governor's Rooms.

"We should carry out the original intention," she told him. "If I use this space, we can cut back on the rent we pay uptown. A win-win game."

Eldon was more than a little confused. He had been vaguely aware that the suite in question was called the Governor's Rooms, but he had never been inside it. And certainly no governor he remembered had used it. Now he was confronted with the prospect of having a politician who loathed him sitting practically on his lap.

"Randilynn, I don't think this is such a great idea. You have your offices uptown and in Albany, I have mine here. Why make confusion? And if there's any formal agreement to make the space upstairs available to you, I'm unaware of it. No, Randilynn, the more I think about it, no. I don't have to do it, and I won't."

"Okay, Mr. Mayor. Have it your way. But when I walk out of here, I'm going straight to Room Nine, to the reporters. I'm going to tell them that all your talk about economy and saving money is bullshit. Presented with a practical suggestion for saving a few thousand—in state money, not city, I grant you—you turned it down. Instead you declared war on the governor. That what you want?"

Eldon needed time, which he now asked for.

"Can I get back to you? I really have to think this through."

"Twenty-four hours. Then I go to the mattresses."

"Randilynn, I'll call you tomorrow."

In a hurried conference with Jack Gullighy after the governor had left, the two men agreed that she had them "by the balls," as she would have put it. If he persisted in turning her down, the two men knew *The Post-News* would fan the flames and turn the petty dispute into a civil war, a blood feud. And she would yap interminably about the money Eldon refused to save.

"Let Randy Randy use the goddam rooms," Eldon concluded. "It's not worth putting up a fight. Just one condition—her people have to call us whenever she leaves the building, so that I never have to run into her."

THIRTEEN

One of Mayor Hoagland's campaign proposals had been to find ways and means of increasing tourism in New York City. Money exacted from tourists was an effective and efficient way of pumping up the local economy, he had argued: increasing revenues through the sales and hotel taxes, enhancing the city's status as a cultural hub for the world, promoting employment among less privileged citizens—actors and artists, busboys and bartenders.

Some residents, strolling in midtown, wondered if the promotional efforts that Hoagland intensified had gone too far, confronted as they were with regiments of foreigners marching five across. But Eldon persisted and his persistence had paid off in healthy increases in the revenues attributable to the tourist trade.

His Office of Tourism had sponsored a poll to find out just who was coming to visit and spend. The results were hardly surprising: Europeans and Asians and Latin Americans, of course, but newly prosperous residents of the Third World as well. Domestically, Southerners and Midwesterners dominated, with Californians, presumably content with the Disneyland they called home, lagging far behind.

There was one strange incongruity—residents of upstate New York tended to avoid the metropolis. Reviewing the results with Esther Henriques, his commissioner of tourism, Eldon theorized that the upstaters had been brainwashed by the Sodom-and-

Gomorrah rhetoric of their parochial legislators. And he urged Ms. Henriques to find ways to correct the anomaly.

Having given this command, he was hardly in a position to object when Esther informed him that she had arranged for a "New York City Day" at the annual State Fair in Syracuse, just before Labor Day. She had half-promised an appearance by the mayor and he felt, albeit reluctantly, that he could not refuse.

Edna declined to accompany him. She had recently volunteered what spare time she had as a dermatologist at a Bronx AIDS clinic, where she quietly and without publicity undertook the unpleasing but necessary task of treating the raging skin eruptions of HIV patients. Eldon could hardly argue that this work was less important than an excursion to Syracuse.

The mayor asked Commissioner Henriques to accompany him, along with Jack Gullighy. The latter was not overjoyed at the prospect—he claimed he broke out in a rash once more than 25 miles outside the city limits—but as usual he acceded to the mayor's wishes.

The mayor was not encouraged by the hour's delay on his commercial flight.

"Would have been faster to go by the Erie Canal," he muttered.

He was not comforted by the briefing sheet on Syracuse that Esther handed him once they were in the air: industry leaving, population falling, family income well below the national average.

"You sure the citizens aren't rioting in the streets?" he asked.

"No, Eldon. Be calm," Gullighy said.

"We go directly to the fairgrounds. For three hours. That's it," Henriques added.

At the fair, the mayor was greeted by a band from a Queens high school. He pronounced the band members' performance "magnificent" though he knew it wasn't. (He'd played the clarinet in a school band back in Minnesota that was the pride of the state. We played Sousa, for Christ's sake, he thought to himself, not this simple do-re-mi stuff.)

After the ruffles and flourishes there was a tour of the fair exhibits and a picnic lunch with the local mayor—a Democrat, Eldon was pleased to note, though the area was known to be very Republican.

Then came the event that memorialized the visit. On the way back to his car, the mayor's party walked through the tents where prize cattle were on show.

"Can you milk a cow, Eldon?" Jack Gullighy asked casually.

"Of course I can. I'm a farm boy from Minnesota, remember?"

"Bet you can't."

"Dammit, I'll prove it."

It was late afternoon and the cows' udders were full. Jack, to call his friend's bluff, told a young farmer watching the visiting celebrity pass that the mayor wanted to milk a cow. Magically a stool and a pail materialized and Jack pointed to the docile Holstein in front of them.

"Watch now. I'll show you!" Eldon said. He sat down on the stool and, to the wonderment of the crowd, began stroking the cow's teats and, mirabile dictu, produced milk.

This unusual event did not go unrecorded. A photographer snapped a beautiful shot of the mayor, hard at work but smiling. The photo even showed the milk dribbling into the pail.

"See?" Eldon said to Jack, getting up. "Some things you never forget."

The rest of the trip was uneventful. Describing it to Edna, he somehow forgot to mention his prowess in dairy land. So the next morning she let out a shriek from the dining room that Eldon could hear upstairs while he was shaving. He rushed down, half dressed, to see what had set her off.

There, in living color on the front page of *The Times,* was the picture of Eldon, seated at the side of the cow, who was apparently named Florence. The same picture even made *The Post-News,* though on an inside page. The City Hall clipping service later found out that the picture had appeared in papers across the country, and the following Monday it was on the "People" page of *Time.*

The Times ran a somewhat facetious editorial but concluded that "Mayor Hoagland, with this one gesture, probably did more to humanize the face of the city to upstaters than any local politician in memory." *The Post-News* called it "grandstanding" and wondered how Eldon had been able to "spare a day away from his duties for this publicity junket."

The mayor's e-mail about the picture was heavy. City dwellers loved it—"You sure showed those apple-knockers, Mr. Mayor!"— though there was also a negative response or two. "New York City milking the upstaters once again," one dissenter grumped.

Edna had the last word. "Good grief, Eldon, do you realize you would have been the laughingstock of the country if Florence hadn't cooperated?"

. . .

A week after the triumph in Syracuse, the Hoaglands held a small private dinner party at the mansion for several friends. They tried to do this at least once a month, though it was not easy, given the public demands on the mayor's time. At this particular event, the guests were Senator George McTavish and his current girlfriend, Leaky and Carol Swansea and Eldon's corporation counsel, Noel Miller.

The evening opened, as it always did, with drinks from a self-service bar in the downstairs living room, the self-service part being another of Eldon's small economies. (He had pointed out to his wife that Amber could perfectly well serve as a bartender on these occasions, but Edna had vetoed the idea; still suspicious that Amber was gathering material for a book, she didn't want her overhearing the cocktail hour conversation.)

Swansea was the first to arrive and made himself a stiff martini. His wife, Carol, had come in especially for the mayor's dinner. Otherwise she would have been in Southampton working on her tennis. At the moment she was brown as a berry, suntanned to the point where her skin had cracked, as if she'd had a face-lift that had been pulled too tight. For all of that she was the healthiest-looking person in the room.

"Glad to see you're still serving decent gin," Leaky told the mayor. "Schoolchildren may not be getting their hot lunches, but there's a good gin supply at Gracie Mansion."

"I pay for it myself, thank you," Eldon said. "And what do you know about good gin, anyway? I remember the industrial-grade alcohol you used to drink at Princeton."

"Oh God, Princeton. You're not going to sing that awful song for us, are you?" Carol asked.

"Shut up, my dear. What do you want to drink?" Leaky asked her.

A Kir was the answer, but there was not any cassis with which to make it.

"Sorry, we gave the cassis money to the school lunch program," Eldon explained, so Carol settled for a simple glass of white wine.

(Eldon was grateful that there was no such thing as New York City wine, since he would then have had to serve it. It tickled him that Governor Foote was stuck with a wine cellar limited to the New York State product.)

Noel Miller and Senator McTavish and his latest friend arrived at the same time. Noel looked the part of a prominent and successful Wall Street lawyer, which he had been before taking the city job at Eldon's urging, if not insistence. Fair-haired and in his late fifties, he was even taller than the mayor. Many thought he looked down on the world both literally and figuratively, but he was really an open and democratic sort.

Noel had been worried that the strange world of municipal law might overwhelm him, but he came to the job of the city's top lawyer from a tough mergers and acquisitions practice and, thus trained to expend boundless time and energy on his work, was able to keep ahead of the game. Being called a workaholic would have surprised him; he just did what he had to do and if that took every night and weekend, that's the way it was. Besides, there had never been a Mrs. Miller to occupy his time or attention.

The senator's "new" find (she had been in residence in his Watergate apartment for three months) was the object of close scrutiny. She had been described in the gossip columns as a "budding actress"; up close she looked more like a buxom waitress in a not too upscale restaurant. She was introduced as "Casey," though later it turned out she spelled her name "KC." Her first question to Edna was whether she could smoke. Edna looked sympathetic and nodded her head. "Don't ask, don't tell," she told KC, producing an ashtray from inside a cupboard.

Obviously briefed, KC said she understood that Edna was a dermatologist.

"That's right."

"Then you could clear up Ricky Martin's acne scars," KC said.

"Perhaps," Edna replied noncommittally, not knowing who Ricky Martin was.

(As they had conferred about the evening's guest list, Edna and Eldon had laughed about their senior senator's way with the ladies. There was always one in residence, but they changed as often as two or three times a year. The Hoaglands reflected on "how times have changed."

"Remember Adlai Stevenson in nineteen fifty-two?" Edna asked her husband. "He had to apologize because he went to church one Sunday wearing a blazer, not a suit!"

"Yes, and the divorce business really hurt him. And can you imagine the uproar if he'd been living with someone?"

"George would have been in hot water all the time back then. Probably driven out of office," Edna added. "Assuming he ever got there in the first place.")

The senator, a bourbon in hand, congratulated Eldon on his "brilliant" performance upstate. "You did in one day what I've been trying to do for twenty years—get the yokels to trust me. I'm up there six or seven days a month; thought about getting one of those SUVs, with a gun rack on the back, and driving around in that, but it's too out of character for me. So I just walk around in my shirtsleeves, shake hands with everybody, take the maple syrup and cheddar cheese they give me and hope for the best. Thank God it's worked for me, but I got worried every time I ran."

The guests moved on to the dining room for Julio's paella. Edna realized that most of the guests present had had the dish before, but it seemed to be the one concoction he could not destroy, so here it was again.

Over the dinner table, conversation about the cow milking continued. The senator, sitting next to Edna, shouted down to Eldon at the other end that he'd heard the governor was furious. "'He's invading my territory,' she's been telling people."

"*Me* invading her territory!" Eldon snorted. "Have you heard what she's done to me?" He recounted to his incredulous guests Randy Randy's demand for access to the Governor's Rooms.

"You know, it's terrible, but I understand the Democrats up in Albany have started the rumor that Randy Randy's really a man," Senator McTavish said.

"That's funny!" KC commented. It was to be her last remark of the evening.

The mayor called a halt. "Look, I know I'm among friends, but I'm not going to comment on what George said. I'd be likely to say something so outrageous that you'd all be tempted to repeat it. I have enough problems with Randilynn already. So please, let's move on to something pleasant."

Edna came to the rescue, asking McTavish who would run for his seat two years hence.

"Well, you know the usual suspects, Edna. The comptroller, Congressman Canale or Rosie Malloy, Westchester's gift to the Legislature."

"Out in Southampton they're talking about a local lawyer named David Bowen," Carol Swansea said.

"Oh, yeah, forgot him," McTavish added. "He's been a hard worker for the party out there. Don't know much about him as a lawyer, though. Do you, Noel?"

"Never dealt with him. He has a one-man office in Riverhead as I understand it. Probably handles dog-bite cases."

Edna for an instant looked as if she had been struck, then recovered when she realized that the Incident was not involved. Eldon had much the same reaction.

"Speaking of dog bites," Leaky Swansea said, after downing the last of the second martini he had quickly made for himself in the living room. "I'm getting damn sick of those crazy cold calls you get every night—selling you stocks, magazine subscriptions and every other goddam thing."

"And I'm afraid even soliciting campaign contributions sometimes, for me or Eldon," McTavish added.

"Yes, I suppose that's right. But most of these calls are just plain asinine. Why, the other night some damn fool called from that gossip sheet, *The Surveyor.* I told him I had a subscription already, but he tried to keep me on the line with some cock-and-bull story about a dog murder. Couldn't make any sense of it at all. But these people will try anything!"

"We have it in the country," Carol added. "Chimney sweeps. They call all summer long."

Neither Edna nor Eldon really heard what was said about chimney sweeps. Or any of the rest of the talk around the table as the evening wound down. Their thoughts were elsewhere as they somehow got through the rest of the dinner on automatic pilot.

· · ·

The next morning, at breakfast with Gullighy, their friend did not even get a chance to specify how he wanted his eggs done before the first couple brought up the Incident.

"I knew it, I knew it. Operation Blockhead is going to collapse. That has to have been a reporter who called Leaky."

"Yep. You're probably right," Gullighy said. "But what's he going to find out? Nothing from your friend Swansea, and I'll bet nothing from anybody else."

"I hope not. I hope not," the mayor kept saying, almost as a mantra.

"We're doing all we can, Eldon. Just have to play it cool. We'll stonewall if it comes to that. Meanwhile, our little P.P. project seems to be right on course. Betsy Twinsett's got the guest list almost ready. We're going to have a festival the likes of which St. Francis himself couldn't have put on."

.   .   .

Betsy had solicited the names of guests from each of the Coalition for Animal Welfare organizations and had duly collated them into a master invitation list. As a formality, she presented a preliminary, annotated version, giving everyone's affiliation, to the mayor in his office the next afternoon. Four hundred people in all, with a flexible policy about allowing invitees to bring a guest. A whiskey distributor who had recently branched out into wines was providing the spirits for free. And Eatable Edibles, a new catering outfit owned by a confirmed cat lover, was donating the food. The only expense would be the wages of the wait staff, which Betsy assured the mayor would not make a very substantial dent in the mayoral entertainment budget.

"Four hundred people, God almighty," Eldon had said, groaning. "Are there really that many animal nuts around?"

"It's the best we could do, Mr. Mayor," Betsy informed him. "We had to invite all the board members from the seventeen CAW organizations, and we had to do some incentivizing by letting them add more names. We want to be welcoming, don't we?"

"Bosh. Let me look at that list." He picked it up impatiently and scanned down it, until he came to Randilynn Foote's name.

"What's this, Betsy? The governor's being invited? Christ, she'll take over a bedroom in my house while she's at it. The answer's no. Take her off."

Twinsett protested, saying that the Humane Society was adamant about inviting her. It seems she had appeared in one of their adopt-a-pet ads, holding a small Labrador puppy to which she had allegedly given a home.

"Poor creature," Eldon said. "It would be better off living out its life at the pound. But you're going to have to tell the Humane Society no. Explain to them that this is a city, not a state, event. This whole festival is horrendous enough without having that woman jumping in to take credit. Okay?"

"You're the boss, Mr. Mayor," she said dejectedly.

Eldon got to the fourth page before he spotted Sue Nation Brandberg's name. He was trapped. What reason could he give for not inviting her? (Unlike some of his predecessors, who vetoed invitations to Gracie for those who had dared to give as much as $50 to an opponent, he had a sense that, within reason, he had to act on occasions like this as the mayor of all the city and not just as the titular head of the Democratic Party.)

He hesitated, took off his black-rimmed glasses and looked out the window. But he simply could not cook up an excuse for crossing off Sue's name. He handed the list back with a sigh. Maybe she'll be back visiting the reservation or in Italy or something, he thought, though he didn't really believe it.

·   ·   ·

Governor Foote was in residence in her new City Hall quarters that afternoon. At the very moment she was being excised on the floor below, she sat thumbing the latest issue of *Time*, with Eldon's milk picture staring back at her from the "People" page.

"That crazy egghead bastard wants my job," she muttered to Pedro Raifeartaigh. "Milking an effing cow, for God's sake. Well, all I can say is he'll have a fight on his hands if he fools around upstate again. I'm going to get him. I don't know how yet, but I'm really going to get him."

FOURTEEN

Ethan Meyner had been so pleased with Justin Boyd's debut year at *The Surveyor* that he had presented him with a new maroon Bentley sedan (complete with driver) on the first anniversary of his editorship. The mix of scandal and innuendo that Justin had concocted, coupled in some instances with some genuinely solid and tough reporting, had pleased Meyner, even though the weekly was still losing money at an astounding rate.

Boyd loved his Bentley and often, when riding in it alone in the backseat, he thought of his former colleagues in London, using the Underground and chivvying their expense accounts to cover up five-pound taxi rides. Life in the New World (at least in a Bentley) was good. So good that Justin took to doing much of his editing and phoning while in the car. It had become an extension of his office, and perhaps even of himself.

Thus it was that the editorial conference about Scoop Rice's first crack at the Wambli story took place in the Bentley (the glass partition closed to prevent Boyd's driver from hearing the conversation).

Scoop thought he had hyped the story as much as possible, having sweated over it for three days, almost without sleep and sustained with large doses of Snapple lemonade. It was a *"The Surveyor* has learned" piece, that being the only way Scoop could figure out to handle the factual roadblocks he confronted—the inability to name his source and the "No comment" from the owner of Wambli. (The "No comment" had come in a phone call he had made to Mrs. Brandberg. This had been his only contact with her, and as a result of Boyd's coaching, she had limited herself to that terse response, eager though she was to tell Scoop the whole terrible narrative, the details of which he, of course, knew already.)

This was Scoop's first excursion in the Bentley and he was awed by the array of communications equipment aboard—a phone (with three lines), a small TV, a notebook computer permanently affixed to the back of the front seat and even a small printer. Air Force One had nothing on this, he thought.

While Scoop was examining the gadgets, Boyd read the story, peering through his Ben Franklin half-spectacles. Using the car's reading light was not necessary. It was a sunny morning and the glass in the Bentley's windows was clear. (This had not originally been the case; the car had come equipped with one-way windows that shielded the privacy of the occupant. Justin had decided that if he was going to have this magnificent chariot, the masses should be able to see him as he rode past. The Darth Vader windows had been replaced at great cost, the expense hidden somewhere in *The Surveyor* accounts, where Boyd hoped the generous Meyner would not discover it.)

Boyd made little noises in his throat as he read, Scoop listening carefully as he tried to interpret their significance. Finished, the editor rustled the copy pages with a flourish and pronounced the product "very good."

Scoop was relieved and rose up just a trifle—not quite puffed up with pride—from his deep, plush seat.

"You've got some good stuff here—the monks, the dope dealer angle. Just a few things. First, you've got a little syntax problem in that dope-dealing graph. Possibly implying Sue is a dope dealer herself. Can't have that or I'll never be invited back." He laughed dryly at his miniscule joke.

"Then, your man 'G.' Albanian. Not much sex appeal there. No one cares about Albania. What about Kosovo? Isn't there a Kosovo angle?"

Scoop allowed as how Genc had said he did have relatives in Kosovo. And didn't like Serbs.

"Excellent! Was he in the army over there by any chance?"

"He said he was. Drafted."

"That's it! Kosovo freedom fighter . . . flees bloodshed in his native land only to find it on the streets of New York. . . . . *A*-number-one perfect!"

"What else?" Scoop asked.

"A minor detail. You quote your freedom fighter as saying the dog was urinating. You can't use that word in *The Surveyor.*"

Can't say "urinate" in print? What kind of prudery was this? Scoop wondered. What the hell was he supposed to say, "micturate"?

"Scoop, you have to understand that *The Surveyor* is a family newspaper. We want to appeal to all ages, all members of the family, and we have to keep that in mind with everything we write. 'Urinating' is a turnoff for the twenty- and thirty-something readers. 'Pissing' is the word you want. 'Pissing,' 'shitting,' 'fucking.' It's the only language they're comfortable with. You have to sully the breakfast table if you want to keep ahead in this business, my boy."

Scoop absorbed this new wisdom, or at least tried to.

"One last thing. We have all this stuff about Sue's dog. Nothing about her. I think we have to work around her, get quotes from those she may have talked to. No—maybe not. Don't want to offend her, as I said. Let's go with the blind story and see if it stirs the pot. Fix it up and we'll run it."

.   .   .

The fixes were easy, and by the end of the day Scoop had turned in a revised version, which appeared the following Thursday:

HUSH-HUSH PARK AVENUE MYSTERY: WHO SHOT SOCIETY QUEEN'S DOG?

Mysterious Kosovo Freedom Fighter Reveals Midnight Shooting of Pit Bull

Owner Not Talking; A Gangster Error?

By Frederick P. Rice

The Surveyor has learned that a prize Staffordshire bull terrier, owned by heiress and charity maven Sue Nation Brandberg, was shot and killed gangland style around midnight on August 16th.

The 18-month-old dog, named Wambli, was killed in a hail of bullets outside the posh apartment building at 818 Fifth Avenue. The alleged assailants were three men in black suits, who pumped several bullets into the animal before speeding off in their black car.

At the time, Wambli was being walked by a 26-year-old Albanian refugee for its mistress, the well-known hostess and former Native American beauty queen.

The circumstances of the cold-blooded murder were related to this reporter by the dog's walker, who would identify himself only as "G."

G stated that he was walking Wambli at midnight when two men emerged from the front door of 818 Fifth. One ordered him to get out of the way as they headed for an unidentified black car parked at the curb, its motor running. This was impossible, G reports, because the dog was pissing at the time.

As the men approached the dog, one lost his balance and stepped on its leg, possibly breaking it. The dog reacted violently and bit the man, whereupon his companion opened fire. He was joined by the driver of the car, who also began firing at the animal, which was writhing in pain and moaning in the piss-and-blood-stained gutter.

G, fearful for his life, fled across the street into the bushes in Central Park. He looked back and saw that the men were still firing.

Nothing else is known of the incident. Cornelius Barry, the doorman on duty at 818 Fifth the night of the shooting, was apparently on a break when the incident occurred. He denies any knowledge of it.

None of the prominent owners of expensive cooperative apartments in the building (including three CEOs of Fortune 500 companies, Mayor Eldon Hoagland's wealthy friend Milford Swansea and the actress Myrtle Weston) has come forward to acknowledge hearing or seeing any sign of a disturbance at the crucial hour. Police at the 17th Precinct, which covers the neighborhood, have no record of the incident.

Mrs. Brandberg herself offered only a terse "No comment" when contacted about the matter, although she sounded tense and grief-stricken before she hung up on this reporter's call.

The young G was reluctant to discuss his personal background. He did say that he had served in the Albanian army and had relatives in Kosovo. While he did not acknowledge it directly, it is thought that he was a freedom fighter in the Kosovo Liberation Army who possibly fled to the United States to avoid the violence in that troubled province—only to encounter a bloody melee on the streets of New York.

There has been no sign of the dog's body, which was presumably carried off by his assailants. Staffordshire bull terriers, commonly known as pit bulls, are frequently trained as fighting dogs, although dogfights are illegal in New York.

The principal breeder of this species of pit bulls is, bizarrely, a small community of monks, the Order of St. Eustache, based in Armonk. It was originally a French order, and dog breeding and processing honey provide the income to support their community.

When contacted by telephone, Brother Aloysius, who is in charge of the dog-breeding operations, objected strongly to use of the term "pit bull" in reference to Staffordshire terriers, though they are commonly known as such among most breeders.

"Staffies are courageous, dependable animals. They are not street fighters and I've never heard of a case where one bit a human," he said. "Although in the odd circumstances you describe, it is possible that one did so.

"All I can say to the killers of that dog is, God have mercy on them," Brother Aloysius added.

He refused to confirm whether Mrs. Brandberg had purchased her Staffie from the monks, as G believed.

Two theories have been advanced to explain last week's bloody event. Quite possibly G, the exiled freedom fighter, was suffering from combat-related trauma and imagined the whole incident. (He told this reporter that he had seen gangsters kill a dog in his native Tirana merely for the sport of it.) Until Mrs. Brandberg confirms or denies the death of her pet, this conjecture cannot be dismissed.

The other is that the incident was a case of mistaken identity and that the three assassins were drug dealers intent on sending a warning to a competitor by shooting his dog. Credence for this theory is the known fact that pit bulls are the dogs of choice of drug traffickers, pimps and street thugs.

The mystery may never be solved. But if G's story is to be believed, there's a man somewhere in the metropolitan area walking around with a severe bite mark on his right calf.

FIFTEEN

The night *The Surveyor* came out, Scoop stopped in at Elaine's for a nightcap. Several of his journalism buddies were there. They'd had dinner and a good deal of wine, and now were quietly sipping whiskey, waiting for the evening to evaporate. The new arrival brought them to life. The comments ran like this:

"Scoop! Where's G? Thought you'd bring him around for a glass of slivovitz, or whatever the hell Kosovo freedom fighters drink."

"Never met a member of the KLA. Was looking forward to it."

"You really think you got a story there? Your man G wasn't stepping on your hind leg?"

"The squaw princess is going to have your ass if you're wrong."

"Scoop, you didn't make this one up, did you? That's a no-no—even for Justin Boyd, though don't hold me to that."

Scoop took the kidding in good grace but realized now more than ever that he really had to uncover all the facts and write "30" to the story.

. . .

Jack Gullighy was coming from lunch with a friend and (had he not been working for the mayor) potential client—a newly minted computer billionaire who thought he might like to run for the Senate in Colorado—when he spied the "Hush-Hush Park Avenue Mystery" headline on a newsstand copy of *The Surveyor*. He grabbed it up and devoured the story, ignoring the gentle admonition of the Middle Eastern newsdealer that reading unpurchased publications was not permitted.

Jack slammed down the one-dollar cover price and continued reading as he walked along, attracting dark looks from the two people he jostled while turning to the breakover page. His reading concluded, he found a quiet recess in the lobby of an office building he passed, pulled out his cell phone and called Mayor Hoagland's hot line (something he had previously done perhaps twice in the time he'd been associated with the mayor).

Eldon himself answered and Gullighy told him straight off that he "mustn't panic," though the slight quiver in his voice did not inspire calm.

"What the hell are you talking about?" the mayor asked, perplexed.

Gullighy described the story and read parts of it aloud, over an undercurrent of small groans from the other end of the phone. "You *must not* panic," he exhorted again. "There's no mention of you or your heavies, no hint that they're on your trail. Quite the contrary, it seems. It was gangsters, Eldon, gangsters who did the dirty deed. And that dog walker's clearly afraid of talking. So shut up and stay cool."

"I'll try, Jack," the mayor said weakly.

. . .

Tommy Braddock and Gene Fasco were on duty that night, waiting for the mayor and Mrs. Hoagland to emerge from a dinner at their friend Wendy's. Braddock walked around the corner to get coffee at a deli for the two of them when he, too, saw *The Surveyor* headline. He bought the paper with his coffee but refrained from looking at it until back in the safety of the mayor's car. He scanned the story quickly and then read excerpts to Fasco, much as Gullighy had done with the mayor.

"So that *Shouesh! Shouesh!* was Albanian. Interesting," Fasco said, trying to remain calm.

"Forget the language. Brother, don't you feel some hot breath on the back of your neck?" Braddock asked him.

"Yeah. Hot, ugly dog breath."

. . .

Brendon Proctor did not much resemble the stereotypical trusts and estates lawyer. He did not have a slick appearance, a comforting baritone voice or a wardrobe of elegant Savile Row suits. Instead he was bumpy and roundish, balding with unruly tufts of hair surrounding a shiny bare spot, and a high, almost squeaky, rapid-fire voice. Not to mention an undistinguished wardrobe of suits and shirts that always seemed to be rumpled and often spotted, too tight or too loose.

His lack of superficial charm notwithstanding, he was the trusted lawyer and confidant of an impressive stable of wealthy clients, who saw beneath the surface a lawyer of high intelligence and ingenuity. And when he conferred with them as clients, speaking rapidly and flapping his hands, they realized, appreciatively, that the hyperexuberance he displayed was all directed to understanding and solving their special problems.

Proctor had for years been Harry Brandberg's lawyer and now managed Sue's legal affairs. This particular afternoon he did not look forward to the prospect of tea with her. Despite his outward show of enthusiasm, after 40 years as a trusts and estates lawyer with the old-line firm of Chase & Ward he was becoming weary of hand-holding rich widows. Most, like Sue, preferred to confer about their affairs at home; whether office settings frightened them or merely gave them the feeling that they were less in control, he had never figured out.

Transmitting wealth from person to person and generation to generation, with a minimum of fuss and taxation, was Proctor's specialty. But he often also served as the discreet intermediary, when necessary, between his clients and the less elutriated members of the bar expert in such coarser specialties as divorce and immigration law.

Today he was such an intermediary, and he did not relish giving Sue bad news. Especially since she had implied rather strongly that if he did not solve this particular problem to her satisfaction he might not have the luxury of solving others, and charging her for doing so.

Once inside the Brandberg residence, seated across from the portrait of Wambli, he hemmed and hawed and finally came to the point: there seemed no legal way of keeping Genc Serreqi in the country. Granted he was an electrical engineer, an occupation much in demand amid the construction boom around the nation, but that cut no ice with the immigration authorities. Nor did the fact that he came from an impoverished, troubled Eastern European country. The naked fact was that he had overstayed the term of his tourist visa and was now illegal and subject to deportation.

"I'm very disappointed in you, Brendon," Sue told him. "I expected more. Some imagination, or some pressure applied in the right places."

"I can't change the law, Sue."

"Isn't there *anything* that can be done? *Any* way to keep Genc here?"

"I'm afraid not, my dear."

"Thank you, Brendon. Thank you very much," Sue said coldly, abruptly getting up and making clear that the interview was over, along perhaps with Brendon's tenure as her legal adviser.

Then, just as he reached the door, Proctor turned back to his client. "Of course, Sue, there is one way. But it's too ridiculous even to mention."

"Well, what is it?"

"You're an American citizen. You could marry him."

.   .   .

Alone once again, Sue poured herself a drink. Marriage. What a preposterous idea! A man a quarter of a century younger than she.

But then she thought of OOOH! SHPIRT! How she would miss those passionate shouts if Genc had to leave the country. Maybe, just maybe. . . . No it was absurd. She'd be subject to subversive ridicule. Or would she? she mused. If people laughed, they would have to do so surreptitiously, lest they cause her to stop the flow of her many benefactions.

Could she bear mean, behind-the-back cattiness? Or perhaps more to the point, could she bear lonely nights without those screams of OOOH! SHPIRT!?

Absurd as the idea was, she'd have to think about it.

.   .   .

Two days later, Sue called Betsy Twinsett's office and asked if she could bring a guest to the St. Francis Festival. Not for a moment realizing how she was directing fate, Ms. Twinsett said yes, by all means.

So Sue would surface Genc, on a very public occasion. Just to see how it went.

. . .

The day of the St. Francis Festival, Mayor Hoagland tried to hurry through the day's business at City Hall so that he could meet at home with Gullighy and Betsy for a final run-through before the great affair occurred. The concentration required also took his mind off what he was certain would be a distasteful event, at least for him. It was times like this that made him long for the surface tranquillity of the university.

He did stop hurrying when he met with Lucille Barnes, the chairperson of the City Art Commission. He had called her in because he wanted to discuss what he saw as a problem—the care of the numerous works of art in City Hall.

"Lucille," he greeted the costume-jeweled blonde, "I've been thinking. We've got a terribly valuable collection of art here in this building, do we not?"

"Absolutely, Mr. Mayor. Some of the paintings are next to priceless."

"What I thought. Are they properly insured, do you know?"

"Oh yes, we've seen to that."

"And what about caring for our patrimony—cleaning the canvases, that sort of thing?"

Ms. Barnes sighed. "Oh, Eldon, I know. Some of our pieces are in terrible shape. But we just don't have the money to do what's necessary."

"Well, I propose to fix that. I'll make available whatever you need from my contingency fund. But I think you should get on with the job, before things crack and crumble some more. Could you start right away?"

"We'd probably do the cleaning and restoration at the Met. I'd have to check to see how busy they are."

"Will you do that? Tell them I'm very concerned about this. And Lucille, do you agree with me that our biggest treasures are those up in the Governor's Suite? Those Trumbull portraits of Jay and Hamilton and Washington, the Vanderlyn, the Sully and so on?"

"Absolutely, no question."

"So I would start by taking them down and shipping them up to the Met just as fast as possible. And what about those two huge chandeliers up there? They within your jurisdiction? Yes? Then I'd replace them temporarily and get them cleaned, and probably rewired."

"Mr. Mayor, this comes as a very pleasant surprise. We've been urging refurbishment like this for years."

"Well, now that Governor Foote's using those quarters—for the purpose they were originally intended—I think the art up there should be in tip-top shape."

"I'm delighted, Mr. Mayor, just delighted. And I guess I'm going to see you at the mansion in a little while."

"Yes."

A good piece of work, Eldon thought. Let the Honorable Randy Randy look at the bare walls. Perhaps by candlelight.

.   .   .

Back at Gracie, Betsy Twinsett handed the mayor, Edna and Jack Gullighy copies of the final invitation roster.

Eldon swallowed hard when he once again came to Sue Nation Brandberg's name. "Who's the guest?" he asked, seeing Betsy's penciled notation by her name.

"She didn't say," Betsy said.

"Some pretty boy, no doubt," the mayor noted.

"What are you wearing to this event?" Edna asked her husband.

Before he could answer, Gullighy had an inspiration.

"You know, Eldon, what would be great? Show your humanity? Informality?"

"No, what?"

"Why don't you wear Bermuda shorts? It's a beautiful day, not too cool. Lighten things up, stress the informality."

"Are you out of your mind?" Edna said. "Remember that *The Surveyor—*" She stopped quickly, suddenly realizing that the innocent Betsy was present.

But Jack got the message, remembering the reference to the man with tooth marks in his calf walking around free in New York. "Forget it, forget it."

"I think shorts would be cute," Betsy added. "A real cool touch. Surprise everybody, Mr. Mayor. Do it!"

"I'm wearing the dark business suit I've got on. End of subject."

No one was prepared to argue, so Eldon turned to another matter.

"Gene Fasco and Tommy Braddock came uptown with me. I assume they're on duty all afternoon. Call them in here."

The two detectives were found and came into the living room.

"Boys, this damn festival is going to be a mess, I'm sure of it.

Dogs and cats crapping all over the place, people tripping on leashes and so on and so on. Why I ever agreed to do this I don't know. But let me get one thing straight—I want you boys beside me the whole time. I don't want to have to pet any dog, any cat or any of God's other goddam creatures. I don't want little Nippy jumping up on me.

"In other words, just make believe those animals are terrorists and keep them away from me. Understood?"

Fasco and Braddock nodded dutifully.

"Okay, I'm going to shave. Then into battle."

SIXTEEN

At four o'clock on October 4th, the feast of Saint Francis, a bright sun seemed to bode well for the festival. The mayor and his wife, flanked (as directed) by Fasco and Braddock, came down the front steps. They walked to the far edge of the property, the East River in the background, where they could see the arrivals as they came around the side of the mansion onto the immaculately kept lawn. The three bars were in place, rows of glasses gleaming on white tablecloths. Interspersed were tables covered with trays of canapés. It was a movie set for a proper English garden party.

The good-looking young wait staff, both men and women wearing white jackets, maroon shirts and green neckties, waited in anticipation. Almost all were aspiring actors (the remainder were playwrights and novelists) waiting for their big break, which, if it came, was likely to be a supporting role in a soap opera or a detergent commercial.

Arriving guests had their names checked off at a table next to the sentry booth on the York Avenue side, then passed by two uniformed policemen who scrutinized them discreetly.

The earliest visitors were largely distinguished presbyters from the most established of CAW's constituents—the ASPCA, the Humane Society, the Animal Hospital. Among them were

Mr. and Mrs. Stuyvesant Duncan and Spotty (a Dalmatian)
Mr. Emerson Brown and Trixie (a calico)
Mr. and Mrs. Max Gunther and Horace (a Pekinese)

Mrs. Henrietta Pelton Tomkins with Flossie (a Maltese in a
  Vuitton carryall)

Dr. George Englund with Pepsi (a dachshund)

Mr. Carlyle Dawson (unaccompanied)

Mr. and Mrs. Northrup Jaspers with MacBeth (a collie)

And so it went.

Bearers of old New York names and possessors of old money,
they were the sort who made it a practice to be prompt. Not being
members of more vocal and conspicuous minorities (though the
city's demographics had actually made them a minority) regularly
asked to Gracie Mansion functions, they were glad to have been
invited. Many had not met the mayor and they were pleased to do
that, too.

The men mostly wore flannel slacks and tweed jackets, the
women unpretentious woolens and single strands of pearls. If it
was not an English garden party it was a tailgate picnic at a Harvard or Yale football game.

Eldon greeted the guests politely, air-kissing the ladies he knew
but shying away from the pets, which, to his surprise, were behav-
ing in an exemplary manner. Edna was more forthcoming and remarked on the cuteness or size or other redeeming qualities of the
animals.

The decorum was broken for a few moments when Commissioner Lucille Barnes made her entrance, a brightly colored parrot,
called Manfred, perched on her shoulder. The dogs yipped and the
lone cat then present arched its back, but the owners succeeded in
shushing them.

A cordon of three press photographers and as many reporters, plus a single television crew, came to life when 90-year-old Victoria Lawrence, the acknowledged doyenne of New York society, came around the corner with Stephen, her Airedale. Wearing gloves and a hat (the only woman so attired), she had some trouble controlling Stephen as she crossed the lawn—in part because the dog was on a long, retractable leash, in part because of her mature and slightly unsteady gait. (Her limousine driver had helped her get a grip on the handle of the leash and propelled her forward in the direction of the party, hoping for the best.)

In midfield, Stephen pulled on his leash and lunged for the single cat, the fat calico, Trixie. A waiter tripped over the dog's leash as he tried to separate the two brawling animals. Order was restored and the hapless Samaritan was helped to his feet—and Mrs. Lawrence was kept on hers—by the timely intervention of three of the guests. As this mishap occurred, Jack Gullighy passed by the mayor, who gave him an I-told-you-so look.

The crowd gradually expanded, with more colorfully and less conservatively dressed arrivals. Gullighy, surveying the crowd, correctly sized up the latecomers as the likely money supporters of animal-related charity events, rather than the more traditional trustees and directors. The differences were reflected in the women's dress—chic designer versus Smith College—and in the sometimes flamboyant garb of the accompanying pets: leads and collars decorated with flowers and ribbons, even a tiny jacket or two (despite the Indian summer weather).

An even more amazing splash was made by a young man, apparently under the misapprehension that the event was a costume party, who came dressed as an organ-grinder with a small rhesus monkey on a chain. The fellow didn't have a hand organ, but he did have an accordion, which it turned out he was quite adept at playing, as the monkey dutifully sought contributions (unsuccessfully in this crowd) with a tin cup.

A much needed racial seeding came when Estes Broadwood, a black assemblyman from Queens, came in with his black rottweiler. Broadwood was that rarity, a Republican legislator from the city, and had been asked in accordance with Eldon's nonpartisan, nonvindictive invitation policy for Gracie events. He embraced the mayor—the two genuinely liked each other—and the photographers snapped the bipartisan hug. (Eldon was especially pleased at this. After Eldon's vaporizing of Otis Townsend in the mayoralty race, Broadwood was conceded to be the ranking Republican in the metropolitan area. The picture, if it ran, would surely spoil Randilynn Foote's breakfast the next day.)

At this point another young man, sanely dressed in a shirt and unstructured jacket and carrying what appeared to be a violin case, passed the sentry booth. Once inside, he stripped off his jacket and shirt, opened the violin case, and produced a good-sized boa. He draped the snake around his heavily tattooed chest and plunged into the party. The assembled quadrupeds were properly intimidated, as were most of the bipeds.

He was followed, more sedately, by the cardinal, utilizing the invitation exacted from Jack Gullighy as a condition for his episcopal acquiescence to the festival.

New Yorkers were still getting to know Virgilio Cardinal Lazaro, named archbishop of New York by the pope two years earlier and a prince of the church a year later. In contrast to the tall, serious Irish prelates the city had become used to, Lazaro was more compact and had been born in the Philippines. Brought to the States by his parents, he had later become a priest and spent his entire career within the archdiocese.

His appointment to a post that Irish-Americans thought belonged to them by entitlement had caused many resentments, not only among the Irish but among the Italians as well, who thought it was about time they had an archbishop, too. (The cultural crosscurrents were confounded by the fact that Cardinal Lazaro spoke with what could only be described as a brogue; he had learned English in a Philippine missionary school where the teachers were Irish Christian Brothers.) But despite the mild discord his appointment had caused, he was becoming more and more a popular figure: jolly and outgoing yet gentle, manifestly intelligent and tolerant.

The prelate was dressed in simple black clerical garb, though one of his more ostentatious predecessors might have worn full regalia, given the St. Francis connection. His round gold-filled glasses and his pectoral cross gleamed as he approached the mayor, accompanied by his secretary and Gullighy's friend, Monsignor McGinty.

"Good afternoon, Mr. Mayor, Mrs. Hoagland," he said, eschewing the first-name informality common to his predecessors. "Beautiful day you have."

"I assume you prayed for it," the mayor replied, smiling.

"You don't have a pet," Edna remarked.

"No, only Monsignor McGinty." The secretary gave a tight smile and the First Couple laughed.

"You don't have a pet, you have a flock," Eldon noted.

"Quite true, my son. But I do have pets. As I believe St. Francis himself said 'all creatures great and small.'"

The group was joined by Rabbi Harlan Friedman, who presided over a Reform Jewish synagogue in Manhattan. Middle-aged and as affable as the cardinal, he was widely respected in the Jewish community—he somehow managed to avoid the internecine rancor that often beset his rabbinical colleagues—and in wider circles as well. His straightforward liberalism, articulated splendidly but not stridently, appealed to New Yorkers.

A confidant of the mayor's and a friend of Cardinal Lazaro, he was greeted enthusiastically.

"Your Eminence, St. Francis was a Jew, you know," he said to his fellow cleric. The two men had an easy rapport, as became two powerful figures of goodwill in a highly pluralistic city.

"Yes, Harlan. If you say so. And Jesus Christ was a Filipino, I suppose," the cardinal retorted.

"I'd always understood they were both Buddhists," the mayor added. "But I went to a very strange Sunday school."

Busily conversing with the two clergymen, Eldon did not notice the entrance of Sue Nation Brandberg with an Armanied Genc, but no animal, at her side. The knowing in the crowd, having read *The Surveyor*, took this to mean that her dog had indeed been murdered. And speculated whether the buff stud at her side had taken its place as her pet.

Genc had not wanted to come—too public an exposure for an illegal. Sue had assured him that her lawyers were well on the way to a solution of his problem and also indicated, by the tone of her voice, that it was a command performance. So there he was, surfaced in polite society for the first time. To those she talked with she introduced him very properly as Genc Serreqi. She used no identifying description other than "my friend," but one or two deduced that he might be the mysterious "G."

At this point the organ-grinder/accordionist was playing "O Sole Mio" and several of the bystanders, having drunk heartily of the barely palatable (but free) Long Island wine—Ronkonkoma red and Whalebone white—and eaten copiously of the much more flavorsome Eatable Edibles hors d'oeuvres, joined in singing. The animals by and large were quiet and content. It was shaping up as a merry afternoon.

Then, like the appearance of the wicked fairy in *Sleeping Beauty*, the tone suddenly changed. The catalyst was the approach of six seemingly innocuous twenty- and thirty-somethings, neat in button-downs and khakis, except for one girl in what appeared to be farmer's overalls. Their names were on the list, under the aegis of Friends of Animals, and the guards had thought nothing of their attaché cases and what they took to be an advertising portfolio, innocent accoutrements to the uniforms of young professionals. They were wrong. Before one could say abracadabra, they had moved to a corner of the lawn and set up a visual display of photographs and leaflets. The pictures were provocative: vivid depictions of vivisections, hunting traps and other beastly cruelties. A large sign screamed MEAT IS MURDER, the letters red and dripping with blood-red paint. And a poster board headed NO MORE ANIMAL EMBRYO EXPERIMENTS contained a lengthy text.

Before people realized the import of the incursion, one myopic young man with a small goatee began leafleting the crowd on behalf of the group's organization, the Animal Liberation Army. The gist of his handout was the brutality and cruelty of keeping a pet—or a companion animal, as he put it. As the recipients of the pamphlet, mostly owners with their leashed beloveds beside them, realized its import, they turned on the crusader and a shouting match ensued. Cries of "Moron" and "Creep" were met with ripostes of "Neuter your dog!" and "Slaveholder!" The last brought an outraged Assemblyman Broadwood into the fray, and at least for a moment, it seemed as if his rottweiler—his presumed slave— would take an emancipated chunk from the ALA proselytizer. The TV crew recorded the increasingly angry exchanges, which ended only when the young man, perhaps thinking (rightly) that he was in danger of grievous bodily harm, retreated to the company of his comrades.

At the same time this confrontation was taking place, one of his colleagues, the girl in the rustic farmer's getup, accosted a petite blonde waitress and asked her what was in the canapés on the tray she was passing.

"Delicious foie gras," she replied innocently. "On slices of apples. Try one."

"Are you kidding?" the ALAer shrieked. "Do you know how they make foie gras? How they force huge tubes of food down geese's throats to enlarge their livers? Sister, I pity you." She seemed about to upend the waitress's tray when an irate gent came between them. He conspicuously picked up a canapé and stuffed it down, followed quickly by a second, glaring at the protester the whole time. "Delicious!" he proclaimed loudly, through a mouthful of the offending substance. His adversary moved off in disgust.

The mayor, some distance away, was unaware of these scuffles. He was busy working the crowd, flanked by his omnipresent body-guards, and actually seemed to be relaxing. Approaching Commissioner Barnes, her parrot perched on her shoulder, he asked, "Polly want a cracker?" in the artificial high voice he might have used to speak to an infant. They were the first words he had uttered to a nonhuman all afternoon.

For his pains, the parrot cackled back, "Noaw . . . Polly want crack! Crack! Crack!"

Ms. Barnes explained with amusement that it was believed that her Manfred had once belonged to a narcotics peddler.

Meanwhile Dr. Englund, a research professor at Rockefeller University, led his dachshund, Pepsi, to a bush at the end of the property so that the dog could take what the professor discreetly called a "pee." (No Boydisms for him.) Returning, he passed the ALA's setup and, as a world-class, Noble Prize–winning embryologist, fixed on the embryology display. Having been the recipient of hate mail—and a couple of ugly threats—for his own animal research, he was irate; he also knew the cost to the university of the increased security such threats required. Mild mannered by nature, he had kept his laboratory work and his abiding love for Pepsi in separate compartments of his formidable brain. But now he exploded, forcefully informing the army members that their protest was wrongheaded, that advances in his field required animal experimentation and that the animals under his care—more often mice than dogs—were treated humanely.

His listeners now included Amber Sweetwater, who had joined the ALAers and was apparently their friend. They would hear none of the embryologist's arguments. He was a speciesist (a word he had not heard before) and just possibly a criminal. As he spoke, Cardinal Lazaro and Rabbi Friedman, in an ecumenical stroll through the crowds, came up behind him. They were confronted by another army member whose particular specialty seemed to be an antimeat crusade.

"I suppose you gentlemen eat meat," he accused. Slightly overweight, it was clear that he ate something in some quantity, but evidently not animal flesh. The prelate and the rabbi looked at each other and smiled, ignoring the youth's hectoring tone.

"It's not funny!" he said. "Have you ever been to a slaughterhouse? Ever seen conditions there?"

Rabbi Friedman, for some years after his ordination, had done so in connection with kosher inspections, and now said that he had.

His accuser ignored his response and ranted on. "Animal Auschwitzes, that's what they are! An animal Holocaust!"

Rabbi Friedman looked dumbfounded, but the tirade continued. "Yes, Holocaust. Worse than the Holocaust! Six million Jews were killed in that, but slaughterhouses kill six *billion* chickens *in a single year!*"

"My son, that's very strong language and I'm sure offensive to Rabbi Friedman," Cardinal Lazaro said gently but firmly, nodding at his colleague, who was too astonished to speak. "I'm sure you can make a more acceptable argument for your case than that."

The ALA soldier did seem cowed at this, but his sidekick, a pigtailed, freckle-faced girl, sought to bail him out by attacking the cardinal, whom she recognized.

"Bishop, isn't this the St. Francis Festival?" she asked accusingly.

"I believe so, yes."

"Didn't St. Francis preach to the birds?"

"Oh, yes. Or so tradition has it."

"Doesn't that mean that birds—animals—have, like, souls?"

"My child, I'm afraid that's a mite extreme. The love of God knows no bounds, and it surely extends to animals. But immortal souls? I'm afraid not." Vatican II had wrought many changes in his church, but not that one.

The girl wanted to continue the argument but Rabbi Friedman cut her off.

"Virgilio, I think we should be going," he said.

"Yes. Can I give you a ride downtown?"

They turned to leave and as they did so Rabbi Friedman muttered, "These children are crazy."

"No, just misguided, Harlan. Like most of the world. It's fun to go to events like this in New York, isn't it?"

The two clergymen found Monsignor McGinty, talking with a former parishioner, and made a hasty exit after thanking Edna and apologizing for not waiting to hear Eldon's remarks. Jack Gullighy, drinking with an acquaintance, an indecently rich and not very smart young whelp who wanted to be, for reasons that eluded Gullighy, a city councilman, saw the retreat in progress. His instincts told him something was amiss, but the men of the cloth had departed before he could reach them.

Dr. Englund was still engaged in spirited conversation. "What about insulin? Wouldn't have it without animal research. And AIDS—probably started in monkeys, you know, and primate research is absolutely essential if we're ever going to find a cure."

Eldon, escaping from Manfred, the crack-loving parrot, came up beside him and did not realize the ferocity of the debate going on. In fact, when he saw Amber in the assemblage he did not suspect he was confronting the ALA's guerilla tactics.

"Mr. Mayor, what do you think about embryology experiments involving animals?" Dr. Englund's adversary asked.

Here was a question that the mayor, well versed as he was in most public policy issues, had never confronted. But in keeping with what he thought was the pacific tone of the festival, and to give at least some answer to the question, he made what he thought was a light remark, that "we must watch out for all God's creatures, great and small," repeating the words the cardinal had used earlier. The reporters, hoping for a confrontation, crowded beside him and his protectors and strained to hear what he was saying. And the TV crew recorded his words.

"You tell 'em, Mr. Mayor!" one of the ALAers shouted, raising his fist. Dr. Englund listened incredulously and then, stony faced, walked away.

Eldon did, too. As he and his little entourage strode along, they came face-to-face with Sue and Genc. Eldon maintained his equilibrium and air-kissed her.

"I've read horrible things about your dog," he told her, with a deviousness he had not employed since smoothing over petty faculty disputes as a Columbia department chairman. "Was that *Surveyor* story correct?"

"Yes, Eldon, the story's true. And I'll tell you straight out that I've been going to call you to give you a piece of my mind about the things that go on in this city."

He sighed. "It's part of urban life, I'm afraid."

"Part of urban life? To have dogs murdered in the street? To terrorize poor innocent foreigners like my friend Genc?" She turned to her companion for support, but he had fled. Angry and annoyed, she scanned the crowd to spot him, but he had hurriedly penetrated as deep as he could into a cluster of people around one of the bars.

Concentrating on handling his delicate encounter with Sue, the mayor had not noticed the astounded and flabbergasted looks of recognition that had simultaneously appeared on the faces of Genc (before he bolted), Fasco and Braddock.

Gullighy signaled the two detectives that it was time for the mayor to speak. They relayed the message by physically propelling Eldon away from the irate Mrs. Brandberg and toward the mansion steps. Over his shoulder, Eldon said he hoped to talk to Sue again later on. He was glad of the excuse, but no more so than his escorts.

The organ-grinder/accordionist burst forth with "New York, New York" as the mayor went up the steps and stood before the microphone that had been set up. His remarks were brief. A small joke about how sorry he was that no one had brought a cow for him to milk, then some Gullighy-crafted sentences about how much New Yorkers (and by calculated implication, he himself) loved animals and how fortunate the city was to have first-class zoos with animals who were well treated and first-class donors who supported them. Nothing about New York as the country's leading center for medical research, or the estimated quarter million rodents and other animals who contributed, if that is the word, to that effort.

The party broke up soon after the mayor spoke, the ALA contingent exiting quickly, having made their protest, but leaving their paraphernalia behind. The organ-grinder was the last to leave, playing "Arrivederci, Roma" as he walked toward the sentry box. One of the cops put a dollar—the day's first contribution—in the monkey's cup.

SEVENTEEN

Well, the ark got ashore without anyone drowning," Eldon said as he drank a scotch, feet up, at a postmortem in the Gracie living room. Edna, Gullighy and Betsy were sitting with him.

"Yep," Gullighy said. "That was damn good Preemptive Prophylaxis." Betsy gave him a puzzled look and he realized his gaffe. "Just a figure of speech, Betsy. Good civic event to prevent municipal unrest."

"But how did those so-called Liberationists get in?" Edna asked, looking sharply at the mayor's scheduler.

Betsy looked downcast, and with a soft blow pushed a strand of her blonde hair back. "It's not my fault, Mrs. Hoagland. I checked the guest list, and they were put on by a secretary at Friends of Animals. She must be a secret member of the ALA."

"It doesn't matter," Eldon said. "They livened things up, if the truth be known. No great harm done. They tried to give me a hard time, but I just mumbled something noncommittal and walked away."

"They somehow managed to piss off the cardinal and Rabbi Friedman," Gullighy said.

"Yes, something must have happened," Edna said. "They left in a terrible hurry and, now that you mention it, seemed a bit frosty when they said good-bye."

"That's all right. I'll call them in the morning. Can't be anything very serious." Eldon helped himself to another scotch and asked how the wine at the party had been. "I didn't touch it myself."

"I had some of the Whalebone white. Tasted as if it had been made from whalebones," Edna said.

"Glad I was spared."

"Who was that jerk in the organ-grinder outfit?" Edna asked.

"His name is Louie Kohane," Betsy explained, brightening. "He got rich on Wall Street in his twenties and now spends his time playing jokes like that. He gives a lot of money to the Animal Shelter."

"Was that his monkey? Or did he rent it somewhere?" Edna wondered.

"Rented, I'll bet. You can rent or buy anything in this city, Edna," Gullighy said.

"Including a dope pusher's parrot," Eldon noted. He told his fellow drinkers about Manfred, then asked Jack if he thought the festival would make the evening news.

"Maybe the late news."

"What will they use? My speech? Embracing Estes? The guy with the snake?"

"Yes, who was he?" Edna asked, turning on Betsy once again.

"You got me there. But remember we've never had an event like this without at least one crasher."

"Yeah, remind me to commend the police commissioner on the security arrangements," Eldon said, heavy sarcasm in his voice. "Though thank God for Fasco and Braddock, who kept me from being bitten."

"Again," Edna interjected, then realized *her* gaffe. "Since the time when you were a paperboy," she added quickly, before Betsy could take in her unguarded remark.

Gullighy had a dinner date and said he had to take off. Betsy joined him, leaving the First Couple to a quiet if inedible dinner: cocido magico de mollejitas de pollo.

. . .

"Why did you leave me?" Sue asked Genc as they rode home in her hired car.

"I was upset."

"Why? You were wearing that new suit I bought you, everyone was being nice—there's no excuse."

Genc looked forlorn, but not because of Sue's reproach.

"I have something to tell you, Miszu. Something very strange."

"Oh, for heaven's sake. What?"

"Miszu, the three men who killed your dog?"

"Yes. What's the matter, you feeling sorry for them?"

"The three men, the three men in black suits. I saw them at the party."

"WHAT?" The "what" was now pitched several decibels higher.

"The mayor and his bodyguards. The mayor stepped on Wambli's leg and the other two shoot him."

"WHAT?" Even higher decibels.

The driver turned back toward them, glad that he was about to be rid of this hysterical lady. She left the car, Genc tailing after her, without saying another word until she was inside and up the stairs, standing in front of him and looking straight at him.

"Are you sure, Genc, about what you are saying? Are you *sure?* This is very serious."

"Miszu, I tell you. I recognize them. The black guy, the little guy, the drunk guy. There they were."

"Genc, will you marry me?"

146

Her companion's mind went blank, as it had that fatal night in Central Park. Is this woman crazy? he asked himself.

"Miszu, Miszu, calm down. Please."

"No! Will you marry me, or won't you?"

"I don't understand."

"You dimwit. Let me draw a map. You say the mayor of this city and his men killed my dog. You're the only witness. And you can't speak because you're a goddam illegal alien. So we have to make you legal and there's only one way to do that. Marry an American. Marry a Native American, for God's sake. Marry me!"

Genc's mind raced. Was this what she had meant when she said there was a solution to his problem? He hesitated, not because he ruled out the idea—not at all; it seemed like a solution to his green card dilemma—but for the simple reason that he had left a wife behind in Tirana. But who would know thousands of miles away? And couldn't he always leave Sue once he was legit? He gave her a melting smile.

"Yes, Miszu, if that is what you want."

She did not respond with any of the gestures or endearments one might have expected at such a moment. "Good! Let me call Justin Boyd and that reporter of his. But you're sure?"

"Yes, Miszu, I'll marry you."

"No, no, you're sure that the mayor's men killed Wambli?"

"I am certain."

. . .

After their chicken gizzards magic stew and a nightcap to deaden the taste, the Hoaglands went up to the master bedroom and turned on the ten o'clock news on New York One, the channel that had sent a crew to the festival. Eldon sprawled on the bed while Edna sat in a chair beside him. The teasers came on, and the very first one was: "Mayor Supports Animal Extremists."

"Queer way to put it," Eldon remarked.

Soon the pert Hispanic anchorwoman came on with the full story:

"Mayor Eldon Hoagland this afternoon at Gracie Mansion strongly endorsed the stand of a militant animal rights group against experimenting on animals as part of medical research. Our reporter Andy Hartwell has the story."

Hartwell, with the Gracie lawn, strewn with debris (not to mention an unspeakable amount of animal droppings) as a backdrop, elaborated:

"The scene was a reception for officials and guests of the Coalition for Animal Welfare and its constituent organizations to coincide with the feast day of that greatest friend of animals of all time, St. Francis of Assisi. Those attending were invited to bring their pets, and many did." (*Pan to Manfred the parrot and the anonymous snake owner*)

"The tranquillity of the occasion was broken when six members of a militant animal rights organization, the Animal Liberation Army, broke into the party. According to a spokesman for the group, it is against the keeping of pets, the slaughtering of animals for food and their use in medical experiments. The interlopers set up a series of displays, including one condemning the use of animal embryos in research laboratories.

"Mayor Hoagland surprised—if not shocked—the crowd by forcefully endorsing the ALA antiembryo stand when confronted by one of the militant protesters."

(Pan to ALAer) "Mr. Mayor, what do you think about embryology experiments involving animals?"

(Pan to mayor) "We must watch out for all God's creatures, great and small."

(Pan to ALAer raising his fist) "You tell 'em, Mr. Mayor!"

"We asked Dr. George Englund, a Noble Prize–winning embryologist at Rockefeller University, when he was leaving the party, what he thought of the mayor's stand."

(Pan to Dr. Englund, standing on York Avenue) "It's contemptible. The mayor is a smart man, but it's clear he doesn't understand the first thing about embryological research. Not that he should, mind you, but he ought to keep his mouth shut about matters he knows nothing about. To endorse those young extremists was disgraceful, truly disgraceful."

Dr. Englund's remarks were the only follow-up to the mayor's "strong endorsement," and the news went on to the story of a truck overturning in Brooklyn.

"I don't believe it!" Eldon said. "Did you see the way they cut that? Mouthy bastard—click!—then me!—click!—then another mouthy bastard. Strong endorsement, my foot!"

"You should have kept still."

"Thank you, Edna. I thought I avoided the whole subject with that quote from St. Francis. Damn!"

He had taken an audible groan from his wife during the news segment as protest at what she was hearing. But now he learned he had been wrong.

"I assume you saw your favorite during that segment," she said.

"What do you mean?"

"Amber."

"Amber?"

"Yes, Amber. The little minx you're so protective of. Didn't you see her standing there in the middle of that bunch of loons? Her nose ring shining in the sun?"

"No, no I didn't. Are you sure?" But now he remembered that he had seen her, back in those halcyon moments before he made his "endorsement."

"Look, there's no mistaking that girl. Those darling Pre-Raphaelite curls. She's one of them! Or at least she's a fellow traveler."

"Now that you mention it, I did see her. Didn't think anything of it at the time."

"You wouldn't. She's history, Eldon. I'm going to fire her in the morning. Get her out of here."

"You do what you have to do, Edna," he said sadly. "But what do I do about this bear hug I supposedly gave those animal rights people?"

"Don't call it a bear hug, for starters. Maybe the papers will have a different take on it. Then you can ignore the whole thing and it will blow over."

"Maybe, but don't count on it. You want a drink?"

.   .   .

Eldon had recently been of the view that print journalism had changed rather drastically since his days as a paperboy in Minnesota. Back then, "news" meant stories of what had happened not later than the day before and were detailed in scope; he recalled vividly delivering an extra edition of the *Minneapolis Star* on the day Franklin Roosevelt died, mere hours after the president's death

had been announced. Now it seemed that only hurricanes, Far
Eastern train wrecks, large school shootings and earthquakes were
extensively covered on a timely and complete basis; other stories
were printed only when an editor got around to doing so, or were
reduced to short-paragraph bites in summary columns or collec-
tions of personality items.

His theory proved correct the next morning, when he scanned
The Times over breakfast. It had only a short squib in the "Public
Lives" column that began, "There were no cows, but a variety of
other animals, in evidence yesterday when Mayor Eldon Hoagland
entertained supporters of the Coalition for Animal Welfare at
Gracie Mansion. . . ." The ALA invaders were mentioned, but in a
light and benign way. *The Times* played the festival story just about
right, Eldon thought, and certainly had not twisted his "all God's
creatures" remark out of shape.

Then he got to *The Post-News*. In his theorizing about what stories still grabbed an editor's attention, he had forgotten that not
only disasters received up-front coverage but, at least in the case of
editors like those at *The Post-News,* stories embarrassing to politicians on their enemies list as well. So it was that the front page
blared forth:

ANIMAL LIBS MAKE ZOO OF
MAYOR'S GARDEN PARTY

Hoagland Backs Liberation Army Militants

With, of course, a picture of the ALAer with fist raised as he stood
at the mayor's side, and a page-three story taking the same slant as
the previous evening's TV report.

"Those bastards," Eldon muttered to the not-as-yet-fired Amber as she cleared the breakfast table.

. . .

Jack Gullighy, who had missed the New York One newscast, saw *The Post-News* and realized that his clever exercise in Preemptive Prophylaxis had probably been less than a complete success. And had ignited a raging fire that had to be smothered. After the cow-milking triumph, why this? He taxied down to City Hall to await the mayor's arrival. And probable wrath.

. . .

On 62nd Street another sort of breakfast was taking place. The night before, Sue had managed to reach Justin Boyd, in his Bentley, and told him it would be "worth his while" to come to breakfast, with his ace reporter in tow. Boyd in turn had reached a bleary Scoop—out of sorts because he had lured a prospective conquest from Squiggles to his playboy pad and did not need interference from his boss.

Sue appeared tired when the *Surveyor* team arrived at eight o'clock. She had been so keyed up after Genc's revelation that she had not been able to sleep. Nor had she responded—most unusual for her—to Genc's attempts at lovemaking. Lovemaking with his wife-to-be that he had approached with the ardor he thought the occasion demanded. After all, one did not get engaged that often; he had done it only once before.

. . .

Seated around a coffee table in the library, Sue made Genc recount his tale of discovery to the two journalists, after telling them, without further explanation, that Genc was prepared to talk on the record. Boyd in particular cross-examined him intensely.

"The dog was pissing and the mayor stepped on his hind leg. Right?"

"Yes sir."

"And the dog bit him?"

"Yes sir."

"Which leg?"

"The right."

"And then?"

"He said to 'off' the dog."

Boyd smiled contentedly.

Scoop was more distracted, wondering if he had somehow missed the story—had there been enough clues for him to have pieced it together, to have figured out who the men in black were? He thought not, but he wanted to reflect on the matter very critically since his competency as an investigative reporter, and therefore his very reason for being, as well as his self-esteem, were at stake.

The two men left without any commitment as to how they would handle the story, but Sue had enough confidence in Justin's instinct for the melodramatic to feel sure that he would do justice to Genc's tale.

. . .

"What do you think?" Boyd asked, looking over at his reporter in the backseat of the Bentley.

"He sure seems certain."

"Certain enough for me. Will you start writing this morning?"

"Sure," Scoop said but then, after a moment's silence, added, "I'd feel more comfortable if I had a second source for the story. Didn't Woodward and Bernstein say they always had two sources for everything?"

"Yes, but those were anonymous squealers. Here you've got a live one who talked on the record."

"I guess so," Scoop said, not entirely convinced. Then he asked Boyd how this story would square with the latter's obsequious support for the mayor in his bid for election.

Boyd was only half paying attention. Drumming on the plush armrest next to him, he was savoring the consequences of the Wambli epic for *The Surveyor*. It would be the story of the year, a clear beat on the laggard daily press. Might it just be the jumpstart needed to convince Ethan Meyner to go daily? The possibilities were delicious.

"What?" Boyd asked, still preoccupied.

"You've been very pro-Hoagland. Can you just, um, reverse field now?"

"My boy, the first law of journalism is that you have to follow the story. Take it where it leads you, and then print it. Let the devil take the hindmost."

"But *The Surveyor* was his biggest backer," Scoop persisted.

"That was before I knew the man was a dog murderer," Boyd told him.

. . .

While he waited outside the mayor's office, Gullighy fiddled with a computer and read the morning e-mail (he had the privilege of access to Eldon's account). The thunder had begun already:

My father's life was saved by insulin injections. Insulin was devel-

oped in experiments on dogs, right? Why would you want to kill my
father?

I've been told that apes are essential to the search for an AIDS vaccine, since the disease probably started with them anyway. Is is really better to have thousands of AIDS victims die rather than use a
few apes in experiments? Get real, Mayor.

Thank God there is someone in public life with a sense of balance.
Close the laboratories! If experiments are so important, do them on
doctors!

And so it went. Seventy-three missives, all polarized and vehement.
Then Gullighy got a message on his pager. Fasco was calling,
from home. He dialed him back.

"Mr. Gullighy, remember the conversation we had about that
dog? The one we terminated?"

"Of course."

"Well, I've been thinking about it all night, and I think I better
talk to you."

"Shoot," Gullighy said, before realizing that was perhaps not the
most apt choice of word.

"That dog belonged to Mrs. Brandberg, okay? And she was at
that lawn thing yesterday, okay?"

"Yes and yes."

"Well, did you see the guy she was with?"

"Didn't really notice."

"It's the one who was walking the dog that night."

A painful quiver circumnavigated Gullighy's middle.

"Did he recognize the mayor? Did he recognize you?"

"I'm pretty sure he did. We ran into him head-on out there on the lawn."

"Jesus. Well, thanks for the good news, Gene. I'm outside the mayor's office now and I'll tell him. But not a word of this to anyone else, understand? And that goes for Braddock, too."

"No problem."

"My best to your family, Gene. I'll be in touch."

.   .   .

Eldon was all business when he arrived. "Listen, Jack, you've got to help me draft a statement. I've got to put this damn-fool animal thing to rest. It's the worst misquotation since I was elected. Totally irresponsible. Absolutely wrong. I want a statement saying I have no sympathy for the ALA or whatever the hell that outfit's called and that I fully support responsible medical experiments on animals. As far as I'm concerned the docs can use their damn embryos any way they please. Period. Full stop."

"Until ten minutes ago I would have agreed with you."

"What happened then? Your stomach get upset from drinking coffee from that slop machine outside?"

"No sir. Not that simple." He reported what Fasco had told him. "Holy shit."

"Well put, Mr. Mayor. I'm afraid the holy shit is about to hit the blessed fan. But remember what I said right from the beginning— you might have to resort to a first-class stonewall if the cover-up comes apart."

As Eldon recalled their earlier conversations, Gullighy had said that *we* might have to stonewall, but he let the thought pass.

"You're not in stonewall mode yet, but you'd better be prepared for it. Prepared to deny, deny, deny. Which shouldn't be hard since you were so drunk your memory wasn't functioning at the time of the Incident anyway."

Eldon looked hurt and defeated.

"But stonewalling may not be so difficult. Remember, we thought he was an illegal, and when he wouldn't even give his name to *The Surveyor* that sort of confirmed it. He may disappear. And even if he doesn't, it'll be your word, and Fasco's and Braddock's, against his."

"Well, first things first. Let's get started on my animal rights statement," the mayor said.

"Hold on a minute, Eldon. You remember the purpose of the festival was to establish your great love for animals, just in case. Just in case. A harsh statement right now would not be the best idea."

"But I've got to say something," Eldon protested.

"Okay. Say that you were misquoted, that you didn't endorse the ALA's antiresearch stand. But don't say outright that they're wrong—or crazy. Just say that you're not a scientist, the issue's very complex, blah, blah, blah."

"You're the master here, Jack. If you say so."

.   .   .

The mayor's statement, following Gullighy's approach, was given out before noon to the press and put on the mayor's Web site. Meanwhile, he called Rabbi Friedman and Cardinal Lazaro to smooth their ruffled clerical feathers.

Rabbi Friedman was highly critical of the ALA's presence at the festival. "These are ignorant people who probably don't appreciate how grossly offensive their rhetoric is," he told the mayor. "They're free to express their hateful views, but that doesn't mean you have to give them a platform."

Eldon explained that they had tricked their way into the party and the rabbi accepted his explanation.

Cardinal Lazaro downplayed the Liberationists' presence and also accepted Eldon's version of what had happened. But then he commented on the mayor's position in the embryology controversy.

"If I may be very frank, Mr. Mayor, your support for their position on animal embryos is very misguided."

"I didn't—don't—have a position, Your Eminence. That was totally fabricated by New York One and *The Post-News*."

"I accept what you say. But what you must do is unequivocally condemn their position. It is wrong and without moral justification."

Eldon paraphrased his statement, which had already gone out.

"Not strong enough, Mr. Mayor. Don't you understand the implications of condemning research with animal embryos?"

"Perhaps I don't."

"Embryological research, the doctors tell me, is important— breakthroughs in treating leukemia, et cetera. And if they can't use animal embryos, they will use human ones."

"You obviously have given some thought to this matter, Your Eminence."

"I certainly have. You must know my position. A human embryo is a living being. To kill it is murder, pure and simple."

"You mean it's like abortion?"

"Precisely."

"Oh."

Eldon graciously thanked the cardinal for sharing his thinking and ended the conversation as quickly as possible.

Abortion? Oh my, the mayor thought to himself as he put down the phone; so far in his public career he had managed to avoid that black pit of an issue. Should he revise his statement? Too late. Put out a new one, then? No, matters were quite confused enough already.

.   .   .

Dr. Englund, whom the mayor had known slightly over the years, was frosty. He, too, did not blame the mayor for the presence of the ALAers but, like the cardinal, asked Eldon to make a strong statement criticizing their position. The mayor responded with what was becoming a litany, his lack of enough scientific knowledge to get on either side of the controversy.

"That may be, sir, but you are an important public figure. Equivocation on your part can only lend credence to a very wrongheaded view of what our research is all about. You must speak out."

Eldon dimly recalled that the professor had been quoted on New York One as saying that he, as a layman, should simply shut up. But he did not raise the point.

"What's the alternative to animal research?" Eldon asked.

"Human embryos, of course," Dr. Englund replied, as if addressing a not terribly bright student. "There's no reason you should know it, but that's a red-hot issue down in Washington. Congressmen go crazy over using human embryos in research. That's why we try to avoid it.

"I've got a tank full of fish here at the lab—zebra fish, medaka fish from Japan. I've even got eggs in incubators, on their way to becoming chicks. What am I supposed to do? Kill the fish? Eat the eggs for breakfast? Your cockamamy statement would suggest that I should. You've got to hit those Liberationists and hit them hard."

.   .   .

While City Hall was ablaze, Amber Sweetwater sat fuming in her makeshift bedroom back at the mansion, bent on revenge. Edna, without a great deal of tact and with a certain amount of zest, had fired her after breakfast and told her to move out before the day was over.

No legitimate reason had been assigned for her dismissal, just what she regarded as petty, middle-class gripes one might expect from a professor's wife—her bare feet, the nude sunbathing, the fraternizing with her ALA friends. She had pointed out that it would be expensive to replace her—no one else would work for her substandard wages—but the city's first lady was not moved.

Amber idly flipped through her diary; Edna had been quite right that the idea of an upstairs-downstairs exposé had not escaped her. She was made even angrier when she realized that her employers, as far as she knew, had led a pretty dull existence, and she had observed very little behavior of the sort that sold confessional books. (A city councilman's groping of a minor screen star might have qualified, but the fingered actress's career was already in decline and she was likely to be dimly remembered history by the time a book appeared.) And no one, probably, would really care that she disliked Edna.

Maybe she should get some more expert advice. A writer more clever than she ought to be able to shape her raw material into a book, or at least a magazine article. What about that hotshot reporter she'd met at Squiggles? Had a funny name. Scrooge. Scope. No, Scoop. And who did he work for? *The Inspector, The Examiner,* something like that. She would have to track it down and give him a call, but first she had to let her friend Gretchen know that she was moving in, at least temporarily.

. . .

Later that morning Dr. Englund placed a call to Governor Foote, to caution her about the tack her health commissioner had been recently taking regarding greater accountability for the expenditure of medical research funds provided by the state. The previous winter there had been a minor scandal at a medical school upstate, where skiing equipment had been purchased out of moneys earmarked for an obesity study. The hapless director of the project had defended the purchase on the grounds that *(a)* the equipment was for cross-country and not downhill skiing, *(b)* his team was interested in finding out if cross-country skiing, one of the few non-fat-inducing activities available in the rural areas, could help in weight reduction and *(c)* his overworked and underpaid staff could use the equipment, thus improving their morale, when their corpulent subjects were not.

The upshot of this embarrassing comedy, when it was revealed, had been a declaration by the health commissioner that supervision of grants under his jurisdiction would be tightened. Dr. Englund, like every other research doctor in New York, believed with confident arrogance that he was pushing forward the frontiers of science and that he should be funded in this remarkable work with few, if any, questions asked; his televised admonition to the mayor to shut up pretty much summed up his attitude toward any potential critic or inquisitor.

He had been deputized because of his lofty reputation to give the governor an early warning that her commissioner might stir up unnecessary contention if he tried to breach the protective walls of the city's preeminent research institutions.

He had met the governor socially on a number of occasions, but not nearly often enough to call her Randilynn. He had asked at an earlier lunch at the common table of his club whether she was "Madame Governor" or simply "Governor" and had been advised that "Governor" would do.

The conversation, actually a short monologue by the Nobelist, was proper and polite. At the end the governor said she had seen him on television the night before and agreed with him completely.

"They tell me I shoot my mouth off all the time," she said, "but I certainly wouldn't stick my hand in that bucket of worms, if I can use that phrase. What do you suppose got into the mayor?"

"I am at a total loss, Governor. He called me this morning and said he was misquoted, but it was not a satisfactory conversation."

"Is he losing his mind?" she asked hopefully.

"That's a trifle strong, Governor, but he certainly showed bad judgment."

When the conversation ended, she turned to Pedro Raifeartaigh with a cackle. "Listen to this, Raifeartaigh. The most eminent scientist in the Empire State thinks Eldon's losing it. I felt like saying, 'Fuckin'-*A* right he is,' but you know I only talk that way to you, sweetie."

"Yes, Governor." (And, "Three bags full, Governor," he murmured to himself.)

EIGHTEEN

After she had moved her things to her friend Gretchen's, Amber Sweetwater went to the nearest newsstand and looked over the display of front pages, seeking the name of Scoop's publication. There it was. *The Surveyor.*

She called the paper's number, wondering if the operator would know who Scoop was. Fortunately the nickname had been in sufficiently wide use that she did and Amber was put through.

Scoop had been tempted to tell the operator that he was on deadline and to refuse the call, but when he was told it was Amber calling he instantly changed his mind; he remembered that she was the girl from Gracie Mansion.

"Hello."

"This is Amber."

"Yes. You work for the mayor, right?"

"Hmm. Yes."

Before Scoop could ask if he could see her—might not she be the second source he wanted?—she requested a meeting with him.

"I need some advice," she explained.

Scoop had a dilemma. His Wambli story was not going well and was due at noon the next day. But he thought he'd better spare the time to see the girl, just in case she could reveal something that might help him.

They met at Humpty Dumpty's, a bar on Second Avenue. It was deserted at three o'clock in the afternoon, so they could talk freely. Amber told the story of being fired and her desire for revenge.

"Were you mistreated?"

"No, not exactly. She was a real bitch to me but no, I wasn't."

Scoop thought a bit, sipping on a beer. "You a city employee? Civil service? I don't know anything about it, but can't you bring a grievance?"

"I dunno. I wasn't a member of the union. Julio, the chef, joined but I didn't. Couldn't afford the dues on what I was paid."

"Which was?"

"Room and board and a hundred and fifty dollars a week."

"Slave labor! There may be an angle there if you want to go public."

"I'll carry a banner through the street. Naked. If I can get back at them. Specially her."

"Let me think about it."

Amber tentatively brought up the matter of her diary. "You know anything about publishing?" she asked.

"Not much, but I can find out. Why?"

"Well, I did, like, keep a diary of what went on at the mansion."

"You did?" Scoop asked, a light suddenly going on. "Like what happened the night of August sixteenth?"

"Sure. But I don't know anything went on that day."

"Late that night—did the mayor come home with a dog bite on his leg?"

"Gee, I don't remember anything like that. But I'd have to look to see what I wrote."

The pair hurried off to Gretchen's, several blocks away, where the diary was stashed in a box of Amber's meager possessions.

"What was the date again?" she asked, once she had retrieved her bound notebook.

"August sixteenth. A Monday."

"Let's see . . . lunch for Mrs. Hoagland and some people from Ronald McDonald House. We'd been told no hamburgers, so had some kind of tortillas instead. . . . Then she had dinner alone. Ate the rest of the awful chicken gizzards from the night before, I remember. . . . Wait, let's see . . . 'That black jerk Tommy Braddock came down to the kitchen after midnight and woke me up while he searched around for first aid supplies. Said the mayor had a cut on his leg. Very unfriendly. Mayor may have been drunk. . . .'"

"You wrote that? Let me see!" Scoop shouted.

He read the passage and pulled out his own notebook.

"Can I copy this?"

"I guess so," Amber said, puzzled at his excitement.

"Anything else you can tell me about that night?"

"Let me think. Braddock came back later, I remember, with that other creep, Gene Fasco. They sat and drank coffee and had a long conversation. I could hear them, but not much of what they were saying. Except Braddock did raise his voice once, shouting about garbage bags, I think it was."

Scoop wrote this down; were they looking for a garbage bag to dispose of Wambli's body, perhaps?

"Any mention of a dog?"

"Dog? No, I don't think so."

"I've got to go, Amber. I'm on deadline. But let's do Squiggles some night. Can I call you here?"

"Sure. And you will find out about publishing for me, won't you?"

.   .   .

Publishing, indeed. *He* was about to break the story of the year. He returned to the newspaper office and began phoning. Leaky

Swansea. Was the mayor at your apartment on August 16th? ("I don't remember.") Did he get drunk? Slam went the phone.

Gene Fasco and Tommy Braddock (if Amber had their names right). "I'm sorry, it's against department rules for members of the mayor's security guard to talk to the press," the Police Department press officer told him. "But I'll be happy to try and get an answer to any question you may have."

Scoop decided not to pursue the Police Department lead. No point in having the NYPD up in arms before the story ran. Instead he called a press corps buddy from Elaine's, a reporter for *The Post-News,* and asked him if he could find out Fasco's and Braddock's full names. It took his more experienced colleague one phone call to get the information; little did he know he was helping put together a news beat that would acutely embarrass his own paper.

Working through the night, Scoop had a draft ready for Justin Boyd when he appeared in the morning. Boyd scanned it eagerly and announced that it "really kicks Hoagland in the achers."

"Achers?"

"Sorry. Britspeak for 'balls.' Or as I suppose you'd prefer to say, 'testicles.' Be that as it may, I have a few quibbles.

"Park Avenue Pit Bull, the freedom fighter angle, thunder from Jack Gullighy—all that's fine. And that girl, Sweetwater, excellent. But you're too fond of 'appears' and 'apparently,' my boy. Step up to the plate. The mystery doesn't *appear* to be solved, it is solved. And the mayor didn't *apparently* tell his men to shoot the dog, he *did* tell them.

"Then, later, you have him emerging from the apartment building. How about emerging 'unsteadily'? I think we can get away with that."

"By the way," Scoop asked, "you want me to work in something about the animal rights thing?"

"No, no. We'll put a graph or two about that inside, to cover ourselves. But no point in touting the competition's story."

"Don't you have a problem with that? Mine says the mayor ordered his men to shoot Wambli, the other will say he so loves animals that he sided with the ALA."

"That's for him to puzzle out, not me. Isn't it just possible he's a hypocrite?"

. . .

Scoop's story went to press that night, but before *The Surveyor* appeared on the newsstand the following noon, *The Times* was heard from. Contrary to Eldon's belief that the "Public Lives" item would be the end of its coverage, the editors did a full-court press on the ALA controversy, obviously miffed at *The Post-News*'s purple reporting. Under a front-page headline, "Mayor in Bitter Animal Rights Dispute," *The Times* story began: "Mayor Eldon Hoagland yesterday was between the Scylla of the support he gave the militant Animal Liberation Army's position against research involving animal embryos and the Charybdis of the city's medical establishment, vocally opposed to the mayor's stand."

The story, which was restrained and fair, recounted the details. Then it ran quotes from a dozen diverse, and polarized, sources, including Cardinal Lazaro, Dr. Englund, the heads of the National Institutes of Health and the National Right to Life Committee, Barbra Streisand, a spokesman for the National Abortion Rights League and two congressmen embroiled in the embryology-funding controversy in Washington.

The paper also ran three sidebars: a history of the animal rights movement, a status report on the current work being done in embryology and what can only be described as a history of the embryo. The last feature stretched back to quote Galen's second-century treatise *The Formulation of the Fetus* and reproduced a Leonardo da Vinci drawing of a fetus in utero along with a photograph showing a chicken's egg in the third day of gestation. All that was lacking was a pronouncement from the editorial board.

. . .

The Hoaglands, oblivious to *The Times*'s new tack, were spending a quiet evening at Gracie watching *Titanic* on the VCR when Gullighy burst in, copies of the newspaper in hand.

"The fat lady has sung."

He handed over one to Eldon, one to Edna.

Eldon read the whole coverage without comment. Edna did, too, but remarked, "Well, Eldon, this is certainly educational. I know much more about embryos than when I started. And I'm a doctor."

"I don't know what we do," Eldon said, in a toneless voice. "We've got this, and from what you told me earlier, Jack, a piece in *The Surveyor* as well. I'm going back to Minnesota."

"It's gonna be tough, Eldon," Gullighy told him. "But keep cool. You're still the mayor of the greatest city in the world."

"Yes, tonight."

. . .

Scoop's story appeared on schedule on Thursday:

PARK AVENUE MYSTERY SOLVED:
MAYOR'S MEN SHOT PIT BULL

Kosovo Freedom Fighter Recognizes Assailants

Mayor Ordered Cops to "Off" the Dog

By Frederick P. Rice

The brutal killing, reported here last week, of the Park Avenue Pit Bull outside 818 Fifth Avenue on August 16th has been solved. The killers of the dog were two bodyguards of Mayor Eldon Hoagland, acting at his direction.

Last week The Surveyor reported the midnight murder of heiress Sue Nation Brandberg's prize Staffordshire bull terrier, named Wambli, outside the exclusive Fifth Avenue apartment house. The dog's walker at the time he was killed, who originally identified himself to this reporter only as "G," has now come forward to accuse Eugenio R. Fasco and Thomas N. Braddock, two members of the mayor's security detail, of the killing.

Originally, "G" was unwilling to talk on the record but Tuesday, the day after attending the St. Francis Festival on the lawn of Gracie Mansion, he changed his mind. Here are the facts.

"G," identified only by his initial and his past as a soldier in the Balkans fighting for Kosovo's independence, has agreed to go on the record: he is Genc Serreqi, a 26-year-old Albanian who works for Mrs. Brandberg.

Mr. Serreqi attended the mayor's festival for officials and friends of the Coalition for Animal Welfare as a guest of his employer. Previously he had identified the dog's killers only as unknown "men in black suits" that he took to be gangsters. But at the

Gracie Mansion fete he recognized two of the "gangsters" as the mayor's bodyguards—and the third as the mayor, Eldon Hoagland, himself.

It is believed that the mayor was visiting his former Princeton roommate Milford Swansea at the Fifth Avenue address the night of the tragedy, although Swansea, when contacted by this reporter, refused to confirm or deny this.

When the mayor emerged unsteadily from the apartment building, he lost his balance and tripped over the hind leg of the dog, who was pissing at the time. The animal reacted violently and bit the mayor on his right calf.

At this point the two bodyguards opened fire, sending a hail of bullets into the helpless dog's body, presumably killing it. Mr. Serreqi, fearful for his life, as was earlier reported, ran from the scene into the comparative safety of Central Park.

At the time of the fracas, Serreqi alleges, he heard the mayor tell his men to "off" the dog, and their shots were in response to his command.

Additional confirmation for this account comes from the testimony of Amber Sweetwater, 24, until this week a nonunion employee in the kitchen at the mansion.

Sweetwater told this reporter that on the night in question Officer Braddock came down to the kitchen, after he and his partner had brought the mayor home, in search of first aid supplies. Later, he and Sgt. Fasco had a long conversation over coffee in the mansion kitchen. Sweetwater, who slept in a small adjoining room, could hear their voices but not what they were saying, except for a reference to "garbage bags"—possibly as a means of disposing of the dog's body.

Last Tuesday, Sweetwater was abruptly fired from her job in the Gracie Mansion kitchen by Edna Hoagland, the mayor's wife, for unspecified reasons. It is not known whether her dismissal was related to knowledge she may have had of the dog's slaying.

Neither Mayor Hoagland nor his wife was available for comment concerning Serreqi's grave allegation. However, John R. Gullighy, the mayor's press secretary and close political confidant, said that the allegations were "absolutely untrue" and "somebody's hallucination."

"I have no idea what happened to that dog, if anything," he told The Surveyor. "All I know is that Mayor Hoagland spent that evening with an old friend and came home, as was customary, with his bodyguards." He acknowledged that the two plainclothesmen were Fasco and Braddock but said he had no way of knowing whether they had been dressed in black.

"You better be careful with this one, young man," Gullighy warned this reporter. "I think you've got an unstable young fellow on your hands. You'd better be sure of your ground."

The Public Affairs Bureau of the Police Department refused to let the two suspected murderers talk to this reporter. Nor would the bureau spokesman confirm or deny whether the police had any record of the shooting, or if a Firearms Discharge Report had been filed, as is required whenever a police officer's weapon is fired.

Asked if there had been a cover-up, Gullighy angrily dismissed the idea. "To have a cover-up, there has to be something to cover up. That was not the case here."

Ms. Brandberg, a former Native American beauty contest winner and widow of billionaire industrialist Harry Brandberg, said that she believed her employee, Serreqi, "completely." "I'm out-raged. All I can say is, I hope the mayor and his goons will be brought to justice."

Ainsley Potter, chairman of the Coalition for Animal Welfare, also expressed shock at the charge. "The mayor very hospitably en-tertained us last Monday and appeared to be a friend of animals. But if this charge is correct, it is reprehensible."

Will the mayor have to resign? this reporter asked. "If the allega-tion turns out to be true, I would certainly think so."

[The mayor's bad week: embroils himself in animal rights con-troversy. Story, page 3; editorial, page 6.]

Justin Boyd's editorial was hard-hitting:

LIFT YOUR PANTS LEG, MR. MAYOR

Mayor Eldon Hoagland has a crisis on his hands. We aren't refer-ring to his pusillanimous dispute with a bunch of animal rights cra-zies over the esoterics of embryological research, but the serious charge of dog murder leveled against him by a young Kosovo free-dom fighter, Genc Serreqi.

As our front-page story today details, this brave young man, fresh from bloodshed in the Balkans, was walking a young dog on Fifth Avenue when it was cold-bloodedly shot by three men he has since identified as Mayor Hoagland and his two bodyguards. The shoot-ing took place, according to Serreqi, after the dog bit the mayor on his right leg and the mayor ordered his men to shoot.

This is a serious charge, going to the question of the mayor's judgment and character. As one of his earliest and most enthusi-

astic supporters, we would be both shocked and saddened if Serreqi's tale were true.

The mayor's spokesman has emphatically denied the story, and further denied that there has been any attempt to cover up the incident.

Who should we believe? We need to know the truth. And there
seems to us a sure way to determine that truth: permit an indepen-
dent physician to examine Eldon Hoagland's right leg for signs of a
dog bite. If the telltale evidence is there, we are owed an explanation. If it's not, we'll be the first to apologize to him.

Lift your pants leg, Mayor Hoagland, and let's see the truth!

. . .

"All right, Jack, what do we do about *this?*" Eldon demanded, drumming his fingers on the latest *Surveyor*.

"Keep your pants on. Literally and figuratively."

"Very funny."

"What's your choice? Deny, deny, deny. You're going to have to
do it in person very soon, you know. You can't hide behind my
skirts forever."

"Hmn."

"As for the take-off-your-pants thing, you can ignore that. It's a
silly, undignified demand. Justin Boyd sensationalism."

"I don't understand Justin. He was my biggest supporter. Why
would he turn on me like this?"

"He's a journalist."

. . .

After leaving his distraught employer, Jack Gullighy turned his attention to another idea. If this Albanian freedom fighter *The Sur-*

veyor wrote about was an illegal, as everyone seemed to believe, why not get him deported? Pursuing the mayor would be a lot harder if the principal witness were back in the Balkans, he reasoned.

To that end he called an acquaintance in the Immigration and Naturalization Service information office. The latter had not seen *The Surveyor* story, so Gullighy filled him in.

"If he's a wetback, and we think he is, it doesn't look too good for you guys—an illegal alien getting these headlines," Gullighy explained and then, helpfully, supplied his contact with Sue Nation Brandberg's address.

A long shot, Gullighy realized, but with calamity just around the corner it was worth a try.

.　.　.

That morning, before *The Surveyor* story appeared, Sue Brandberg had called Brendon Proctor and asked him to come and see her. The lawyer, aware that he was in at least temporary disfavor with his client, said he would come by as soon as he could that afternoon. Her intention was to work out the details of her marital arrangements with Genc. Then, after she had read Scoop's article, she began to have second thoughts. The story of her dog's assassination was out; it seemed only a question of time before Eldon Hoagland would be brought to account. Was Genc necessary to the process? Perhaps he was. But what if he was not? Did she really care if he was deported?

After a few minutes' reflection, she decided that she did indeed want him around, with those cries of OOOH! SHPIRT! So when Proctor arrived, she told him that she was going to marry Genc Serreqi.

The wisps of hair on Proctor's bald head were sticking out, as usual; had they not been, her announcement would certainly have propelled them outward.

"Mrs. Brandberg, you are serious?"

"Absolutely. He's a charming young man. And I think I love him."

"I certainly hope you're going to have a prenuptial agreement."

"That's what I wanted to ask you about. Do I need one?"

"*Need* one! He's penniless, I'm sure, and you have millions. If you should die, he could get half your estate." He didn't add that given the discrepancy in the lovebirds' ages, it was probable that she would predecease Genc.

"What about children?" Proctor asked.

"Children? At my age?"

"You might adopt."

"Most unlikely."

"Well, you might want to cover that. I assume he's some sort of Muslim or Mohammadan or whatever. And I'm sure you'd want your children to be raised as Christians."

"Not necessarily. There are Native American religions, you know." She enjoyed making Proctor uncomfortable.

"Oh yes, I see."

"But I don't think I need to pay for a lawyer's time to draft clauses about our children's religion. The money, yes. I understand that part of it."

"I'll need a schedule of your assets. But I guess I can put that together for you."

"Fine. The sooner the better."

"He spells his name *S-E-R-R-E-Q-I?* No 'U' after the 'Q'?"

"That's right."

"Most odd. Are you absolutely sure, Mrs. Brandberg, that you want to go through with this?"

"Yes, Brendon. As certain as I am that I want you for my lawyer."

NINETEEN

The flow of e-mail to Eldon kept growing. And there was no middle ground in the messages received:

You halfwit! Go back out west, where the gun is king! We New Yorkers are more civilized, in case you hadn't noticed.

First your police kill my people, now they kill animals. Watch out when we turn our guns on you!

Only one message (secretly) pleased Eldon:

Good for you! If I had my way, I'd shoot every dog in New York City. The crap on the streets, stupid owners who can't, or won't, control their little—and big—Fidos. I wish I could say you've shown us the way, but the bleeding hearts would never let us get away with it.

The Surveyor may have downplayed *The Post-News*'s coverage of the embryology controversy, but the daily gleefully picked up on the Wambli scandal the morning after Scoop's second story appeared. Giving its weekly rival a boost was of minor significance when there was such a delicious opportunity to attack the mayor. THUGS KILL PUPPY AS MAYOR STANDS BY, the front page screamed, beside a stock photo of a Staffordshire bull terrier (not Wambli). Except for changing the Park Avenue pit bull into a lovable puppy, the story was basically a rewrite of Scoop's.

The editorial in the same edition was something else again:

THE BLOOD ON ELDON
HOAGLAND'S HANDS

New Yorkers are used to shocks and scandals, but seldom has the city been shaken as profoundly as by the revelation that two armed thugs in the employ of Mayor Eldon Hoagland brutally shot a helpless puppy in the supposedly safe precincts of upper Fifth Avenue. And shot the defenseless animal at the direction of the mayor himself.

The shooting, described in our story beginning on page 1, terrorized the young Albanian freedom fighter who was walking the dog, Wambli, when the ferocious assassination occurred. It ought to terrorize the rest of us, too: employees of our city wantonly slaughtering a tiny animal at the behest of the mayor. Granted Wambli was not pumped full of 41 bullets as in the infamous police-shooting case our readers will remember, but the fusillade was nonetheless gruesome enough.

The mayor continues to deny any involvement. We frankly don't believe him. But if he is innocent, there is an easy way to prove it. As another publication opined yesterday, all he has to do is let his leg be examined for evidence of the bite that supposedly led to the killing.

If, as we believe, the mayor is lying, we are of the opinion that he has little choice but to resign. We cannot tolerate a first magistrate who does not tell the truth, or who condones the outright killing of a pet beloved by one of our city's most socially conscious citizens, Sue Nation Brandberg.

Mayor Hoagland, do not cover up any further. Uncover, and let us have the true facts. We await your decision.

. . .

"It's certainly nice to be trusted by one of the two biggest newspapers in your city," Eldon told Edna at breakfast.

"Postnewspaper, dear."

"Now I know how Bill Clinton must have felt when that Jones woman's lawyers wanted to examine his prick. 'Distinctive characteristics,' I believe they were looking for."

"Well, you've certainly got them. That bite is still ugly."

"And nobody's going to see it."

. . .

"You've got to have a press conference," Gullighy told his boss later that morning at City Hall.

"Let's wait another day, or better, over the weekend. Or still better yet, next Wednesday, after the Columbus Day holiday. Let things settle down."

"All right, but I'm afraid it's not going to get any better."

"You're not thinking I should do what the *Post-News* says, are you?"

"Hell, no. You've got *some* dignity left to protect."

"Thanks," Eldon said, not much liking his aide's emphasis on "some."

"By the way, the wound's not fully healed, I take it?"

"No, dammit. And it itches."

. . .

It was a rare occurrence, but leaving City Hall that afternoon the mayor and his entourage ran smack into Randilynn Foote and hers as they came down the stairs from the Governor's Rooms. Surface politeness prevailed, but the surface was very thin.

"Hello, Governor."

"Greetings, Mr. Mayor. Nice suit you got on there. I especially like the pants. Mind if I feel them?"

Eldon backed away, defensive and horrified.

"Just kidding, Mayor. Just kidding."

. . .

The mayor was on his way to a ribbon cutting at a garment factory in the Bronx. The new enterprise was exactly the sort of project he had tried to encourage: a new business creating jobs in an economically deprived area, unionized, free of mob influence and not a sweatshop. As an added dividend the owner was a dynamic—and attractive—Hispanic, Laura Cata, who had been an ardent supporter in his election campaign, not least because of his commitment to helping start-up businesses.

After the bruising he had taken for days, he was gratified at his reception: a sensuous buss from Ms. Cata (no air-kissing here) and rousing cheers and applause from the rainbow crowd of workers—mostly women—Asian, Hispanic and black. They were all wearing bright yellow T-shirts inscribed CATA, INC.; he was presented with one and, when he handed it off to Gene Fasco, the onlookers protested. So he took off his jacket and put it on over his shirt, to even more shouts of approval.

He hoped that the pool photographer accompanying him would get the right picture—the smiles of the owner and the local Bronx politicians in attendance, the enthusiastic crowd. Send *that* to *The Post-News!*

Ms. Cata's introduction was fulsome. Eldon rose to the occasion with some short, graceful remarks—even working in a reference to *ciudad grande*. Then, after a glass of the sparkling wine being passed and shaking hands all around, he headed back toward his car with his hostess, pleased and exhilarated. Suddenly, out of nowhere, a large golden retriever ran out and nuzzled Ms. Cata, its owner. She was as affectionate as she would have been with a small baby and introduced the creature, Miguel, to the mayor.

Mercifully there were no jokes about canine homicides, and Eldon, steeling himself, even made a tentative gesture to pet the dog. The crowd applauded some more, the photographer snapped away and the mayor left in friendly triumph.

"Better than last time," he muttered to Fasco and Braddock as they headed back to Manhattan.

．　．　．

Maybe better than last time, but it turned out only marginally so. The next morning's *Post-News* featured the photograph of Miguel and Eldon—the cheering crowd cropped out—on the front page, revealing a dogphobe's steely smile that scarcely concealed underlying fear and loathing. "Better Watch Out, Doggie," the caption began. And in the upper left corner of the front page was a black-bordered box—

BITE   *Day 2*

WATCH

—presumably referring to the mayor's reluctance to lift his pants leg.

• • •

"Can't win 'em all, Mr. Mayor," Gullighy told his boss helpfully Wednesday morning.

"Thank you."

"I've scheduled the press conference for two o'clock. You want to make a statement, or just get up and stonewall?"

"I want a statement about that embryo business. That I'm un-equivocally in favor of properly conducted, responsible research on animal embryos. The rest I'll handle. Okay?"

"You got it."

"Meanwhile, if you will permit, I have a meeting with the Technology Zone Task Force. It will be nice to do some substantive work around this place for a change."

• • •

The meeting with the task force should have been a triumph. The chairman, Don Mead, was Eldon's commissioner of economic development. He was a former Wall Street investment banker with both a brain and a social conscience. He had been in the Peace Corps in Nigeria and had an idealistic view of the world that he had managed to retain even while rising to the top at an aggressive Wall Street banking house. He could be brash and tough—he had had to be in the brutal internal wars within his own firm—but he had avoided the seduction of regarding the ever-expanding accumulation of personal wealth, formerly known as greed, as his ultimate goal in life. He was that interesting and rare phenomenon, a true liberal who was also a multimillionaire.

Like Eldon, he shared the view that good could be done for—and more important, with—the poor, mis- and uneducated, often dysfunctional underclass. Eldon had spotted him on one study commission or another, and easily, as it turned out, persuaded him to join the Hoagland administration.

Mead's brief from the professorial Eldon had been to put aside the (failed) clichés of the War on Poverty, Urban Renewal (with a capital "U" and a capital "R") and the other nostrums for dealing with urban deprivation.

"I know they say if you teach a man to fish he will eat for a lifetime," Eldon had told him. "But that ignores that the waters he will fish in are polluted, his fishing gear is likely to be stolen and his family will soon tire of an all-fish diet. We need new approaches, Don, and you're a tough enough son of a bitch to develop them. The technology zone first and foremost."

Mead had accepted the challenge, at a cut in income that meant little to him, and assembled the Technology Zone Task Force from within and without the city administration. They were all present today in the mayor's conference room: Sal Miskovitz, an extraordinary number cruncher and municipal budget expert from the comptroller's office; Mina Gordon, Mead's cool assistant and an alumna of another downtown banking firm; Jared Vaughan, a black economist from the Finance Administration who had actually visited (or more precisely, grown up in) one of the desolate areas that were the task force's concern. The three staff members were two Ph.D. candidates from Columbia whom Eldon had supervised, Mary Palucci and Christopher Lehrman, and a young intern, Garry Spiller, from the Public Affairs Program at NYU.

This serious group rose as one when Eldon entered the room, which he circled, shaking hands. There were empty coffee cups amid the papers on the table, but no one had left exposed a copy of the morning *Post-News* (which they had all read avidly).

"What have you got for me?" he asked as he sat down next to Mead.

"Mr. Mayor, we hope we have a doable technology zone proposal and one that won't break your budget."

"Good. That's what I like to hear."

Spiller handed Eldon a stapled set of pages that duplicated the sheets on a flip chart at one end of the long conference table. Then he went and turned the title page on the visual display.

"Here it is in a nutshell," Mead explained. "One billion spread over five years to start the highest-technology state-of-the-art complex anywhere. That includes the construction of a high school building and a new City College branch at the site. As you will see, the potential is for a minimum of five thousand high school and college graduates within eight years and a minimum of forty-five hundred new jobs at the end of five."

"The schools. I hope they'll teach computer skills and not just how to change a spark plug."

"Yessir. That's a later chart. You'll see that."

"What about tax breaks for the industries coming in? You include them as a cost in your billion?"

"No, we do not. Hopefully the tax deals will be at a minimum and the chance for skilled labor in a convenient location will be enough to attract plenty of high-tech upstarts. We don't want tax considerations to be the tail wagging the dog."

Mead, intent on his presentation, did not realize his unfortunate choice of metaphor. Jared Vaughan did and hastily covered his mouth, though it was unclear whether to conceal a look of amazement or a grin. The others sat stock-still with pursed lips. Eldon stared intently at the chart.

"Show the map, Garry," Mead instructed. "As you can see, the location we have picked in the South Bronx is conveniently located next to railroad sidings and arterial highways, as well as subway and bus lines."

The exposition went on, and Eldon tried desperately to focus his attention on what was being said. The subject was a favorite one— he saw the zone program as the capstone of his administration— but his mind kept going back to the Incident, to the morning's headlines, to the upcoming press conference.

He realized he must "compartmentalize," as they had said so recently in Washington, putting Wambli in one part of his brain and this bold new program in another. It was nearly impossible and he now realized, as he had only suspected back then, that compartmentalizing was a fiction; if your adversaries were trying to wreck your house, it was damn hard to sit in the living room insouciantly sipping a cocktail. Your survival instincts fought against attempts to focus on anything other than the imminent danger that threatened to destroy you and your reputation.

Eldon could not let his feelings show. His task force had worked hard and had, as near as he could tell in his agitated state, done a masterful piece of work in realizing his vision of a "technological Radio City" for the new century. So with great force of will he tried to be attentive, asking questions that he knew were perfunctory and that he would have treated with some disdain in a seminar back at Columbia.

After 45 minutes, Mead, with justifiable pride, concluded by saying that the study, if implemented, "could turn this city around for good." He democratically asked his colleagues if they had comments to add. They didn't, except for Miskovitz, who said the projected numbers were solid, and Mina Gordon, who said there had been an "amazing" amount of agreement within the group on the recommendations being made.

"This is great work, Don, and I thank all of you," Eldon told them. "You've given me lots to think about. I'll get back to you just as soon as I can, then let's finalize this thing and get your report out. Agreed?"

They all did, and the meeting broke up.

TWENTY

Gullighy was waiting outside the conference room where the task force meeting had taken place. "Here's the embryo statement. What else do you want? Shouldn't we do a practice Q & A?"

"What the hell for?" Eldon snapped. "You keep saying I should deny, deny, deny. Stonewall. What difference does it make what the damn questions are?"

"Okay, okay. I'll be in my office if you have fixes to the statement."

"Fine. Right now I just want to be left alone. I'll have lunch at my desk. Have them get me a roast beef on rye. Rare, raw animal meat, please."

. . .

Eldon entered his office and closed the door. Normally when he was organizing his thoughts he looked at the passing scene outside his window; today he stared at the portrait of Fiorello La Guardia that, in a spirit of nonpartisanship, he had ordered placed over the mantel. Had the Little Flower ever stonewalled? he wondered.

At length he reviewed Gullighy's draft. It was fine. Unequivocal. No animal would be safe from embryological research after the statement was disseminated. Then he pulled out a legal pad and began writing his statement about the Incident. Although he was computer literate, the printer for his PC was outside by his secretary's desk. What he was writing he did not want examined in advance, hence the legal pad. After tearing up two false starts, he began again. Satisfied with the result, he ate his sandwich, which was properly bloody, and drank a diet iced tea.

By the time he had finished, Gullighy was knocking at the door and was summoned in.

"You ready, Mr. Mayor?"

"Ready to be fed to the lions, you mean? Or should I say the dogs?"

"It's standing room only in there. All the TV outfits. The London papers, for Chrissake."

"They love animals over there."

"Must be a hundred bodies in all."

"Let's go."

"You sure you don't want a quick Q & A practice?"

"Nope. Come on."

As they walked across to the Blue Room and toward the crowd overflowing out into the hall, Gullighy inquired in a low voice, "What are you going to say when they ask you to lift your pants leg and show the bite?"

"What my grandfather would have said back in Minnesota: *Kyss mig i arslet.*"

"What the hell does that mean?"

"'Kiss my ass.'"

"Don't say it, please."

. . .

The Blue Room was so crowded that Eldon and Gullighy had difficulty reaching the podium. People tried to move aside to let them through, but progress was still difficult in the crush. All the cameras, still and TV, seemed to be pointing down toward the mayor's legs.

188

Eldon pulled his papers from his suit pocket and smoothed them out on the podium. "I have three statements," he began.

"First. I spent this morning with Don Mead and the members of his task force studying the question of a technology zone for the city. He and his brilliant group have given me a preliminary report, which I'm not prepared to discuss until it has been finalized. But I can say that the task force has done a splendid job, and we should have something for you very soon. I'm excited about the report and maybe even you cynics will be, too.

"Second. I want to clear up any possible misunderstanding about my views on embryological research on animals. Through what I can only call some careless editing of the tapes of me at the St. Francis Festival at Gracie a week ago, it was made to appear that I am against such research. I was not and am not. New York is one of the great medical research centers in the world and it is certainly not the mayor's place to do anything other than stand in awe of the wonders that are accomplished here. The proper treatment of animal subjects is, I am certain, more than adequately handled by surveillance committees at the various research institutions. They do not need me interfering, and I have not done so. Is that clear?"

There were desultory murmurs from the pack of reporters and several hands were raised seeking recognition.

"No questions. Let me go on to the third matter. That is the killing, by my bodyguards, of Mrs. Sue Nation Brandberg's dog."

This simple declaration, acknowledging what had theretofore only been speculated about, was met with an excited buzz. Gullighy had a beet red, I-don't-believe-what-I'm-hearing look on his face. Eldon raised his hand for quiet and then spelled out how he had "accidentally" stepped on the dog "while it was relieving itself." The animal had reacted by biting him "quite viciously," and his two police bodyguards, "fearful for my safety," shot Wambli.

"I sincerely apologize to Mrs. Brandberg for what happened. And I apologize to the citizens of New York for not bringing this matter to an end sooner than I have. It is now my hope that we can move forward and not let a dead dog divert our attention from where it belongs: on the technology zone program and on our other initiatives for moving this city forward. And perhaps now you gentlemen and ladies can once again start reporting the news, instead of what I like to call postnews.

"Thank you. There will be no questions today."

Pandemonium broke out as Eldon headed out of the room. Many raced to the door to relay the news, others dialed their cell phones and began dictating their stories in the Blue Room itself. And all microphones were directed at Eldon. He ignored the questions shouted at him. "Have you talked to Sue Brandberg?" "Are you going to pay her?" "What happened to the dog's body?" "Have you had a rabies shot?" Everything except whether he believed that Wambli had gone to heaven.

· · ·

With Gullighy running interference, Eldon got back to the safety of his office.

"Sorry to disappoint you, Jack."

"It was your call, Mr. Mayor."

"I just had to put an end to all the nonsense. This city would have come to a halt if I hadn't. I've cleared the air and we can go on to other things."

"I hope you're right. I hope you're right."

. . .

Scoop Rice had attended the mayor's press conference. Most of the reporters present did not know him but one or two who did congratulated him as they filed out. "See what you started?" one said. "Great job."

Taxiing back to *The Surveyor* office, he was less sure that the "job" had been so great. Sure, he'd broken the story that had preoccupied the local media for over a month. But what had he really accomplished? Making the world safer for democracy? Uncovering corrupt skulduggery in high places? No, he told himself, he had caused great pain—obvious from Eldon's subdued and sober demeanor—to a guy who got caught up in a minor and silly incident. Involving a dog, for shit's sake. Was this what investigative reporting was about? Woodward and Bernstein wouldn't have bothered. It was *National Enquirer* stuff when you came right down to it.

And even if it was investigative reporting, he hadn't exactly covered himself with glory. He had missed leads that in hindsight seemed obvious, and the reality was that the story broke only because Genc Serreqi had recognized Wambli's killers at the mayor's festival—an event he had not even attended. His reportorial digging had not been responsible.

Furthermore, what about his boss? Shamelessly boosting Eldon Hoagland for months and then turning on him when the chance for a hot headline came along—is that what journalism was about?

Back at the office he tried to convey some of his thoughts to Justin Boyd. Unlike his fledgling reporter, Boyd had no reservations about what he had done. "My boy, as sure as eggs is eggs you've uncovered the story of the year. Nobody's going to top it. So what if it embarrassed the mayor? He never should have been in politics in the first place, if you ask me. You're just having a little postpartum depression. Go have some drinks with the boys at Elaine's. You're a full-fledged member of the reporters' club up there now. Bask in the glory!"

Scoop was still troubled, and headed off instead to Squiggles. Maybe by this time some of the girls would have heard of the Wambli scandal and, he hoped, his part in it.

TWENTY-ONE

Wheels within the Immigration and Naturalization Service office moved slowly, but on the day of Eldon's confession, the seed planted by Jack Gullighy sprouted. Immigration enforcers liked the idea of bagging an alien prominent in the public eye, and Genc Serreqi qualified. Their computer searches had determined that he had long overstayed his tourist visa so that midmorning two agents paid a call at 62nd Street.

Luckily Sue had sent Genc off to get a haircut, less because she objected to his fulsome locks than because he needed a good professional shampoo. So she was alone when the government operatives appeared at her door.

Showing their badges, they explained that they were inquiring about one Genc Serreqi. Did she know him?

"Yes," she said warily.

"Can you tell us any more about him?"

"He works for me. He's my houseboy."

"Is he here? We'd like to talk to him."

"No, he's out at the moment. Can I ask what this is about?"

"Our records show that Serreqi is here illegally. His visa expired months ago. He must leave the country. And I should also warn you, Mrs. Brandberg, that you are subject to penalties for employing an illegal alien."

"I see," she said calmly, secure in the knowledge that her impending marriage would solve all problems.

"Where is he, Mrs. Brandberg?"

"He's been away." Thinking quickly, she told them he was visiting an old pal from her designing days. "He's with my friend Barbara Hopson up in Westchester."

The gumshoes looked dubious.

"He's an accomplished gardener, you know," Sue invented. "He's working temporarily for Barbara."

"What town in Westchester?"

"Bedford."

How could she get them out of the house? Genc might return, shorn, any minute.

"I do have the telephone number," she said eagerly. "Let me get it."

Sue retrieved her Filofax from the bedroom—quickly—and gave her questioners the number.

"If he returns, will you let us know?"

She nodded but said nothing.

Each of the Immigration agents gave her his card.

"I'll certainly let you know," she told them. "But right now you'll have to excuse me as my trainer will be here any minute."

"Fine, Mrs. Brandberg. I trust you will keep us informed about Serreqi's whereabouts."

The two men left before Genc's return, a mere five minutes later. He found her talking in an agitated way to Barbara Hopson, arranging a cover for her prospective husband. She put down the phone as he inquired whether she liked his new blow-dry hairdo.

"Yes, yes. It's gorgeous. But we have something else to talk about. The Immigration people are after you. We've got to go to the barricades."

"Barricades?"

"Shut up. Listen to me. I'm getting you a room at the Carlyle

Hotel. Under the name Gene Brandberg. You go there until I call you. Don't talk to anyone. The room will be paid for, so you don't have to do anything except to register under that name. Meanwhile, I've got to figure out how we can get married. Like this afternoon or tomorrow."

"That's what you want, Miszu?"

"Yes. Now hurry. You know where the hotel is. I took you there once. Madison and Seventy-sixth. Go there, lock yourself in your room and keep your trap shut."

"Trap?"

"Oh, Genc, just cooperate. Otherwise you'll be on the plane to Tirana before you know it. Call me and let me know your room number right away. Take a small bag with you so they won't ask questions."

"We are really going to get married, Miszu?"

"Yes, today, if I can arrange it."

. . .

Once Genc had left she called the Carlyle. The hotel, she was told, was fully booked, except for the Presidential Suite ($4,000 per night). She had no choice but to reserve it, asking the self-styled "reservationist" to have the bill sent to her.

"I'll need a credit card reference, Sue," the hotel operative said, affecting the first-name familiarity one associated with motel chains, not the Carlyle.

"Listen. I don't think you know to whom you're speaking. This is Sue Nation Brandberg, and if your credit manager doesn't know the name he's an idiot."

"Can you hold for a moment, Sue?"

In increasing fury, Sue listened to a canned version of the *Doctor Zhivago* theme as the reservationist put her on hold.

"Mrs. Brandberg?" she said when she came back. "Of course we will send you the bill. Twenty-nine East Sixty-second Street, is it? We look forward to welcoming Mr. Brandberg."

Officious airhead, Sue thought. Then she called Brendon Proctor.

"Brendon, that prenuptial agreement. Can you have it ready this afternoon?"

Proctor's face tightened, but this being a client he wanted very much to retain, he answered affirmatively.

"And Brendon, will you please tell me what one has to do to get a marriage license? I need to know that now. Call me immediately."

Proctor deeply resented her request. In his years as a trust and estates lawyer, he had often been jerked around by wealthy clients, but seldom as peremptorily as this. And to find out information that in his lofty but wide and varied practice he hadn't a clue about.

Reluctantly he called Chase & Ward's managing clerk, who possessed, or knew how to obtain, such esoteric knowledge. Proctor had visions of a rumor sweeping the office within minutes that he, the perennial and contented bachelor, was about to tie the knot. But there was nothing he could do about that.

The answer came back in minutes: both parties had to appear in person at the Municipal Building downtown with unexpired picture IDs—passports were best—and documents relating to any prior marriage. Plus a money order for $30.

"*Money order!* Nobody's used a money order since the Second World War!"

"That's what they said, Mr. Proctor. No cash, no checks, no credit cards. Money order only."

"For Christ's sake."

"And there's a twenty-four-hour waiting period after the license is issued."

"Thanks. Thanks a bunch."

"Oh, and a blood test is no longer required."

"Will miracles never cease?"

. . .

Proctor relayed his newly acquired knowledge to his client. She was not fazed by the document requirements: surely Genc had a passport and she had hers. And she knew her marriage certificate and poor Harry's death certificate were in the safe upstairs in the bedroom. But the money order requirement flummoxed her, as it had Proctor. As did the 24-hour waiting period.

"Look, Brendon, you get the money order and come to the Carlyle Hotel, with that prenuptial agreement, at three o'clock. No later. Ask for Mr. Gene Brandberg. Oh, and Proctor, get a car. We have to get to the Municipal Building before the Marriage Bureau closes. And I'm sure there's some way that twenty-four-hour requirement can be waived. I'll tell them I'm about to give birth."

"I doubt we can do that, Sue. Got to give the prospective newlyweds time for a final day's reflection. And who, by the way, is going to perform the ceremony?"

"I don't give a damn, Proctor. Cardinal Lazaro perhaps. Can't they marry you right there at the license place?"

"I assume so but I don't know it," Proctor answered testily, angry with himself that he had not asked that question of his managing clerk. "But you're going to have to wait twenty-four hours, I'm sure of it."

"To use an old Native American expression, Proctor, eaglefuck!"

. . .

Eldon had no idea what had gone on that day in Sue Brandberg's life when he called her after his press conference. He felt he had to make a personal apology to bring closure, as the postmoderns say, to the Wambli affair.

"Sue, it distresses me to tell you this, but those newspaper accounts of your dog's death are pretty much true. Your dog *did* bite me quite badly, after I accidentally stepped on him, but shooting him was wrong."

"Thank you, Mr. Mayor, I appreciate the call, though Wambli's death was probably the single worst thing that has ever happened in my life."

"I understand. What can I do to make it up to you?"

Sue, still upset and confused about her plan to save Genc from deportation, had a brainstorm.

"You can perform marriages, can't you?"

"I think so. I've never done it. But yes, I'm sure I can."

"Eldon, in a little while I'm going for a marriage license and I want to get married today."

"And who are you marrying?"

"Genc. The man who was walking Wambli."

Eldon swallowed hard but then offered his congratulations, improbable as the union seemed.

"There's only one problem," Sue told the mayor. "There's apparently a twenty-four-hour waiting period after you get the license. But I'm sure you as the mayor can waive that. Can't you?"

"I have no idea. But I'll find out. If I can do it, I will."

"Then we can let bygones be bygones, Eldon. Can you find out and let me know in, say, an hour?"

Eldon told her he would do his best and took down the number at the Carlyle. At once he called Noel Miller, his corporation counsel. Thirty minutes later the lawyer called back.

"I can't give you a clear answer," he informed the mayor. "The statute says twenty-four hours. But it is at least arguable that you can exercise your inherent powers as mayor to give a waiver."

"These days I'm not sure I have any powers, inherent or otherwise."

"The best thing to do would be to have your couple wait. What the hell is the emergency?"

"I can't say for sure," the mayor said.

"Well, I don't think you'll go to jail if you waive the requirement, but it's not a great idea."

.　　.　　.

Miller's lukewarm blessing was enough in the circumstances. He called Sue at the hotel and relayed the news.

"Can you marry us at five o'clock? Brendon Proctor tells me the Marriage Bureau is across the street from you."

"Sue, I obviously owe you one. Come at five o'clock, to the back entrance on the Court Street side. I'll have Jack Gullighy meet you."

.　　.　　.

The mayor called in his press secretary and told him the situation.

"Great! You think you can get her to say all is forgiven? This place is still crawling with reporters and she could make a statement. First break you've had in a long time, Eldon."

"Yes."

. . .

At the Carlyle, luxuriating in the velvety splendor of the Presidential Suite, Sue told Genc and Brendon of the plan to have the mayor perform the marriage. The lawyer, at his most businesslike, explained the intricacies of the prenuptial agreement he had drawn up. He was especially careful to explain the provisions to Genc; he was nervous that the young man did not have his own lawyer, but there wasn't time for that.

He was not the only one nervous. Genc's stomach was churning. He had assumed the marriage ceremony would be a quiet one performed by a functionary in the registry office, or whatever it was called. Not one performed by the mayor of the city, and one sure to attract publicity that just might get back to Tirana. The prospective groom also little understood Proctor's legal exegesis of the prenuptial agreement. What was he getting into?

"The one thing we need, Mr. Serreqi, is a list of your property to be attached to the agreement."

Genc shrugged.

"My sneakers? My jeans? My suit?"

"No, no. Bank accounts, investments, real estate. That sort of thing."

"Nothing, sir. The only valuable possession I have is a ring, which is back at Mrs. Brandberg's."

"What ring, Genc? I've never seen you wear one."

"I don't wear, I keep. It is a family ring."

Prompted by the lawyer he described it as a simple gold band, but with some small diamonds embedded in the front.

Proctor wrote in the description on Exhibit B (Exhibit A consisting of 98 pages inventorying Sue's more valuable assets).

After signing, the trio took off in the car Proctor had hired. There was a quick stop at 62nd Street, where Genc changed into his Armani suit, recovered his Albanian passport from under his mattress and took down the prized ring from the back of the top closet shelf in his room. He stared at the ring for a long moment before slipping it into his pocket.

Back in the car he showed the ring to Sue, who was now wearing a well-tailored but simple green dress (her usual black somehow had not seemed appropriate for the occasion).

"It's beautiful," she said, though it was much less ostentatious than any of her jewelry. "My God. We need a wedding ring! Can we use this one? Will you give it to me, Genc?"

Serreqi seemed hesitant, but then said, "Of course, Miszu."

Proctor hurried them along, warning that time was running out.

.   .   .

At the Marriage License Bureau, Genc and Sue sat side by side filling out the obligatory forms. When he came to the question about previous marriages, he leaned over and whispered to Sue, outside of Proctor's hearing.

"Miszu, there is something I must tell you. That ring I have? It was my wedding ring."

"I know," she said impatiently. "We already agreed we'd use it."

"No, it is *my* wedding ring. You see, I have a wife in Albania."

"You what?"

"I'm sorry. I had to tell you. Greta, my wife. She is in Tirana. We were separated before I left, but we never were divorce-ed. Here is a picture." He pulled out his wallet and extracted a faded snapshot showing a couple in the back of a rose-bedecked donkey cart— Genc in a dark jacket, the woman in a white dress.

"Fine time to bring this up! I don't believe it. You had a steady girlfriend. You lived with her. But you were not married," Sue said, denying the pictorial evidence before her. "And no children, for God's sake?"

"No, no children. But we married. Greta and me."

"Well, maybe in Albania. By the communists. Nobody would recognize that marriage here."

"Are you sure, Miszu? Should I ask Mr. Proctor?"

"No! Take my word for it. So there, where it says, were you ever married, the answer is *N-O*, no." She pointed to the space on the form in front of Genc.

Genc looked dubious but complied. A green card was a green card. But would this lie on an official form trip him up somehow, green card or no green card? The churning in his stomach did not cease.

As they left the bureau, license in hand, Sue spoke sternly to her husband-to-be. "I never want to hear about this Greta again. Do you understand me? Never."

"Yes, Miszu."

.   .   .

As Eldon had advised, Sue, Brendon and Genc slipped into the back door of City Hall, but not before Genc had impulsively bought his bride a small bouquet of autumn daisies from a street vendor. The mayor was ready for them, having obtained from Miller a copy of the form of words he was to use for the ceremony. He greeted his guests with what warmth he could muster in his exhausted state.

"Mr. Mayor, are you sure you can do this—that you can waive the waiting period? I haven't researched the matter," Proctor said. He wanted to cover himself, especially since he was certain he'd be pressed into service as a witness.

"I'm assured that I can. So shall we proceed? Oh—witnesses. You, I assume, Brendon. But what about a bridesmaid?"

Betsy Twinsett was hastily summoned from her downstairs office. She arrived out of breath but with enough wind left to blow a loose blonde lock out of her face.

She recognized Mrs. Brandberg and was sure her intended was Wambli's walker—the man who had recognized the mayor. What on earth were they doing here? But she didn't ask questions and remarked only that "weddings are fun."

The ceremony, utilizing Genc's "family" ring, was brief. Gullighy was absent on a sneaky errand—alerting the Room Nine press that something of interest was afoot. He returned just as the groom kissed his bride.

Eldon kissed her, too, and wished them both happiness. "Am I forgiven, Sue?" he asked.

"Yes, sweetie. You're forgiven. You did an awful thing, but you were man enough to 'fess up and apologize. In the end."

He smoothly guided the newlyweds out, this time through the main entrance of City Hall and straight into the army of flacks.

Sue was shocked as the photographers blazed away. Genc was terrified; might a photograph end up in Albania? Greta watched the international news program faithfully every night. His worst fears were being confirmed.

It was impossible to get past the inquiring phalanx. Why was she at City Hall? Who was her husband? Did she have hard feelings toward the mayor?

To Gullighy's relief, she pardoned the First Dog Killer as the cameras clicked and ground away.

Aided by Proctor and Gullighy, and shielded by her new spouse, Sue finally extricated herself and reached her waiting car without answering more questions barked at her by her pursuers.

Once safely inside, she instructed the driver to go to the Carlyle, knowing that her own house was probably besieged by even more reporters.

"We'll spend the night at the hotel. In our Presidential Suite. And I'm going to expect four thousand dollars' worth of damn good fucking."

Genc gave her a weak smile.

.　　.　　.

Over dinner and a bottle of champagne—to celebrate the end of the Incident—Eldon described to Edna the bizarre events of the afternoon.

"It sounds like your political psoriasis has dried up, dear."

"Yes, I feel cured." Eldon took a deep swig of his champagne. "You know, Edna, those restaurants, places that have done a lousy job, how they post a sign, 'Under New Management'? Well, tomorrow we start our restaurant with new management. A brand-clean joint. With no dogs allowed."

TWENTY-TWO

The new management found itself confronted with a mixed press reaction the next day. *The Times*, albeit with a front-page picture of a troubled Eldon Hoagland, ran a forthright account of his press conference. Reference to Sue and Gene's wedding was buried in the story and termed an "odd twist," without any other comment. An accompanying editorial noted that "the silly season is over" and the Wambli incident forgotten, "notwithstanding the not very clever behavior" of the mayor and his bodyguards.

This view was not shared by *The Post-News*. RESIGN! its cover headline read, over a story beginning:

> **Mayor Eldon Hoagland yesterday lifted his pants leg, figuratively at least, and admitted his complicity in the killing of Sue Nation Brandberg's Staffordshire terrier puppy. In a crowded City Hall press conference, the mayor acknowledged what had been rumored for days—that his black-suited bodyguards, at his behest, killed Wambli, the hapless and helpless animal.**
>
> **Hoagland's press conference came as the cover-up engineered by his administration had started to unravel. It was unclear whether New Yorkers were more stunned by the killing or by the mayor's attempt to conceal the sordid details.**

The story went on to quote "respected" animal rights leaders, including a spokesman for the Animal Liberation Army, to the effect that Eldon's conduct had been "barbaric," and questioned whether it was appropriate for such a man to remain in office. And his officiating at the marriage of the victimized dog owner in the "pomp" of a City Hall ceremony was declared to be nothing more than a "craven" attempt to silence Mrs. Brandberg.

The Post-News's editorial was rabid (as befitted the subject matter):

The revered Mahatma Gandhi once said that "the greatness of a nation can be judged by the way its animals are treated." The same could be said of our city. So what does it say about ourselves when we are led by a First Citizen who cold-bloodedly orders the shooting of an innocent puppy belonging to one of our most distinguished citizens?

What it says is that Mayor Eldon Hoagland must resign. His conduct in the dog murder that has riveted the attention of law-abiding citizens for so many weeks is unspeakable, unconscionable and uncivilized. The fact that the dog's owner, bedazzled both by love and the prospect of a City Hall marriage, has forgiven him does not mean that we have to.

Mayor Hoagland has set us a terrible example. He must go, and go now. Nothing he said in his press conference—cheap politician-and-dog remarks reminiscent of Richard Nixon's infamous Checkers speech—gives us grounds for forgiveness. He has committed his crime and must suffer the consequences. Go, Mayor Hoagland, and spare your city further embarrassment.

The morning's e-mail was no more encouraging:

Dear Swedish Meatball: Some of us love dogs, some of us don't. But we don't run around killing them. Archie Meehan

**Dear Mayor Hoagland: Please don't come to Staten Island, ever
again. I don't want to have to lock up my dear Rusty when you're in
the neighborhood. Donna Manzoni**

.   .   .

Over the next few days the "crisis"—*The Post-News*'s word—
over Wambli did not go away as Eldon had hoped, but heated up
volcanically. Political psoriasis was no longer in remission.

The band of Animal Liberation Army troops who had disrupted the St. Francis Festival gathered in a grim fifth-floor walk-
up downtown on Avenue C to plan strategy. They had been
summoned by their leader, the goateed man who had passed out
the antipet pamphlets at the festival. His name was Ralph
Bernardo, a perennial graduate student in philosophy. The son of
alumni of the 1968 Free Speech Movement, he had been inculcated with radical and Marxist teachings by his parents. He had
felt the burden of carrying on the family ideological tradition but
had not found a crusade extreme enough to suit him until a girlfriend interested him in animal rights. The cause was perfect: a
way of attacking the bourgeois establishment (pet owners and
meat eaters all) with an ideological jumble of Marxism, utilitarian-
ism and political correctness. The girlfriend had long since left
both him and the movement (in favor of a sexy Tibetan and his intellectual commitments) but Ralph stayed with animal rights, becoming one of the founders of the ALA.

The festival crew was intact: the girl horrified at the serving of
foie-gras canapés (named Stacey), the fat youth who had accused
the attending clerics of eating meat (named Conrad), the baby-
faced towhead who had tricked Eldon into his antiembryo stance

(named Alfred), the boy who had triumphantly raised his fist for the TV cameras (named Lenny) and the girl concerned with animals' souls (named Mary Ann). Plus Amber Sweetwater, the army's newest recruit.

The seven of them sat either on the floor or on a sagging Salvation Army sofa as Ralph exhorted them.

"Hitler Hoagland has got to go," he began as he waved a copy of the morning *Post-News*. "The traitor has gone back on his stand on embryo research. Not to mention the horror of offing that dog.

"But that dog just may be the martyr we need. If we can force Hoagland out of office, we'll put ourselves on the map. We won't be seven people meeting in an apartment but seven *million* people marching for animal rights."

"How do we do that?" Amber asked. "God knows I'm ready to get the bastard."

"We've got to think up guerilla tactics—terrorist tactics. Arouse the public. Bring the city to a halt."

"A big demonstration. Tying up traffic. A mob scene at City Hall. Blocking the Brooklyn Bridge. Like the cops did a few years ago," Lenny said.

"That's brilliant!" agreed Conrad.

"Yeah, brilliant all right. But can we do it? We call ourselves the Liberation Army, but let's face it, there're only seven of us," Ralph said.

"But maybe we can. Stir up the animal rightists on the Internet. I'm for it," said Alfred.

"When should we do it?" Ralph asked.

"Hey, if we could combine it with the Greenwich Village Halloween parade, we'd really have something," Conrad said.

"No, I don't think so," Ralph replied. "Those Village weirdos who dress up on Halloween aren't interested in serious issues like animal rights. Besides, we should strike while this issue is hot. Let's say for fun next Wednesday, October twentieth. Shall we go for it? October twentieth at City Hall. Four o'clock in the afternoon. Just before the rush hour."

"Cool! Let's put it out on the Web right away," Alfred said.

"But we need to do more than that. Guerilla tactics to get attention. Any ideas?" Ralph asked.

The group had plenty of ideas, which became evident in the days before the Wambli Memorial Rally, as they decided to name it.

. . .

Noel Miller called at midday for an appointment. Eldon saw him soon after lunch.

"To what do I owe the pleasure?" Eldon asked. "The animal nuts suing me?"

"Not yet. I was sorry to read about that dog business." Eldon detected an emphasis on the word "read" and perhaps the unstated implication that Miller should have been informed about the Incident before learning of it from the newspapers.

"What I must talk to you about has to do with that. Danny Stephens called to feel me out this morning. What he should do as police commissioner about your bodyguards."

"Fasco and Braddock. Nothing, I should think."

"It's not that simple. Aside from the animal people's outrage at them—Danny's a big boy and can withstand pressure from that direction—there's a rather sensitive technicality.

"You probably already know this, but those fellows never reported that they had used their automatics, as they're required to do. He feels he has to suspend them. I agree, but wanted to pass it by you."

"Look, I've already taken the full blame for what happened and apologized."

"Be that as it may, the department's rules were violated. If he lets them off the hook, no telling what New York's Finest will do next time they shoot a human."

"A widow or child, of course. And black, brown or yellow."

"I'm going to tell Danny to go by the book. He says he'll give them thirty days. It'll shut up the howlers—maybe—and keep the department's skirts clean."

Eldon sighed deeply. "I suppose. Poor bastards did what they thought was right—shot the dog and then dumped him in the East River."

"They did what?"

"Shot the dog and dumped him in the East River," Eldon said crossly.

"They dumped the body in the river?"

"That's what they said."

"Oh, my. Another violation."

"What the hell do you mean?"

"Unfortunately I'm an expert on dumping after that Mafia garbage scandal last year. Under the New York State Navigation Law it's a misdemeanor to put a dead animal in the navigable waters of the state. Penalty is one hundred dollars or a year in jail, as I recall. The district attorney invoked the law against those gangster dumpers."

"I have two thoughts, Noel. First, I don't think the DA needs to enforce the whatever it is, the Navigation Law. And second, if he wants to prosecute my loyal men under that law, he's become even more eccentric than we already know."

Miller pondered these observations, then allowed that only a misdemeanor was involved, so possibly "we can let sleeping dogs lie."

"Noel, if you must use a cliché I'd prefer 'Let well enough alone.'"

It was agreed that Miller would tell the police commissioner to go ahead with Fasco's and Braddock's suspension.

"When you talk to him, please convey my very strong view that they thought they were following orders and therefore the lightest possible penalty should be imposed," Eldon instructed.

"Did you really tell them to shoot that animal?"

"Noel, I find it hard to believe I did, but I can't honestly remember the words I used. It doesn't matter, they thought they were following orders and I'm not going to try to undercut them."

"Yes sir."

"Should I call Stephens?"

"No, I'll give him the message. You understand it means you'll have a new shift of bodyguards."

"Yes, yes. So also please tell him that I want a new pair with Braddock's height and girth, not Fasco's. The way things are going, the taller my security men, the better."

. . .

Police Commissioner Stephens himself phoned later. Eldon took the call impatiently. He was running late for an appearance at a school in Queens.

"Danny, I assume you've talked to Noel Miller. And that he conveyed my views about Fasco and Braddock."

"Yes, he told me. I've given them fifteen days rather than thirty, in deference to you. But that's not what I'm calling about."

"What then?"

"You know those animal righters, the Animal Liberation Army? The ones who made a mess of your festival?"

"What about them?"

"They want to have a rally at City Hall, outside in the park, on October twentieth. The Wambli Memorial Rally."

The beat goes on, Eldon thought.

"Do you want to stop it?" the commissioner asked.

"Of course I want to stop it! I don't want to hear about the god-dam dog, or the ALA, ever again. But I don't see how you can call a halt. Free speech, you know. Right of Assembly. First Amendment. Motherhood."

"Noel could try for an injunction."

"Against a dog lovers' parade? Get real, Danny."

"Well, at least we can block off the steps and walkway outside City Hall."

"No way. Don't forget I promised in the campaign that City Hall would no longer be the Kremlin, as my beloved predecessor had made it. And I said we'd get rid of all the fascist gimmicks he used to suppress dissent. Remember?"

"Yes, that's why a lot of people voted for you, I suspect."

"Those crazies have already made me look like a dithering idiot on the embryo issue and a war criminal worthy of Nuremberg for that dog's death. I'm not going to let them destroy my civil liberties reputation, too. So let them have their rally. As Voltaire said . . . oh, forget it. Just make sure there are lots of cops—and that the cops behave themselves."

212

"Yes, Mr. Mayor."

"October twentieth, you say? I want to write that down in my engagement book. Don't want to miss it. What time?"

"Four o'clock."

"Make them move it back to two-thirty. Maybe we can avoid a rush hour debacle."

"Noted."

.   .   .

Eldon picked up a new security detail as he rushed out of his office. Fasco and Braddock, who normally would have been starting their afternoon tour, were gone. Their replacements, who introduced themselves as Adam Polanski and Rick Leiter, were roughly the size of the tallest member of the Addams family.

The trio got acquainted on the way to Mario Procaccino Elementary School in Queens. Both were married, lived outside the city in Nesconset and came to their new assignments from the NYPD's SWAT team. Eldon knew this was the elite force that protected visiting foreign dignitaries from assassination. He was gratified by this but hoped it did not mean that some new threats on his life had been withheld from him.

The mayor's visit to the school was another attempt at business as usual, despite the distractions of the Incident. It was also a payback to Wendy Halstead. One of her favorite charities was an outfit called SchoolArt, which attempted to supplement the pathetic Board of Education appropriations for art education in the public schools by paying young artists to give classes. This was the 25th anniversary year of the project and Eldon was to visit a class to commemorate and publicize the milestone.

At Procaccino Elementary he was met by Wendy. "Eldon, dear, it was so good of you to come. I know this must be a very trying time for you."

"Yes. And if I'd never gone to that dinner party of yours, I might not have a care in the world."

"Come. I know you'll be impressed with the work we're doing. We're going to see a third-grade drawing class. It's being given by a sweet young artist named Audrey Fine. You'll love her and you'll love it."

Ms. Fine was a delight, at least to the eye. Pert, with long brown hair tied back, she shook hands with Eldon and gave him a dazzling smile. Her fifteen wiggly charges looked on with interest.

"Today we're having a free-form-drawing session. The students have all been thinking about what they might draw for you." Crayons were at the ready before blank pages in the drawing pads. "Go ahead and ask any of them to draw something."

Eldon selected a pigtailed sprout at the front of the classroom. "What is your name?"

"Esther."

"Well, Esther, what are you going to draw for me?"

"My house."

"Wonderful."

The girl set diligently to work and soon had produced a sketch of a housing development high-rise.

"I live *there*," she said, putting an "X" midway up the building.

"Splendid." In short order Eldon had not only a house but a fire engine, a new baby sister and an apple tree rendered for him.

"One more," the teacher said.

"How about you?" Eldon pointed to a ruddy-faced boy with an old-fashioned brush cut. "What are you going to draw?"

"You'll see."

The mayor looked over his shoulder as he began making the outline of an animal. As the sketch developed, Eldon asked if it was the boy's dog.

"No, no. It's Wambli. Can't you tell?"

Ms. Fine obviously did not read the newspapers, as she congratulated the budding artist on his effort. "How nice. A dog named Wambli. How do you spell that?"

"I don't know. I heard it on television. He's the dog that got shot."

Eldon sucked in his breath and managed a tight, very tight, smile. "Good, young man."

Wendy, at Eldon's side, drew him away. "I'm afraid that's all we have time for," she said. Fortunately she was quick enough that the pool photographer accompanying them did not get a picture with the artist and his subject.

"My apologies, Ms. Fine, but I'm running late and must go. But thank you for a delightful time. And good luck to you."

"I'm sorry, Eldon," Wendy whispered as they left the classroom.

"That's all right, my dear. I've got to reconcile myself to the fact that that dog has taken over my life."

·   ·   ·

Coverage of and editorializing about the Incident ceased for the next couple of days. It was clear, however, that the staff of *The Post-News* had been told to keep the issue alive wherever possible, with a tenacity befitting a Staffordshire terrier biting into a human leg. Thus a sports columnist, writing about the glories of attending an autumn game at Yankee Stadium, slipped in, "unless, of course, you'd rather be out shooting innocent dogs." And one of their several self-righteous preacher-columnists, writing as he often did about moral degeneration, managed to make a reference to the evils of "relativism," which would allow one to slay a sentient animal.

.   .   .

The mayor's e-mail had not improved. One bullet was addressed to "You Speciesist Shit" and another wondered if the mayor "would slaughter his pig wife."

"These people are deranged," Eldon remarked to Gullighy, who read the computer's disgorging with him.

The e-mail also included a copy of the ALA's posting to animal rights sympathizers, announcing the Wambli Memorial Rally and urging one and all to attend.

"Well, at least Barbra Streisand isn't going to sing."

"Don't bank on it."

.   .   .

At lunchtime, Gullighy burst into his boss's office.

"I'm afraid there's something out here you ought to see."

Fearing the worst, Eldon followed his press secretary to a front window in the Blue Room. Outside, at the edge of City Hall Park, was an inflated balloon some 18 feet high in the shape of a dog, albeit a spotted one, probably a Dalmatian. Nonetheless it had a large sign around its neck saying WAMBLI and was festooned with black ribbons. It was one of the ALA's guerilla tactics, the guy ropes held by Stacey, Conrad and Alfred, with Amber Sweetwater in front, passing out flyers for the October 20th rally. (Gullighy and Hoagland did not know that Conrad had once worked in the promotion department at Macy's; he had located the New Jersey balloon maker for the Macy's parade and rented out the retreaded Dalmatian.)

"Remember that girl, the one with the leaflets?" Eldon asked.

"Vaguely."

"She used to work at Gracie until Edna fired her."

"Hell hath no fury—"

"Oh, shut up."

. . .

Eldon decided to pack things in early that day. One of the prerogatives of being mayor was that he could set his own schedule; he did not have to work the nine-to-five day of a bank teller or an ordinary civil servant. He was free to do as he pleased, except for the inexorable demands of appearances at events scheduled by Betsy Twinsett and Gullighy. For two nights in a row he had been at benefit dinners she had committed him to attend. Their banal sameness was predictable: an execrable dinner in a badly ventilated hotel ballroom, hackneyed and overlong speeches extolling the honoree of the evening (read: a successful CEO whose corporation had taken two or three pricey tables to support the sponsoring charity), with graceful and appropriate remarks by the mayor at the beginning, middle or end of the dreary affair. It was the exceptional case when anyone enjoyed being at such a dinner; it was mostly you-scratch-my-back-and-I'll-scratch-yours reciprocity— I'll take a table at yours if you take a table at mine. It was a tedious way to raise money for charities, however worthy they might be, but no one had come up with a better method.

Two nights before, he had attended a gala benefitting a Bronx orphanage at which a Silicon Valley hotshot, aged 28, had been feted. (Hope springs eternal—perhaps the attention would lead

217

the nerd executive to turn some of his paper profits to account for the orphans.) Then last night there had been something called a "super supper," prepared by a bevy of New York's hottest chefs, in honor of the nonagenarian Victoria Lawrence, owner of the Airedale, Stephen, who had created a minor disruption at the St. Francis Festival. She, long gloves intact, was being celebrated for still another beneficence from her late husband's fortune, this time to a bilingual literacy program (*"Uno, no. Dos, sí!"*). Eldon, on the defensive, thought there had been a smirk or two when he shook hands with the organizers of these events, but mercifully there had been no cheap jokes at his expense or references to the Incident. (The one exception had come at the Lawrence supper when he had encountered Governor Foote as they found their places on the dais. He gave her the obligatory air kiss—the media would have babbled about a slight or a snub had he not done so—and she whispered, "Bowwow!" as he pressed against her rough cheek.)

No, tonight he and Edna were going to dine at Gracie, quite possibly on one of Julio's greasy olla podridas. So he picked up his security detail and was driven north to the mansion.

"Holy Hannah!" Polanski exclaimed as he drove up York Avenue and approached the mayor's residence.

There on the sidewalk near the entrance was the inflated spotted dog, transported uptown from City Hall. It suddenly became clear that this apparition was going to follow Eldon wherever he might go, as it did for the next few days.

The ALAers jeered as his car entered the driveway, but otherwise there was no trouble. As predicted, dinner was olla podrida. He and Edna choked it down and tried to remain oblivious to the boisterous noise outside.

Both *The Times* and *The Post-News* ran pictures of the inflatable

Wambli the next morning. The latter also had extensive coverage of the ALAers' planned rally, peppered with quotes from Ralph Bernardo about the rightness of their cause and their hopes for bringing the mayor down. The weekly "Critters" column (one of several desperate attempts to attract a more upscale readership, on the theory that pet owners were by and large affluent) ran a feature on the psychology of dog murder; a number of therapists were interviewed, each one with a different theory of motivation for the canine-killing act (examples of actual executions being notably lacking).

And the inflatable Wambli was back outside City Hall.

. . .

Brother Aloysius, the chief dog breeder at the Order of St. Eustache monastery, called George McGinty in the Chancery Office that morning.

"Monsignor, we need the cardinal's help. I don't know how familiar you are with our operation, but we are very dependent on sales of the dogs we breed."

"Yes, I know about what you do. Pit bulls, isn't it?"

"We prefer not to call them that. The, um, connotations of that term are not felicitous. We prefer to say American Staffordshire terriers. Which brings me to the reason for my call. This controversy that's going on about your mayor. It has not helped us at all. People are canceling orders for our newly bred dogs right and left because your mayor has characterized our terriers as brutal and vicious."

"Yes. I'm familiar with the issue."

"Could not His Eminence call him? Ask him perhaps to make a statement that however blameworthy the dog that bit him was, he did not mean to criticize all American Staffies as a breed? You know, sort of the sins of the father being visited upon the sons— the puppies we are trying to sell? Otherwise we may very well have to disband."

"Brother, I will convey your request to His Eminence, but I can't promise anything."

"God bless you."

.   .   .

It was well that Monsignor McGinty had not made a promise to Brother Aloysius. Cardinal Lazaro found the idea "preposterous."

"Why are they breeding dogs anyway? Why don't they make jam? Or invent a new liqueur? No, I take that back. Better stick to jam."

"So I should tell him no?"

"Tell him I am very sympathetic to his plight. I shall pray for the monks. But the mayor, poor man, needs my prayers, too. This whole controversy is so petty—blown up out of all proportion. You don't need to tell Brother Aloysius that, but it's true."

"I'll simply say you don't think it would be prudent to inter-vene."

"Exactly." Then, a tiny smile on his face, he added, "George, just one other thing."

"Yes, Your Eminence?"

"*Cave canem.*"

.   .   .

When Monsignor McGinty relayed the cardinal's gentle rejection to Brother Aloysius, this did not end the matter. Years before, the monk had been in Catholic high school with Francis Xavier

O'Noone, the founder and one of several dozen members of something called the St. Sebastian Society, ready to take the sharp arrows pointed at Catholics by an unfriendly secular world. Anything more radical than a Roman-collared Bing Crosby singing "Swinging on a Star" set O'Noone off; he could find blasphemy lurking in the most innocent artistic expression. His strident charges of anti-Catholic bigotry, often leveled at the most hapless targets, were a constant embarrassment to Cardinal Lazaro, who was not a supporter but nonetheless felt constrained from denouncing him because of his evidently sincere religiosity. As the cardinal once said, paraphrasing Alexander Pope, the worst madman is a saint run mad.

By way of illustration, the SSS's most recent campaign had been against the common appellation for a vodkaless Bloody Mary—a "Virgin Mary." O'Noone had railed against this label as being an undignified evocation of the Blessed Virgin, though it was not clear whether this was merely because the Blessed Mother's name was invoked or because her name was associated with a nonalcoholic drink (O'Noone having some knowledge of spirits himself). In any event, the SSS staged a campaign to eliminate the Virgin Mary name from drink menus in the city's cocktail lounges, the suggestion being that "Bloody Shame" would be a more fitting identifier. This of course quite overlooked the vulgar connotation of "bloody" in O'Noone's ancestral land, but the SSS pressed the matter to the point of scraggly picket lines outside the Plaza Hotel and the Four Seasons restaurant.

The SSS's effort was so ludicrous that both the secular media and the Catholic press ignored it, though many restaurants began substituting "Bloody Shame" or "spicy tomato juice cocktail" on their drink lists. But it showed how truly hyper-sensitive the outfit

221

was and how eager and inventive it could be in finding slights or injury.

Brother Aloysius called his old acquaintance to discuss the Staffie situation.

"Our plight is apparently not of sufficient importance to interest His Eminence the cardinal. But I can assure you, Frank, that our little community is in danger of going under unless something is done."

"That would be a black day for Mother Church," O'Noone replied.

"Is there anything the SSS can do? Sadly, it's not the kind of issue you usually deal with."

"These dogs. Your monastery is the principal breeder of them?"

"No, there are others. But we like to think we're the best."

"So here we have the mayor attacking—slandering, you might say—a breed of dog. And by so doing endangering the future of the best breeding outfit for those dogs—a Catholic monastery."

"Yes."

"That's anti-Catholicism in my book. As far as I'm concerned *indirect* bigotry, which it sounds like we have here, is as pernicious as the direct kind."

"Interesting."

The conversation halted for a few moments as O'Noone pondered the problem.

"I read in the paper this morning that some animal rights people are going to stage a demonstration against the mayor next week. My group could join that, protesting Hoagland's anti-Catholic slur and asking for an apology, a retraction. With luck, we'd get on the news. Give some publicity to the proposition that your Staffords or whatever you call them are not dangerous."

"That's what we want—the mayor to retract his calumny against our dogs."

"We'll do it. We haven't had a good outing since that movie about Casanova and the nuns."

"Bless you, Frank. I knew you would see our dilemma clearly."

. . .

Later that morning, Eldon left City Hall for a luncheon uptown with the president of Brazil. When his car reached the Towers entrance of the Waldorf-Astoria, ALA protesters had preceded him and had the Wambli balloon set up behind a police barricade across the street. Spying the mayor, they began to chant "Dog killer!" and jiggled their inflated canine vigorously. He ignored the taunts, while at the same time marveling at their logistical agility, and quickly ducked into the hotel entrance.

Making nice with the visiting Carioca was all in a day's work for him, but he was tired and did not relish the expenditure of effort that he knew politeness would require. After working the room at a small reception, he went arm and arm with the president to the dais in the ballroom.

As he ate his nondescript fish lunch, he fielded the visitor's questions about the city's subway system, actually glad to be responding to inquiries that did not involve the Incident. But then the president changed the subject.

"You know, Mr. Mayor, before our Carnival each winter, our people get ready months and months ahead. The *escola da samba* practice in the street for weeks and weeks. Is this what is happening here?"

"I'm sorry, I don't know what you mean."

"That dog figure outside. Are they not rehearsing for what you call it, the Ma-cees parade? My family and I visited New York some years ago and saw that parade. Very amusing. The big balloons. But they are getting ready most early, are they not?"

Eldon answered noncommittally. Judging by his lunch companion's English, he guessed—and hoped—that he had not read the newspapers since his arrival.

"Wambli—is that the name I read on the sign? I do not know the cartoon he represents. Is he like Donaldo Pato, or, how you say, Donald Duck? Or Mickey Mouse maybe?"

Reluctantly Eldon explained that he was a symbol of protest for the animal rights movement and that the protest was directed against him.

"And you permit this? It is not right that you should be subject to such ridicule. We have ways of dealing with such matters in my country."

Mercifully the master of ceremonies began the speaking program so Eldon was spared the necessity of delivering a lecture on the First Amendment and freedom of speech. He merely nodded and drew out the notes for his remarks from his jacket pocket. He pretended to study them intensely, though they were of the fill-in-the-blank variety suitable for all such occasions. ("There has always been a warm bond between the people of New York and the people of ———.")

The canine effigy was still outside when he left.

·   ·   ·

Artemis Payne enjoyed his tenure as New York City's public advocate. This strange position, created in the latest revision of the City Charter, had few defined duties, letting the incumbent pick and choose his targets at will. And to stand ready to succeed the mayor if that should ever come to pass.

The public advocate, soon after he was inaugurated, declared war on the city's banks. Unknown to the public, Payne had a history of bouncing checks, dating back to his hand-to-mouth days as a struggling lawyer. He now proposed that the city adopt legislation prohibiting banks from returning a check without first notifying the person who had drawn it. The penalties proposed were severe: a $100 fine for the first check bounced on an account without notice, then ranging upward as high as $1,000. Payne rightly argued that most banks would never return a check for its gilt-edged customers; they would be politely notified of any shortfalls in their accounts, or be automatically extended overdraft facilities.

The proposal drew protesting howls from the banking community; orderly, high-speed computer check-clearance procedures would be impossible as the banks sought to notify wayward patrons.

Payne received no support for his proposal from the press—next there might be penalties for nondelivery of newspapers. Eldon, who realized the impracticalities of the scheme and who did not want to give the bankers another excuse for moving operations to New Jersey, kept silent. So did most City Council members.

Without additional backing, Payne's initiative went nowhere. But it did serve to make him a popular, or perhaps populist, figure in the city's poorer neighborhoods, where bankers had few friends. The city's business leaders were relieved at Payne's lack of success but held their collective breath as they wondered what scheme he would propose next.

Payne had graduated from City College and Cardozo Law

School with respectable, if not spectacular, records and had set himself up in practice in an office near the courthouse in Brooklyn. But he never succeeded in developing a practice that prospered, a hard task for any lawyer without a staff of junior lawyers and paralegals. Thus when a seat on the City Council opened up in his district he went for it and managed to win the Democratic primary. The general election was a cinch and when he later ran for two more terms there was no opposition in the primaries and almost none in the elections themselves.

Payne had already decided to go for the public advocate's job even before Eldon declared for mayor. And then, with Eldon's endorsement, he had won easily.

A large man, friendly and smiling, he had undeniable appeal to the voters (at least those who were not bankers). In his private life he was an inveterate golfer, a game he had mastered as a young man in a recreation program sponsored by the Police Athletic League.

He fully realized that the city owned thirteen municipal golf courses, and as the public advocate, he believed it his duty to "inspect" them regularly on behalf of the city's golfer consumers. This he did conscientiously an afternoon or two a week, to the point where he became widely known in government circles as "Putter Payne."

Putter met for drinks at five o'clock each Wednesday with whatever other black politicians (Democratic ones, that is) happened to be around—state legislators, city councilmen, occasionally a congressman. These gatherings took place at Foley's, an ancient saloon convenient both to his office on Centre Street and to City Hall.

There was never an agenda for these informal sessions, just a chance to share the latest political gossip and review the current state of affairs.

On this particular Wednesday, three councilmen, a state senator and an assemblyman joined Payne. There was, needless to say, much talk about the Incident.

"I'm not sure Eldon can survive this one," Assemblyman Darrel Green opined.

"Oh hell, it will all blow over," Payne said. "*The Post-News* can diss him all they want but he's not going down for the count because of a dead dog."

"I'm not so sure," Senator Bill Tracy said. "Those animal righters are really fired up. I think we're going to see one helluva ruckus on the twentieth."

"So what? They'll make a lot of noise and that will be the end of it."

"And if it isn't," Green said, "he'll have to resign. And you know what that means, baby."

"Yeah. I'll be the mayor."

"You got it, mister," Green said.

The speculation continued as the pols had a second round.

"Wouldn't be so bad to have a black mayor again, you know," Tracy said. "Or for a black man to get a head start before the next election over our Hispanic brothers."

"You're blowing smoke, boys," Payne protested. "Besides, I can't get into the middle of the mess."

"You're probably right, Artie. But let's think about it. If that rally really is a blast, Eldon might just have to get out. What do you think, guys, couldn't we help give it some juice?" Bill Tracy asked.

"I don't see how," Payne said.

"Think about it," Tracy continued. "The dog that got killed was a pit bull, right? And who owns more pit bulls than anybody else in this town? Blacks, that's who. And Hispanics, of course. They should be real angry at what happened. Now I know, Artie, there's nothing you can do directly. You've got to go with the flow. But George, you're a councilman up in Harlem. Couldn't you quietly pass the word that some of the street bucks who own those dogs might want to join the protest? For the honor of the pit bull? You hear what I'm saying?"

George Hayes, the councilman being addressed, looked surprised. He took a deep sip of his rye whiskey as he thought about the matter.

"Yes, I suppose I could," he said finally. "Have to be real careful, though, so Eldon never finds out, finds out that I perpetrated anything. But yes, we can stir something up. Sure."

"Then I say do it," Tracy said. "Quick, fast and in a hurry. Artie doesn't have to know, nobody has to know. Eldon doesn't have to know. It'll just be some homeboys exercising their constitutional rights."

"I didn't hear a thing," the public advocate said as the group broke up. "I'm out. Peace, brothers."

. . .

Early the next morning, shortly after daybreak, Edna Hoagland was awakened by a persistent jangling noise coming from the lawn. She went to the bedroom window to investigate. Then she rushed back to wake her husband.

"Eldon, you're not going to like this, but you'd better take a look out the window."

Half asleep, the mayor got up and did as he was told.

"Good grief!" was his only reaction to the cow lumbering across the lawn with a large sign around its neck reading MILK ME OR KILL ME. In the middle of the night the ALA had struck again, though the security staff managed to spirit the animal away before the press got wind of its presence.

.   .   .

The running story in *The Post-News* described a "groundswell" of support for the Wambli Memorial Rally. An American Staffordshire terrier organization announced that it would take part in the protest, as did a number of fringe animal rights groups, but not the ASPCA or the Humane Society.

The ASPCA was not, however, silent. An embarrassed Gifford Livingston, its local chairman, called Noel Miller.

"Since you're the mayor's lawyer, I wanted to alert you to a little problem," Livingston began. "I don't know how familiar you are with the laws about cruelty to animals."

"Not very. Though animals have been much in focus down here of late."

"Yes, I'm sure. Noel, take a look at Section three-five-three of the State Agriculture and Markets Law. Article twenty-six. It says any person who, quote, causes, procures or permits, unquote, any animal to be killed is guilty of a misdemeanor. Punishable by imprisonment for a year or a thousand dollar fine, or both."

"I'll take your word for it. But Gifford, what are you suggesting? That I should have the police arrest the mayor?"

"Of course not. But there is a slight problem. Section three-seven-one says that, quote, any agent or officer of any duly incorporated society for the prevention of cruelty to animals, unquote—

that's us—may arrest a violator of the Agriculture and Markets Law."

"So one of your people could arrest Eldon Hoagland?"

"Precisely."

"But surely you can forbid your dogcatchers—sorry, Gifford, that's a bit pejorative—from doing so."

"It's more complicated than that. Note that the statute says, quote, officer, unquote, as well as 'agent,' the agents being what you call dogcatchers. We call them humane law enforcement agents. As far as officers are concerned, as chairman I'm one, so I could arrest Eldon."

"But that's absurd."

"Bear with me. There's a faction on my board—not a majority, at least not yet—that wants me to do just that. A visible and symbolic act to call public attention to the animal cruelty problem."

"Good Lord, you wouldn't do that. Would you?"

"No, I'd probably resign first. Eldon's behavior with that dog was disgraceful, but not enough for me to arrest him. But the society's enforcement agents are damn mad and I can't guarantee that one of them won't try something, even if I forbid it."

"Have these, um, agents, ever made an arrest before? Or is this just some crazy law that's never been enforced?"

"Three hundred arrests last year."

"Are they armed? Will Eldon be shot if he resists?" Miller tried to lighten up the conversation.

"They are armed. But responsible."

"All in uniform, I assume."

"No, there are plainclothes agents as well."

Who could sneak up on Eldon unannounced, Miller thought.

.   .   .

Once the ASPCA chairman was off the phone, Miller checked his *McKinney's Annotated New York Laws* and found that Livingston's description of the law had been accurate. The legal authority for the society's agents to make arrests went back to the 1860s. He decided not to alert Eldon to the potential hazard of arrest—poor fellow, he was besieged enough already. But he did call the head of the mayor's security detail.

"I don't know how you identify them, but you should keep the humane law enforcement agents away from the mayor. They want to arrest him."

"Don't worry, Mr. Miller, we can spot them. They all look like beagles."

If that were only true, Miller wished.

.   .   .

Three days after the cow incident, Amber Sweetwater returned to Gracie Mansion with an unidentified, slightly chubby young man. Each one carried two suitcases, which she explained to the guard, with whom she was on friendly terms, were to take away her remaining belongings. The sentry suspected nothing, though he did think it odd when the pair went by his booth only a few minutes later, without the suitcases.

Soon after Amber and her friend departed, Edna Hoagland startled the sentry and the household staff with her screaming. The cause was soon apparent, as the mansion was overrun with tiny mice. Trying to calm herself, she called Eldon at the office. Normally she relayed any message through a staff member or waited until she met up with her husband in person; it somehow seemed improper to her

to interrupt official city business with (usually trivial) personal matters. But this time she called and asked to be put through to him.

"Eldon, I don't know what to do! You have no idea what it's like
up here!"

"My dear, what on earth is the matter? Where are you?"

"I'm at the mansion. And someone has let loose hundreds of
mice—all over the house."

"Good God."

"The housekeeper and one of the guards are beating them back
with brooms, but they're everywhere. I'm going to call the Health
Department unless you've got a better idea."

Eldon felt helpless. What was he supposed to do? As husband?
As mayor of the City of New York? What could he do?

"That sounds right—"

Eldon was interrupted by a muffled cry. "One of them just
started to crawl up my leg," Edna shouted. "It's like a bad science-
fiction movie. Only it's real."

"Let us call the Health Department from down here. Have
them send up an emergency crew right away. You stay calm—or
better yet, go somewhere for lunch."

"These animal crazies are going to be the death of us, Eldon.
They really are."

"Our ALA friends?"

"Yes. They left a note downstairs. 'Today Gracie Mansion, tomorrow the World. The Animal Liberation Army.'"

"How the hell did they get inside?"

"I mean to find out."

The Health Department squad arrived and after reconnoitering
the invading mouse army, advised Edna to vacate the premises.
"What we'll do isn't going to be pretty, ma'am," she was told.

"That's all right. I'm a doctor," she said but then reconsidered and decided to leave. Before doing so, she questioned the guard in the outside sentry booth, who told her about Amber Sweetwater, her pudgy companion and the suitcases.

The mice, stolen as it turned out by the ALA from a laboratory at Rockefeller University, had been in the suitcases, but the tiny creatures had not made any impression on the metal detector at the gate.

. . .

That week's *Surveyor,* under Scoop's byline, carried a story about "animal terrorist" tactics, past and promised, directed against Mayor Hoagland. The story detailed the plans for the Wambli rally but also gave accounts of both the cow and mice episodes at Gracie.

These latter descriptions intrigued Jack Gullighy. No other publication had mentioned the errant bovine or the scurrying rodents. Especially in the case of *The Post-News,* eager for any scintilla of a story embarrassing to Eldon, it seemed likely that the ALA had not alerted the press to their doings. So how did *The Surveyor* come by the stories? It appeared to Gullighy that its reporter had been uncomfortably close to the action, if not a part of it. And Rice fitted the description given by the Gracie sentry of the fellow carrying two of the mice-filled suitcases.

He placed a call to Justin Boyd.

"I see you're still on the animal rights beat."

"Absolutely. Best running story we've ever had—and it ain't over yet."

"How well I know," Gullighy said. "But tell me, Justin, is it not possible your man Rice is a bit too close to the situation?"

"Dogging the story for all it's worth, if that's what you mean."

"Dogging, hmm. 'Badgering,' I think, would be a better word."

"Ha! Ha! To what do I owe this amusing call?"

"Justin, there were two people who staged that mouse attack on Gracie Mansion. My hunch is that your man Rice was one of them."

"So? Let's just say he was tipped off and was on the spot."

"Fine. But he was seen carrying suitcases full of mice into the mansion."

"So?"

"So he wasn't reporting. He was creating a story."

"Oh, Jack, come, come. Such niceties!"

"Let me give you a hypothetical. Vietnam. The Ho Chi Minh Trail. Reporter goes out with a patrol. Quiet. No news. Reporter, who is armed, starts shooting. Next day reports on a fierce gun battle. Ethical?"

"Why not? There was a gun battle, right?"

"But the reporter started it!"

"As I say, Jack, niceties. A story is a story, regardless of who instigated it. You fellows are getting too uptight down there at City Hall. Stay loose, my boy!"

Gullighy slammed down the phone. "Unscrupulous limey bastard!" he shouted, but there was no one around to hear him.

TWENTY-THREE

As the day for the Wambli rally drew nearer, Eldon Hoagland was nearly exhausted: berated in the press and on local TV, threatened with arrest, harassed in his own home by stray creatures, followed all over town by that silly-looking balloon dog. And even his Web site had been spammed with hundreds of identical messages, all repeating over and over: *dogkillerdogkillerdogkiller* . . . Nonetheless he persevered, convinced he was in the midst of a bad dream that would pass.

The day before the big event, he and Gullighy were briefed by Danny Stephens, the police commissioner, and Chief Inspector Whitehall, head of the department's Intelligence Division.

The Post-News had been predicting for days that the intensity of the demonstration would reach at least 9.5 on the Richter scale, and now Whitehall was not contradicting the newspaper's hysteria.

"There appears to be tremendous support for this rally, if the traffic on the ALA Web site can be believed. All the fringies will be turning out, of course, but it's not only them: the pit bulls' breeder association—or Staffordshire terriers, or whatever they are—something called the Vegetarian League of America and God knows who else."

"You're omitting another group, Inspector," the commissioner interjected.

Whitehall was embarrassed but told the mayor that the Patrolmen's Benevolent Association would be turning out as well.

"They're ticked off at the suspension I gave Fasco and Brad-dock," the commissioner explained.

"Does that mean we won't have police protection tomorrow?" Gullighy inquired.

"No, it's not a strike. Just a show of solidarity by off-duty cops."

"You fellows have any good news?" Eldon asked.

"None that comes to mind," Stephens said. "You know, Mr. Mayor, you really ought to let us block off the plaza out front—and the park as well. Make the demonstrators get behind barri-cades on the streets facing the park."

"No, Danny, unless you tell me you can't control the crowd in the park, I want to let them in there. When my trial comes up in the World Court, I don't want suppression of free speech added to the charges."

"We can handle it. We'll let them in the park, and spill over into Park Place and lower Broadway. We won't let them storm the steps of City Hall or block the Brooklyn Bridge. We'll also stagger the barricades, so that we can keep the various groups separate. You know the hours we agreed on—two-thirty to four. No sound sys-tem, but they can use bullhorns."

"By the way, sir, I assume you will plan to stay away from here tomorrow afternoon," Whitehall said.

"Not on your life! I'm going to be right in this office, at work, tending to business."

"That's up to you."

.   .   .

Scoop Rice planned to be at the rally, even though it was taking place on his deadline day. Boyd was delighted at the timing, even if it meant keeping the paper open later than usual; it meant the weekly *Surveyor* could do a fast-breaking color story to compete with the dailies. He wanted it multihued and personally expressed his confidence that Scoop could do the job.

But Rice got sidetracked early that morning, with a call at his apartment from Genc.

"I have very great favor to ask. Sue has thrown me out. Can I come and stay with you—for a couple of days, or until they send me back to Albania?"

"How can they do that? I thought your marriage sewed everything up."

"It is very complicated, Scoop. Can I come over and talk with you?"

Mystified but intrigued, Scoop said yes. An hour later a disheveled Genc was knocking at his door.

"I'm in the middle of great fuckup," he explained. "Sue gave me the bounce last night. I've been wandering the street ever since."

"What happened?"

"I left a wife back in Tirana. And she's here in New York. She saw a picture of Sue and me leaving City Hall after the wedding and flew over here two days ago. She came to the house yesterday and made very loud mess."

"How the hell did she find you?"

"I wrote her a couple of times from Sue's. Though I told her she must never write to me there."

"Does she want you back?"

"Yes. We had a big quarrel before I came to America. I said it was the only way for me. She said no, she wanted to stay in Albania. I came anyway. Were we finished? I don't know. I told her I would come back for her, but she said she might not be waiting. It was open."

"So you didn't divorce her?"

"No divorce. Now she wants me to come back. But she wants money from Sue to keep quiet. A lot of money."

"How much?"

"Twenty thousand dollars."

Scoop found this a modest price but did not say so.

"Sue said no with much force and made her leave. Then she had at me good. Made me get out with only the clothes on my back and two hundred dollars I had saved."

"Jesus, Genc, I'm sorry. What can I do?"

"I need a place to stay for a couple of days." He looked around the tiny studio and then allowed that he would be happy to sleep on the floor.

"I think it will all work out," he told Scoop. "Sue will get over her angriness. And she's got the money to pay Greta off. I think she will do that. She likes having me around."

"And Greta will go home—alone?"

"I think so."

"Your wife—your first wife, Greta—can she be bought off for so little money? And stay bought?"

"Yes. Twenty thousand American dollars is large money in Tirana."

"And you'll stay on with Sue?"

"Yes. At least until I get my green card."

"I don't know, Genc. It's a pretty dicey situation."

Scoop tried to be sympathetic and helpful, but he had very little experience of marital quarrels, let alone bigamous ones.

"What you going to do next?"

"If you let me, I will stay here. Let my wives calm down for a day, maybe two."

"Then?"

"Then I will see them both and we make a deal. Money for Greta and a plane ticket home."

"Where is wife number one now?"

"She's at the Brandywine Hotel. Down on Twenty-eighth Street."

"What about Sue?"

"Give me time and I'll try to make up with her. I know how." Genc smiled for the first time in the conversation.

"Okay. You can stay. It's not much, but make yourself at home. Let me find my extra key."

Finding it, he left to go to *The Surveyor.*

.   .   .

Poor guy, Scoop thought on the bus ride downtown. At the office, there was a message to see Justin Boyd.

Boyd wanted to talk about the multihued color story he had in mind.

"This rally should be a Christmas pudding, Scoop. I want you to eat every morsel—and leave nothing but crumbs for *The Times* and *The Post-News.* I want every poster, every shout about Hoagland. I want details on every grab-ass thing the animal righters say and do. It will be a three-ring circus, and I want you to tell what happens in every ring. Got it?"

"Yes sir. I'll do my best."

"I wonder what Mrs. Brandberg and her child bridegroom will be doing this afternoon. You might check in with them, for more color."

239

"Matter of fact I happen to know there's some trouble there."

"Oh?"

Scoop told his boss about the sudden appearance of Genc's first wife and the consequences that followed.

"Holy Jehoshaphat, man! Forget about the rally! Do you know where this wronged woman is?"

"Um, I think so."

"Then *cherchez la femme!* Get her on the record about her two-timing husband. Ho! Ho! Sue Nation Brandberg a bigamist! And who performed the ceremony? Why, none other than our dear mayor. Trying to pacify her, to keep her quiet. Yes! Yes! Smoking the peace pipe and performing an illegal marriage to stop her very public bitching. Scoop, you're brilliant. If you carry this one off, we'll eat the bloody dailies for lunch once again."

Scoop protested, if mildly.

"Couple of things, Justin. Genc has become a friend of mine and I don't want to put him in jeopardy."

"Friend he may be, but he's a bigamist. Your public—our public—has a right to know that."

"As for the mayor, he certainly didn't know he was presiding over a bigamous marriage."

"So what? Facts are facts, my boy. Here you have the chief magistrate of our great city aiding and abetting—presiding over—an illegal act. Isn't the public entitled to know when its mayor is breaking the law? Undermining the institution of marriage? Get real, young man. You're a reporter, please don't forget."

"And what about Sue? Wasn't she, isn't she, a close friend? Isn't it fair to say you even dated her?"

"You're getting into private territory, Scoop. As journalists we must avoid letting personal feelings get in the way of truth. Stop chewing on this and find that poor and wronged Albanian woman. Got it?"

Scoop was getting it for the second time; again he agreed to carry out the great editor's wishes—with some reluctance.

TWENTY-FOUR

Eldon came to work on October 20th through the City Hall
entrance on the Chambers Street side. He took a look through a
front window before settling into his office. The view was omi-
nous: television camera dollies, miles of coaxial cable, a string of
blue NYPD barricades scattered through the park, plus a large police communications trailer and two arrest vans. Already there was
a phalanx of cops guarding the steps of City Hall, with other operatives communicating with God knows who on their cell phones.

At lunchtime he was told that it would be difficult to order in
lunch. Betsy Twinsett came to the rescue with a plate of macaroni
and cheese defrosted in her microwave. The mayor pronounced it
delicious.

By two o'clock the Wambli balloon had appeared, this time accompanied by a band of ALAers and supporters carrying a black
coffin-shaped box with a large WAMBLI R.I.P. sign attached to it.
They, too, were talking intently on their cell phones. Could they be
phoning up the police? The park was soon full: a group brought by
bus, mostly wearing jeans and plaid shirts, and bearing the sign
AMERICAN STAFFORDSHIRE DEFENDERS; a motley assortment,
mostly men, and unmistakably off-duty cops, with such signs as
JUSTICE FOR FASCO AND BRADDOCK and SUSPEND HOAGLAND
NOT THE COPS.

A limousine pulled up and discharged a group of familiar-look-
ing passengers—a pop singer, two grade-B actresses, a hero from
one of the soaps. Plus Daniel Storey, an actor with a couple of
modest movie successes, who, it was rumored, was torn between

playing Hamlet and starting a campaign for the United States Senate seat that George McTavish would be vacating. Ralph Bernardo, the ALA leader, rushed over to greet them. Then came a yellow school bus, bringing a delegation of young blacks and Hispanics—the grassroots delegation assembled by Councilman Hayes—along with a collection of fearsome-looking pit bulls.

They were not the only ones accompanied by canines. Several of the ALA supporters, looking like the professional dog walkers often seen on upper Manhattan streets, maneuvered a motley assortment of animals. They either were enthusiastic dog owners, had borrowed the mutts from friends or had rounded up strays. (The majority were strays, collected over several days and tethered in Bernardo's apartment.) All told, there were perhaps 150 creatures weaving among the legs of the protesters.

The makers of a dog food called GROW-1, seizing an opportunity, had set up a trailer on the far side of Broadway and four teenagers eagerly foisted sample cans on passersby. Another entrepreneur operated what appeared to be a hot dog vending cart, selling something called cabbage sausages—no meat. There were few takers. A vendor of T-shirts, a picture of Wambli on the back and of Eldon with a large "X" over his face on the front, did better.

Then there were the Veganettes, a troupe of girls tricked out like high school majorettes, offering carrot sticks and chanting, "Meat is poison." Not to mention a zaftig blonde, wearing a short skirt and a tight blouse over a part of her impressive décolletage, carrying a stick festooned with imitation sausages, flaccid and limp, and a placard reading MEAT MAKES YOU IMPOTENT.

At three o'clock, a half hour into the official rally time, City Hall Park had overflowed and the crowd, still growing, began to fill up lower Broadway. A posse of cool black boys, emerging from the

243

J&R music store, got caught up in the throng and began shouting Public Enemy's rap song "Fight the Power." Students at nearby Pace College, emerging from classes, also joined in. They had heard about the troubled sixties (even from their parents) and now delightedly joined in a genuine public disturbance, though most were not fully aware of what the commotion was about.

Then there were the organized groups: Francis Xavier O'Noone and the St. Sebastianites brandishing SAVE THE MONKS signs; a small crew waving the red-and-black Albanian flag and holding aloft a banner identifying them as the Albanian Defense League (HOAGLAND: PICK ON SOMEBODY YOUR OWN SIZE, one of their signs read, with presumed reference to Genc); and another band, wearing feathered bonnets and face paint, calling itself the Native American Protective League (REMEMBER WAMBLI—THE BRAVE EAGLE).

The ALA supplied all who would take them with placards, the most modest of which said NEW YORKERS LOVE DOGS. Others were more provocative: ELDON HOAGLAND—MAN'S WORST FRIEND; EXTERMINATE THE PIT BULL (this under a photograph of Eldon); EUTHANIZE WAMBLI'S KILLER and SPAY HOAGLAND. Plus seemingly hundreds that simply said RESIGN! RESIGN!

．　　．　　．

The mayor had said that there would be business as usual, Wambli rally or no, but he did watch the proceedings, which were televised live on New York One. Gullighy was with him.

Eldon was detached, even though the increasingly more boisterous carryings-on were directed at him. The detachment was not aloof, but instead reflected his belief that he was experiencing some sort of temporary hallucination that would come to an end.

It just did not seem possible that the Incident could have stirred up so much passion.

The roving cameras captured details that would not have been observable to a spectator in the crowd. When a camera panned on the delegation of uptown pit bull owners, there were the usual signs—PIT BULLS YES, HOAGLAND NO or its variant, PIT BULLS SÍ, EL DON NO. But there was one that read GEORGE HAYES DEMOCRATIC CLUB.

"What the hell is that sign all about?" Eldon asked.

Gullighy, his connector cells at work, immediately figured it out.

"Some mischief making by Councilman Hayes."

"But why is he advertising it?"

"Here's my guess. He rounded up those street dudes, had them report to his East Harlem club, where they picked up those pit bull signs. And somebody grabbed the Hayes sign by mistake. George will be furious."

"George furious? What about me? My technology zone plan is the best thing that could ever happen to his district. So why is he organizing against me?"

"Do I need to draw a map, Eldon? If he and his buddies get rid of you—which, of course, they'll never do—Artie Payne becomes mayor, right? And George becomes power broker number one for him."

"Good Lord. And where is our public advocate, by the way? Is he out there, do you suppose?"

"Putter? Hell, no. He's staying as far away from this one as he can. And besides, it's a nice sunny day so he's probably up at Deepdale, getting in a round or two while the weather's still nice."

As the cameras moved about, they picked up the diverse groups in the mob: the St. Sebastianites, now kneeling and saying the rosary, though it was unclear for whom or for what cause they were praying; the hip-hop boys; the Albanians; the Native Americans.

"Where are the Chinese?" Eldon asked ruefully.

"Probably at home eating dog stew," Gullighy wisecracked.

.   .   .

Randilynn Foote watched the goings-on from a window in the Governor's Rooms.

"Raifeartaigh, this is great! Putting the blocks to Eldon. Look at 'em—ever see such a collection of shit stirrers in your life?"

"No, Governor."

"Look at that blonde with the sausages. 'Meat makes you impotent.' Hee! Hee! You think those sausages are meant to be limp dicks?"

"I think so, Governor."

"What will they think of next?"

Foote's adopted Labrador, at her feet, began to whine.

"Shut up, Albert. Look at all your brothers out there. Demonstrating for your rights!"

The governor continued to laugh and shout delighted expletives as she viewed the maneuvers below.

"Raifeartaigh, you think there's a real chance this will bring the mayor down? Will he have to resign? Is that possible?"

"It's all crazy, Governor. Anything's possible."

"That means Putter becomes mayor, doesn't it?"

"I believe so."

"Delicious thought. We could handle him. A whole lot better than Eldon."

She turned to the third person present in the room, her young politics resident, Sheila Baine, who was sitting quietly at an adjacent window. Foote's predecessor had started the politics resident program (carefully avoiding the titillating word "intern") as a means of attracting bright postgraduate students into public service. Foote had continued the custom and picked Sheila from a group of fifty-five applicants, all with astounding résumés. Sheila had both undergraduate and law degrees from Yale and a master's from the Kennedy School at Harvard.

"Opposites attract" must have been the guiding principle that led to her selection. The two women, the governor and her aide, could not have been less alike. Sheila, thin and attractive in a bookish, bespectacled way, was soft-spoken and perhaps even a bit shy. The closest thing to a swearword in her vocabulary was "darn" and it was used sparingly.

As befitted her status, Sheila seldom spoke in the governor's meetings—she attended all but the most private and sensitive— unless called upon; but an observer could tell that she was absorbing everything she witnessed or heard. And when the governor did recognize her, as she occasionally did, her questions and observations were concise, intelligent and to the point—and free of cussing (though she often told her boyfriend that she was getting an additional master's degree in profanity and invective).

"Sheila, just for fun will you check out what happens if Eldon resigns? Does that putz Putter automatically become mayor? I don't get involved, do I? See what you can find."

.   .   .

Below in the streets, Ralph Bernardo was trying to get the crowd's attention. He wanted to speak, and Daniel Storey, at his side, patently hoped to do the same. The barking and howling of the dogs and the crowd noise in general made the effort futile. Even with his bullhorn turned up to top volume, there was no way of causing the din to subside. So Bernardo did the next best thing and got the crowd to begin chanting, "Dog killer . . . resign. Dog killer . . . resign." The bedlam was extraordinary; had anyone had a rope, and had Eldon appeared, he might well have been lynched, strung up from one of the elms or beeches in the park.

By contrast, Governor Foote, with Albert the Labrador on a leash, boldly walked out the front door of City Hall, and was greeted with cheers. The crowd parted and allowed her and Raifeartaigh and Sheila Baine to reach her car, which was then guided by police and demonstrators alike to a clear route uptown.

Eldon observed her exit without comment, except for a constricted sound somewhere between a groan and a sigh.

When the masses tired of their "Dog killer" chant, a sweating Bernardo and his cohorts began shouting "Arf! Arf! Arf!"—a cry that both the humans and the canines took up—a Dionysian cacophony that was frightening.

"I suppose it's better than *Sieg Heil,*" Eldon said, as he observed the frenzied mob on his television.

By now it was four o'clock, the bewitching hour under the ALA's permit, and the police inspector in charge made his way to Bernardo and reminded him of this. Or did his best to do so, over the din.

Bernardo responded by shouting, "To the bridge!" over and over through his bullhorn. He started a surge that was so powerful the police could not stop its flow. Until, that is, they reached the approach to the Brooklyn Bridge and faced what appeared to be an implacable shield of massed police in riot gear.

At this point the ALAers and their recruits began releasing their dogs. In the face of this onslaught, the police shield collapsed. The NYPD's praetorian guard was prepared for human protesters, ready to knock heads and, if worse came to worst, confront the mob with a blast of tear gas. But dogs nipping at their heels and slithering among them threw them into confusion. Soon there were dogs, but not demonstrators, loose on the bridge; traffic came to a halt as drivers attempted to avoid killing the unleashed animals.

Earlier, when Bernardo called for a march on the bridge, Amber Sweetwater, at his side, rang up a number on her cell phone. She was calling a fellow ALA foot soldier waiting with another group—and another pack of dogs—on the Brooklyn side. At her signal, these dogs were released amid the Manhattan-bound bridge traffic, unimpeded by police, who had not foreseen a two-front war.

The ensuing chaos was wild. With the Brooklyn Bridge effectively shut down as the evening rush hour began, traffic backed up throughout downtown Manhattan and soon there was a snarl that spread to the East River Drive and the other spans to Brooklyn and Queens.

The tie-up did not end there. Throughout Manhattan, minibuses ferrying pilots and flight attendants from their hotels to La Guardia and Kennedy Airports were stalled. Countless early evening departures to other American cities and overnight flights to Europe were canceled for lack of crews—or for that matter, passengers, who were also caught in the gridlock. By midevening air traffic throughout the country and in much of Europe was in a tangle rivaling the land-bound one in New York, with incoming flights halted before taking off in Chicago or Los Angeles or diverted to Philadelphia or Boston. The Animal Liberation Army had effectively disrupted a good part of the Free World.

Unable to travel by car to Gracie Mansion, Eldon was hustled out of City Hall and onto the uptown subway by a heavily augmented detail of police. By the time he got home, walking the last blocks from the 86th Street subway station, the blaring of car horns from helpless and angry motorists on the East River Drive was deafening, even inside the mansion with the windows closed. He longed for a drink or two—or more—with Leaky, but realized that would hardly be responsible behavior when besieged law enforcement officers were trying desperately to untie the biggest traffic jam in the history of New York City.

By nine o'clock the worst was over, and traffic again began to flow. Eldon and Edna watched the untangling with relief on television, between telephoned progress reports from Danny Stephens—and a call from the president asking if the mayor wanted federal troops sent in. But there was a slight chill in the room as an elated Ralph Bernardo, being interviewed, vowed to stage a repeat protest a week hence. "We're going to demonstrate every Wednesday until our animal-hating mayor resigns."

TWENTY-FIVE

Through the marvels of modern telecommunications, the newspapers were able to assemble their Thursday morning editions, though newsstand deliveries ran behind schedule. *The Times*'s coverage began with a restrained lead:

> **Every dog must have his day, and approximately 200 of them had theirs yesterday, causing a traffic jam the Police Department called the worst in New York's history.**

Only deep in the story was Eldon's future speculated about:

> **While the purpose of the Animal Liberation Army rally was to rouse support to force Mayor Eldon Hoagland to resign, it was not clear that this objective was advanced. Most political leaders contacted expressed anger at the ALA's disruptive tactics and offered virtually no support for the call for Hoagland's resignation. Many more refused to comment or made themselves unavailable, including Artemis Payne, the public advocate, who would step into the mayor's shoes if he left office.**
>
> **Governor Randilynn Foote, who witnessed the demonstration from the Governor's Rooms at City Hall, offered only a terse "No comment" when she left the building in late afternoon, accompanied by her Labrador, Albert.**

The *Times* also ran an informative sidebar listing previous noteworthy events in City Hall Park, including the first reading of the Declaration of Independence to George Washington and his troops, the antislavery riots, protests by supporters of Sacco and

251

Vanzetti and a more recent police demonstration, which had turned ugly.

The Post-News's coverage was under the headline

WAMBLI REMEMBERED
AND HOW!

Mayor's Future in Doubt

Resignation was right up front in *The Post-News* story:

The entire metropolitan region was thrown into chaos yesterday as more than 100,000 protestors in downtown Manhattan demanded the resignation of Mayor Eldon Hoagland for his conduct in the brutal slaying of the puppy Wambli last August.

The marchers, from an eclectic assortment of animal rights and civic groups, including the Patrolmen's Benevolent Association and the Catholic St. Sebastian Society, united in a persistent chorus, which at times verged on the ugly, of "Resign! Resign!" and later a ridiculing "Arf! Arf! Arf!"

Led by members of the Animal Liberation Army, many in the crowd, bringing dogs along to honor the slain Wambli, let them loose on the Brooklyn Bridge as the rally came to an end. The resulting tie-up on the bridge, at the beginning of the rush hour, soon escalated to all the East River approaches to and from Manhattan. Police, drivers and spectators agreed that it was the worst tie-up in memory or, as one onlooker put it, "since the invention of the automobile."

The disruptions continued well into the evening and were severe enough that, according to the White House, the president called Mayor Hoagland to offer assistance by federal troops.

It was unclear late last night what effect the rally and the immobilization of the city would have on the future of Mayor Hoagland. Could he ride out the crisis?

Ralph Bernardo, head of the Animal Liberation Army, interviewed on television, expressed satisfaction at the day's unruly events and promised that his group would lead a demonstration every Wednesday until the mayor resigns.

While politicians were reluctant to speculate on Hoagland's future, the man in the street was not.

"We've got to get back to normalcy," said Ollie Gilpey, 46, an auto parts salesman from Bayside, Queens, "and we can't do it while this dog thing hangs over us. Hoagland should get out so we can get back to business."

Mona Finca, 28, an executive assistant in Manhattan, agreed. "It's awful about that dog. Hoagland is a creep who has no business staying in office after what happened."

The other respondents in the newspaper's cross-section survey agreed, except for one elderly woman who commented noncommittally that the controversy was "the dizziest thing that has happened in New York since the Collyer brothers."

The tabloid's editorial called on Hoagland to quit "in the interest of domestic tranquillity."

.   .   .

Following Governor Foote's orders, Sheila Baine had gone to the law books first thing in the morning after the rally. Both she and Governor Foote were working at the uptown executive office—it was thought politic to stay away from City Hall for the day.

Baine's research in the City Charter confirmed that the public advocate was first in the line of succession. But she was amazed by something else that she found, both in the charter and the New York State Public Officers Law. She frankly could not believe what she read, so she checked and rechecked her discovery.

Satisfied, she went next door to confer with the governor and Raifeartaigh.

"What's the good word, sister?" the governor asked, feet propped on an open drawer of her desk and sipping a diet soda. Then she took a closer look at her political assistant.

"Are you all right? You look like something the cat dragged in. Or maybe a dog." She guffawed at her own crack as Raifeartaigh winced.

"Yes, yes, I'm okay. But I've found out something you have to know about."

"Spit it out, baby."

"Well, you were right that Artemis Payne would succeed Mayor Hoagland if he left office. He takes over whenever the mayor cannot act. But there is another applicable law that's pretty incredible."

"Like what?"

Baine nervously turned to the law books she had brought with her. "Section nine of the City Charter says, quote, The mayor may be removed from office by the governor upon charges and after service upon him of a copy of the charges and an opportunity to be heard in his defense. Pending the preparation and disposition of charges, the governor may suspend the mayor for a period not exceeding thirty days, close quote."

"Hell and damnation!" the governor yelped.

"Whew!" Raifeartaigh added.

"That's not all, ma'am. Section thirty-three of the State Public Officers Law says that, quote, The chief executive officer of every city—I'm skipping here—may be removed by the governor after giving such officer a copy of the charges against him and an opportunity to be heard in his defense, close quote."

"Let me see those," Foote demanded, reaching across her desk for the statute books Baine was holding.

She put on her glasses, dangling from a string around her neck, and studied the two texts carefully.

"I'll be damned. What the hell does 'charges' mean?"

"There's absolutely no case law, Governor. 'Charges' is nowhere defined. The Charter says that the mayor—here, give me that book back—quote, shall be responsible for the effectiveness and integrity of city government, close quote. The way I figure it, 'charges' would have to allege some violation of that duty."

"Effectiveness and integrity of city government—like the way those morons in the Police Department handled that riot yesterday? But what about the legislature? Wouldn't those rustics get into the act somehow?"

"Not as far as I can see. The removal power derives from the State Constitution and is vested solely in the governor. You, that is. It's not at all like impeaching the president."

"Raifeartaigh, would I dare to do such a thing?"

"I've no doubt that you would, Governor. Whether it would be wise is a horse of a different color."

"I won't make another dog joke. Well, dearie, you sure have given me something to chew on. However, with all due respect for your Yale Law Journal credentials, I want to check this one out with the attorney general. Do we know where he is today? Up in Albany?"

"I doubt it. You know he's always in the city whenever he can be. He hates Albany."

"If you'd grown up in Skaneateles you'd like to be here in the city, too. Raifeartaigh, get hold of that big oaf and get him in here. ASAP. And as for you, Sheila, you may have done for New York City what Mrs. O'Leary and her cow did for Chicago."

"I'm going to go over everything again, Governor. And you're right, you shouldn't just take my opinion. The AG should certainly be involved."

"It's too good to be true, Raifeartaigh. Removing Eldon from office and getting rid of the only son of a bitch who could give me a run next year. Delicious, but I'm worried about the 'charges.' Ordering the execution of that dog? Probably not enough. But by thereby provoking the worst disruption in the history of the city, is that enough? Let's go over to Le Boeuf Bleu and talk about it. Come on, Albert, we're going to lunch."

.   .   .

The traffic disruptions had delayed the newsstand appearance of *The Surveyor,* less technically outfitted than the dailies, until late morning. But when it appeared, a new ingredient was added to the stew, in the form of Scoop's lead story:

MAYOR PRESIDES AT SLAIN DOG OWNER'S BIGAMOUS MARRIAGE

Was It a Payoff?

By Frederick P. Rice

A new twist in the Wambli dog-killing saga has emerged. It now appears that the marriage Mayor Eldon Hoagland performed at the height of the controversy last week between Sue Nation Brandberg,

owner of the slain Wambli, and her houseboy, Genc Serreqi, was bigamous.

This was the allegation made to The Surveyor by Greta Kalo Serreqi, a 25-year-old computer programmer from Tirana, Albania. Ms. Serreqi, who saw a picture of her husband and his new bride on a newscast in the Albanian capital, flew to New York to confront her husband. She spoke to this reporter sitting in the lobby of the modest midtown hotel where she is staying, which she asked not to be identified.

"Genc and I were married in Kruja, a little town outside Tirana where my parents live, five years ago. We were having some difficulties when he left for America, but he promised we'd work them out once he was established here. We certainly were never divorced and never even talked about it."

The striking brunette, who bears a resemblance to Mrs. Brandberg, the former beauty queen and Manhattan socialite, produced a copy of their marriage license, which she translated for this reporter.

She said that she had been in occasional communication with her husband during his time here, and knew of his employment by Ms. Brandberg. He had described to her his household duties, which included caring for his employer's dog, the American Staffordshire terrier Wambli. Serreqi was walking the dog along Fifth Avenue last August 16th when the canine was killed in the altercation with the mayor's bodyguards that has recently gripped the attention of New Yorkers.

On October 13th, the same day the mayor admitted his complicity in the Wambli killing at a press conference, he performed a surprise wedding ceremony for Mrs. Brandberg and Serreqi at City

Hall. Cameramen covering the story of the shooting had crowded City Hall at the time and snapped pictures and made videotapes of the newlyweds. It was an excerpt from one of these tapes that Ms. Greta Serreqi saw on television back in Tirana.

"All I can tell you is, I was stunned," she told us. When asked what she hoped to accomplish on her trip to New York, the woman said that all she wanted was "my husband back."

The woman said she had confronted Ms. Brandberg at the latter's town house but had been asked to leave when she said she was Serreqi's wife. The Surveyor has also learned that Serreqi himself has been evicted from the Brandberg mansion.

It is unclear how this new revelation will affect the besieged Mayor Hoagland.

At the time of the Brandberg-Serreqi "marriage" last week, there was speculation that the mayor had performed the ceremony as a means of pacifying the intense anger Ms. Brandberg has expressed over the death of her dog, including her public statements criticizing the mayor's part in the incident.

Whether or not there was an element of payoff involved, according to lawyers consulted by The Surveyor, the mayor may have violated the New York Penal Law, which classifies as a class A misdemeanor the performance of a marriage ceremony if the official performing it does so "knowing that a legal impediment to such marriage exists."

Neither Ms. Brandberg nor her "husband" would comment for this article. Calls to the mayor's office requesting a statement were not returned.

Sue Brandberg had forewarning about Scoop's bigamy story; he had called her the day before, asking for comment, which she refused to give. She had immediately tried to reach Brendon Proctor, only to find that he was on a quick, one-day trip to Chicago. She requested that his secretary get in touch with him with the urgent message to call his client at once.

Proctor's secretary had failed in her task. The lawyer had already left for O'Hare when she connected to the office he had been at, and since Proctor was a Luddite who did not believe in cell phones, she could not reach him. Then he had been stuck on the ground in his New York–bound plane for six hours, the victim of the international air traffic jam set off in the aftermath of the Wambli rally.

When he finally did get Sue's message the next morning, he called her forthwith and was assaulted by a mixture of hysteria and vituperation.

"Where were you when I needed you? Why were you in Chicago? That worm Justin Boyd and his baby reporter are about to run a story that I am a bigamist. I need a lawyer right now. When can you get here?"

As usual Proctor was annoyed at Sue's peremptory attitude and baffled as well by the reference to bigamy. What next? he thought. First that lightning marriage to her gigolo and now this. But he concealed both his irritation and his confusion and said he would be over within the hour. But not before taking a quick look at the New York Penal Law definition of bigamy. And along the way to 62nd Street picking up a copy of the new *Surveyor*.

.   .   .

"Here it is," Proctor said to Sue, handing her the paper as soon as she opened her front door. Once they were seated upstairs, she read the account and then crumpled up the paper.

259

"Bastard!" was her terse, angry reaction as she got up and paced around her living room. Calming down, she related to Proctor the details of the visit from Greta Serreqi.

"Did you believe her?"

"I had no way of knowing. It doesn't matter. Genc has admitted it." She did not specify when the admission had been made.

"Where is he now?"

"I have no idea. I threw him out."

"I assume, Sue, that you had no reason to believe that Genc was already married?" Proctor was by no stretch of the imagination a criminal lawyer, experienced in steering clients' recollections in the right direction (that is, toward the path of innocence), but he was shrewd enough to make the attempt solely by instinct.

Sue hesitated, stalling by repeating his question. "Did I have any reason to believe that Genc was already married? No." She recalled full well her conversation about a communist marriage and stuck to her nonlegal but perhaps patriotic conclusion that such a marriage was no marriage at all.

"There were no discussions with him about this—before your marriage, that is?"

"No."

"And no hints in anything he told you?"

"I knew he had had a girlfriend back in Albania. I may even have thought he was living with her. But marriage? No." She answered quietly, perhaps because she saw vividly a mental image of that donkey cart bearing the happy—and very obviously married—Greta and Genc.

"Listen to me carefully, Sue. A person is guilty of bigamy if he or she marries another who has a living spouse. In New York it's a so-called class E felony—not murder or grand larceny, but a felony, punishable by up to four years in prison."

Sue rubbed her face in despair as her lawyer spoke.

"As you might guess, I've only done about five minutes' research on this, but it is apparently a defense if a party acted under a 'reasonable belief' that the other person was unmarried. If Serreqi had a wife, that defense won't do him any good. He's guilty as hell. But from what you say, it sounds like you had such a 'reasonable belief.'"

"Yes!" Sue said. She had feared Proctor would press her on whether she *knew* Genc was married; "reasonable belief" seemed to give her some wiggle room, though it would be just as well if no one ever knew about that picture in Genc's wallet.

"Yes, you had a reasonable belief that he was unmarried?"

"Absolutely."

"Well, Sue, you may have a large embarrassment on your hands, but I think we can probably keep you out of Sing Sing."

"What should I do, Brendon?"

"Lie low. And for God's sake, don't say a word to *The Surveyor* or any other reporter."

"Don't worry."

.   .   .

After a steak, shared with Albert, and a martini—white wine was for fairies, she maintained—Governor Foote was in a mellow mood as she strolled back to her office with Raifeartaigh and Sheila Baine. The prospect of offing Eldon Hoagland still intrigued her but she continued to have doubts, which she had expressed again over lunch.

On the way Raifeartaigh spotted the new issue of *The Surveyor* on a newsstand, as well as it's "Bigamous Marriage" headline. He bought a copy and was soon reading Scoop's story aloud to an incredulous governor and Sheila. He had finished as they got off the elevator outside the executive offices.

"Well, well, well," Foote chortled. "Maybe I can squeeze Eldon's balls after all."

TWENTY-SIX

Gullighy had also received a call the day before from Scoop, inquiring about the "bigamous marriage" the mayor had performed. He had hung up on the reporter, after calling him a "crazy bastard." What will they try next? he thought to himself. Once he had been shown *The Surveyor,* Eldon asked the same thing.

"I can't seem to do anything right. The first marriage I performed as mayor and it turns out to be bigamous.

"The Court Street lawyers that reporter consulted said I committed no crime, unless I knew of the bigamy. Well, I sure as hell didn't. But please check with Noel Miller to make sure that 'knowledge' is there in the law. Jack, the way things are going, they'll put me in a black box, like the 'coffin' for that damn dog, and parade *me* around City Hall Park. Why the hell did I take this job, will you tell me?"

It was a question for which, under the circumstances, Gullighy had no ready answer.

. . .

In late afternoon Scoop returned to his apartment, a copy of *The Surveyor* under his arm. Genc was there and, to Scoop's surprise, greeted him cheerfully.

"Scoop, I know you're my friend—about the only one I have over here—but you didn't have to go and see Greta. It was gentle of you to do that. She was feeling very down and felt happy that a friend was supporting her."

Scoop was conscience-stricken. He had told Greta that he was a friend of her husband's and that he would try to help her. But he needed to know the facts before he could. He had failed to mention that he was a reporter, and one writing a story about her husband's marital adventure. She may even have thought he was a lawyer, though his conscience told him—almost—that he really had said nothing to further that impression, though he had carried a briefcase and had taken notes on a yellow legal pad purchased in the stationery store around the corner, rather than his customary notebook. He chose to stay mute as Genc continued to speak.

"You're a good man, Scoop. I thank you. But I think we do not need your help. I've talked with Greta and told her the truth. That my marriage to Sue was for green card. When I have it—I wait two years, I understand—I can get good job, say bye-bye to Sue. Then bring Greta over to have a real life, not illegal's. She understand now, and if Sue pay up, she will go home without her mouth opening."

"Genc, you better read this," Scoop said, handing him *The Surveyor* and pointing to the lead story.

Genc read slowly. "You fucking Gypsy," he said finally, coolly angry and waving the newspaper. "You ruin all my plans! My plans for my *life!*" He put on his shirt and started gathering up his possessions into his backpack.

"Genc, I'm sorry. Really I am. But you must remember I'm a reporter. My first duty is to my paper and my readers. You and Sue committed a serious crime. The public is entitled to know that and it was my obligation to write about it."

Scoop managed to finish his little speech, even while recognizing his priggish and self-righteous tone. More precisely, he heard the voice of Justin Boyd echoing in his own.

"What are you going to do?" he asked as Genc finished his packing.

"I'll think of something. Do not worry. But don't expect to put it down in your newspaper."

Genc headed to the door and, before leaving, bowed with mock solemnity toward Scoop. "Thank you for everything, my friend. My best friend in America!" He slammed the door hard and was gone.

Scoop sat on the edge of his bed, staring for some minutes at the headline—and byline—in the paper Genc had thrown to the floor.

．　．　．

The Post-News once again had to swallow its pride the next morning and parrot *The Surveyor*'s bigamy story; its reporters had been unable to locate Genc or Greta. Sue, as instructed, refused any comment, and Gullighy indignantly denied Mayor Hoagland's criminality. This did not stop the paper's editorialists, who wrote, under the heading "Something Smells":

> We are not going to write about Mayor Eldon Hoagland and dogs today. Instead our subject is the mayor and a fish—a very smelly fish in City Hall. As reported on our front page, the marriage ceremony that he performed uniting Sue Nation Brandberg and her boyish live-in, Genc Serreqi, was a sham. It turns out that the smooth young Albanian who caught beauty queen Brandberg's fancy already had a wife back home in the Balkans. This makes him guilty of good, old-fashioned bigamy—still a felony in New York. And it makes her guilty, too, if she smelled something fishy, so to speak.
>
> And what about the mayor? There was deep suspicion when the

Serreqi-Brandberg nuptials were announced that there was a *quid* for his *quo:* he would preside at her hastily arranged "marriage" if she would keep quiet about the slaying of her beloved dog, Wambli, by the mayor's condottieri.

We have two questions for Eldon Hoagland:

1. Did he make a deal with Mrs. Brandberg to marry her in exchange for her silence? Did that deal involve only the woman's promise to be quiet, or was it more complicated than that?

2. As to the bigamy matter, one is reminded of that question from another ancient scandal: What did he know, and when did he know it?

We need answers, Mr. Mayor, and the faster the better.

The Times, presumably on the quite valid theory that it could not corroborate Scoop's story, was silent for the day.

The morning e-mail was surprisingly quiet. The only message was not, however, especially comforting:

I hope that Native American and her Albanian did have a bigamous marriage, and I hope you knew all about it. Marriage is a dumb irrelevancy forced upon us by religious fanatics. So bigamy should be irrelevant, too. Who cares how many times someone goes through a marriage ceremony? Stand up for sexual freedom—don't let the bastards get you down. Yours in good sex—Bruce

Having not heard from Noel Miller by noontime, Eldon gave him a call. The corporation counsel confirmed that the mayor was not in violation of the law by marrying Genc and Sue, as long as he didn't have knowledge of Genc's marital status.

"That means I'm in the clear, Noel, since I had no idea her young stud had a wife. *The Post-News* doesn't agree with that, if you've seen it this morning, but what do you expect? They're certainly accusing me of high crimes and misdemeanors. What if they were right? Could I be impeached?

"I'd like to know the answer to that. Could you call me? Edna and I are getting out of here and going to Leaky Swansea's, on Long Island, for the weekend. You can reach me there. You have the number? Good."

.   .   .

Eldon was grateful for the chance to leave town; at least the Wambli balloon did not follow him to Southampton. The Swanseas were good hosts, plied their guests with good food and wine and refrained from discussing dogs or dubious marriages.

He and Edna went for a walk on the deserted, windswept beach late in the afternoon. The mild weather, the impending sunset and gently breaking waves were conducive to an intimate chat.

"I don't know if I'm going to make it, Edna. All the insults, the shouting, the innuendos in the damn *Post-News*, they're getting to me. That editorial this morning, practically accusing me of taking a bribe. Not to mention committing a crime."

"It's politics, dear. Of the New York City variety."

"I now understand why no mayor has ever gone on to be president. They all became exhausted trying to keep the melting pot from boiling over."

"They ought to revise the song. 'If you can make it there, you can make it anywhere—if you survive.'"

"I know that things will calm down. The animal righters will run out of steam. It'll be clear I did nothing worse than lose control when that wretched dog bit me. And the idea that I committed a crime is preposterous. Eventually people will understand that."

"You're right—I think."

"The real question is whether it will settle down soon enough— soon enough for me to push the programs I promised. We're all ready to launch our technology zone project, but it needs my full-time attention. I can't give that with all the stupid distractions. It's so tedious and boring."

"You've been through it with nutcases before, dear. Those new-wave upstarts in your department were almost as extreme as the Animal Liberation Army. And that Dean of the Faculty at Columbia made it about as difficult for you as *The Post-News*. Everything's going to be all right."

"Let's hold hands and look at the sunset. As long as we're okay, we'll hang on."

. . .

Noel Miller called early Saturday morning.

"Good news, Eldon. As I thought, there's absolutely no provision for impeaching a mayor. You're in the clear unless you become mentally disabled. Then they can push you out." Miller chuckled.

"Don't laugh. The way things are going I could be round the bend tomorrow. But thanks for the good word, Noel. Not that I was worried."

"You're okay, my friend, absent mental illness or physical incapacity. Otherwise the only way they can get rid of you is if the governor removes you. Which is a pretty preposterous idea."

Eldon felt an uncomfortable tightening in his throat. "She could do that?" he asked incredulously.

"Yep. All by herself. But for God's sake, don't trouble your head about that. Relax and have a good weekend."

The mayor did his best to follow his counsel's advice. But he did spend a restless Saturday night, dreaming, among other things, of quarreling with Randilynn Foote over her B minus and hearing her obscenity-laced anger at the removal of the furnishings from the Governor's Rooms.

.   .   .

Governor Foote had had a brief meeting with Attorney General Mason Mudson on Friday afternoon. An obese, slow-moving (and by more than one account, slow-witted) small-town lawyer, he had been the bastion of the Republican Party in his upstate county seat. Since all of Randilynn's running mates in her campaign for election had been from the metropolitan area, Mason had been picked to balance the ticket.

Mudson had also been able to raise a surprising amount of money for his own campaign. Many business interests, bruised by attacks from a succession of vigorous, populist, proconsumer attorneys general, saw in him the ideal: a dyed-in-the-wool conservative and a lethargic one. Those dreaded words in the heading of legal complaints, "The People of the State of New York *versus* . . . ," would not be *versus* them.

Once elected, he happily discovered that one was not chained to Albany, the state capital, or the snowbound Brasilia, as some called it. Overcoming an upstater's revulsion to Sodom-on-the-Hudson, he had come to like it, though his wife, Prudence, resolutely refused to leave Skaneateles; in her view the people in New York City "smelled funny."

Mudson was an appreciative dais-sitter at fund-raising and political dinners. He thought the food was marvelous, and there was always the VIP attention—gathering with the event's guest of honor and an occasional celebrity in a private room away from the hordes attending the function in question, drinking free drinks and being addressed as "General." They were even more fulfilling than those Kiwanis Club weekly dinners in Skaneateles, though he had enjoyed them, and the mystery-meat entrees, too.

He had a set speech—written for $100 by a *Syracuse Herald-Journal* reporter—about the great Empire State and the benefits that free enterprise could bring to it (the Syracuse reporter, given the meagerness of his fee, had lifted this portion of the text from various right-wing foundation press releases).

Randilynn Foote was grateful to Munson, so eagerly representing her administration at the banqueting events she could not abide. "He likes having his ass licked," she once observed to Raifeartaigh, "and as long as he doesn't get a sexually transmitted disease in the process, that's fine with me."

At their Friday meeting in her office, Governor Foote made it clear that no decisions had been made but that she wanted to "explore all the options." She told her AG that Ms. Baine had done a great job in researching the applicable law, but she wanted to be doubly sure that Mudson agreed with her young assistant's conclusions.

"You make certain you're in synch," she had instructed him, "because if I do anything you're going to have to spread holy water all over it."

Mudson, like everyone else who had looked at the question, was amazed at the power in the governor's hands. But he promised to vet Ms. Baine's conclusions, and the meeting was adjourned until eleven o'clock on Monday.

"I'd meet earlier," the governor explained, "but I'm off on a camping trip to Schroon Lake—assuming that piece of junk they make me fly in can get to the Adirondacks—and I'm not coming back until first thing Monday morning." She reminded Raifeartaigh to write a reimbursement check to the state for the trip; it was a private one, though she said that the state should pay her money for riding in the rickety executive plane.

Now they were back in her office. As expected, Mudson confirmed Sheila Baine's legal research.

The governor, scratching at some ugly bites on her legs—"Why didn't they tell me there would still be blackflies in the sticks in October?" she grumbled—informed her trio of listeners that she still hadn't made up her mind what to do about removing Eldon.

"I'm tempted, that's for sure. Having Putter Payne in there would be perfect. But could I get away with it?"

While the governor had been pondering the issue in an Adirondack pup tent, Raifeartaigh had been doing the same, in the dark Village coffeehouse he frequented.

"If I understand the law correctly," he said, "the governor can suspend the mayor for thirty days while charges are being readied. Right?"

Baine and Mudson nodded.

"So, why don't you suspend Hoagland and announce that charges, and what they consist of, are being prepared? If the outcry is too great, you can back off. If not, you go ahead and remove him."

"Effing brilliant! I knew there was a reason for keeping you around, Raifeartaigh. I'll do it! Mason, you and Sheila get up a letter I can deliver to His Honor telling him he is suspended. And that charges are being prepared to remove him. Raifeartaigh, get hold of that bog-trotter of his and tell him I'm coming downstairs to see the mayor at two o'clock, or whatever time this afternoon suits him. Hot damn! This is going to be fun!"

.　.　.

The mayor, Police Commissioner Stephens and Noel Miller were conferring downstairs while the governor was mapping her strategy. The Animal Liberation Army, true to its threat of having weekly demonstrations, had applied for a permit for a rally on Wednesday afternoon.

"My view is that they've had their say and we should deny it," the commissioner said.

"I'd like to agree with you, Danny. But free speech is free speech. And you have to admit that they haven't achieved their objective."

"Getting you to resign, you mean?"

"Yes. I say give them their permit—but for God's sake ban animals. That's what got your boys into trouble last week."

"Last week won't happen again, Mr. Mayor. Not on my watch. So we grant them the permit—for humans only?"

"Correct."

As they reached their conclusion, Gullighy came bursting in, red-faced and agitated.

"Something's up. I don't know what, but something's up."

"What are you talking about?" Eldon asked impatiently.

"Randilynn Foote wants an appointment to come see you this afternoon. That half-breed Raifeartaigh says its about a legal matter and the governor thinks Noel should be there, too. Mason Mudson will be along."

"She wants to come down here, not me go up there?"

"Correct."

"It must be important. Randy Randy has probably figured out a way of taking over all of City Hall. But tell her I'll be waiting with bells on. And Noel, you'll join us. I'm almost tempted to invite you, too, Danny; not a bad idea to have the police commissioner around when she lets loose."

"Thank you, no. I'll stick to four-legged bitches."

.   .   .

Gullighy came into the mayor's office again a half hour later.

"Raifeartaigh just called back. They think Putter Payne should be at this meeting."

"The more the merrier," Eldon said with a sigh.

Or maybe not so merry, he thought once Gullighy had left. What was it Noel Miller had said over the weekend about removal? But that B minus had been deserved, it really had.

.   .   .

Sue Nation Brandberg was in a sour mood as she opened her morning's mail. She had been to Café Boulud the night before with one of her walkers and had had the feeling throughout that those seated in the banquettes and tables near hers were discreetly gesturing in her direction and talking about her. It had been uncomfortable.

In her pile of mail she came to a letter on the cheap stationery of the Brandywine Hotel, the message crudely written with a ballpoint pen:

Dear Miszu,

I write this letter as good-bye. Greta and I have talked much and decided is better I go back to Albania. We go to start our lives over.

I love America and am glad to have seen some of it, New York especially. But the authorities don't want me and after all that happened, I go back. Maybe someday I come as legal and maybe Greta will come, too. Now is better I go to Tirana. I can work as an engineer, even if for little money, instead of being watched as illegal person.

I put this in the mail as we go to JFK. We fly to Rome tonight, then to Tirana. Thank goodness Greta has a credit card! Our adventure was interesting and I remember you always.

Goodbye, Genc

Sue thought regretfully of the OOOH! SHPIRT!s; she was glad they had been "interesting" for Genc. She couldn't be angry with him. He had, after all, told her he was already married. And with all the publicity, he would probably have been thrown out anyway. Instead, her anger focused on Eldon. Wasn't he the cause of all her troubles? The death of her beloved Wambli. The public and notorious scandal about her marriage, a scandal inflamed by the press hordes outside the mayor's office after the ceremony. (She had concluded that their presence was no accident.) Not to mention the pack of reporters still camped out in front of her house.

Should she seek revenge? What if she told the press that he knew about Genc's living spouse when he performed the marriage? That would make it hot for him! Brendon Proctor had told her she was unlikely to be prosecuted for bigamy. So what was the risk?

Questions, questions, she thought. She needed time to work out some answers.

. . .

At two o'clock on the dot Governor Foote and Attorney General Mudson came down to the mayor's office. Mudson was sweating, either from the effort of climbing down the stairs or from tension. Eldon and Noel Miller were waiting; Putter had been located but would be late, coming in from Queens.

The foursome exchanged handshakes, but there was no small talk.

"Governor, do you mind if I ask Jack Gullighy to join us?" Eldon asked.

"By all means."

The group sat quietly until Gullighy arrived. Eldon sat at his desk, with Noel Miller at his right. Foote and Mudson took places on a sofa at the side of the room. Gullighy stood by the door, possibly to guard it, possibly to be ready for a quick escape.

"Governor, to what do I owe the pleasure?" the mayor asked.

"Mr. Mayor," the governor began stiffly—this was not an Eldon and Randilynn occasion—"I think this letter explains it best."

No one had noticed until then that she had come in carrying an envelope. She opened it, took out two copies of a letter, and handed them to the mayor and Noel Miller.

Putting on his glasses, Eldon read:

Dear Mayor Hoagland:

Last week, on October 20th, the citizens of the greater metropolitan area were subjected to a paralyzing disruption of both air and ground transportation. This was a direct result of

275

a rally staged in City Hall Park, the purpose of which was to call for your resignation as mayor of the City of New York. The New York City Police Department was unable to contain the demonstrators; this resulted in disruptions widely believed to be the most serious in the area's history.

The organizers of last week's protest have indicated, on their Web site and in the press, that a second demonstration will be held this Wednesday. Indeed, they have stated their intention of holding a demonstration each Wednesday until you resign. All signs point to another disruption beyond the control of the police and, quite possibly, one even more severe than the one experienced last week.

I have reluctantly concluded that charges should be brought against you, looking toward your possible removal as mayor. These will be more fully documented forthwith in a detailed statement. In substance they will allege (1) that you have failed to maintain the effectiveness and integrity of city government operations, as required by Section 8a of the New York City Charter, (2) that the enforcement of law and order and the maintenance of the public safety in the city have been endangered by the consequences of your actions, (3) that your personal conduct on the night of August 16th, in connection with the murder of the dog called Wambli, constituted a violation of Section 353 of the Agriculture and Markets Law, with respect to overdriving, torturing and injuring animals, and (4) that you have violated your duty as a magistrate, under Section 8b of the Charter, by performing a bigamous marriage ceremony between Sue Nation Brandberg and Genc Serreqi on October 13th in violation of Section 255.00 of the Penal Law, allegedly to procure the silence

276

of Ms. Brandberg regarding the aforesaid incident involving her dog Wambli.

As you know, as governor I have the plenary power to remove you from office pursuant to subsection 2 of Section 33 of the Public Officers Law and Section 9 of the New York City Charter. It is my intention to make a determination of whether or not to exercise such power not later than 30 days from the date hereof, during which 30-day period you shall have the opportunity, under the laws cited, to present to me whatever manner of defense you desire.

In the meantime, pursuant to the powers vested in me, as aforesaid, I hereby suspend you from your duties as mayor as of midnight tonight.

Very truly yours,

Randilynn R. Foote

Governor

Eldon's hand was shaking by the time he had finished.

"Is there anything to be said? I suppose not. Though I can't refrain from asking you, Governor, whether you are completely serious about this. Or is this a ploy of some kind?"

"No, Mr. Mayor, I'm serious. I've called a press conference for four o'clock to announce your suspension."

"And as for what you call my 'defense,' is there any point in presenting one?"

"That's up to you."

"Mason, are you on board with this?" Miller demanded of Mudson. "You must realize that nothing like this has ever been done before. Aren't you afraid of a rather strong public reaction?"

"Noel, I am aboard. The law is clear about the governor's powers. She is exercising them in what she considers the best interests of the people of New York—state and city."

"Well, I guess that's it," Eldon announced. "Except, Randilynn, would you do me the courtesy of talking with me privately for a moment?"

"Of course."

Before the meeting could break up, Putter Payne made a breathless entrance.

"What's up, guys?" he said jovially, before sensing the tense atmosphere.

Miller handed him a copy of the governor's letter. Putter read it, emitting a soft whistle as he did so.

"Let me get a grip on this," he said when he had finished. "Does this mean I'm the acting mayor after tonight?"

"That is correct, Mr. Payne," Mudson told him. "Until the governor makes her decision about removal—and then, um, possibly thereafter."

"Holy Jesus." Then, after a pause, "I guess I'll have to start dressing up," pointing at his own attire—a polo shirt and khakis. "No more casual Fridays—or Tuesdays, Wednesdays or Thursdays." His feeble sally did not go down well.

Eldon again asked if he could see Randilynn alone, as the others prepared to leave. "And Artie, we'd better talk when I'm through."

"I'll be waiting right outside, Mayor," Payne replied, with just the slightest pause before uttering the word "Mayor."

TWENTY-SEVEN

Once she was alone with Eldon, Randilynn Foote put her feet up on his coffee table. She offered no apology or explanation for the extraordinary action she had just announced, waiting for him to initiate the conversation.

"I guess you deserved a B minus in State and Local Government, as well as my course," he began.

"Eldon, I'm not here to listen to insults."

"The idea of disrupting a democratically elected city administration by a state authority—I guess you must have been absent the day Professor Behr lectured on that."

"Do you have anything germane to say to me, or not?"

"I do, but I doubt that it will penetrate. For instance, you don't have to destroy me politically. I'm no threat to you—and certainly have no thoughts of running against you next year."

"Really? What about that cow? You went upstate to milk her for the fun of it?"

"Do you really think I was pandering for upstate votes? I milked that cow on a bet with Jack Gullighy, who said I couldn't do it."

"I don't believe you."

"Don't. But let me say one thing before you run off—"

"Run off to that shambles of an office upstairs."

"Squatters can't be choosy."

"Fuck you."

"Thanks, but no thanks. Obviously I haven't figured out how

I'm going to respond to your little game, but I can assure you I'll make it as uncomfortable for you as possible."

"Go to it, babe. Just remember I'm the dealer."

. . .

The tête-à-tête with Artemis Payne did not go much better, though he at least expressed regret at the turn of events.

"Are you really sorry, Artie? You know, I saw on television those constituents of your buddy, Councilman Hayes. Carrying signs saying "'Resign! Resign!'" Except there was one that got there by mistake, for the George Hayes Democratic Club. George stirred things up on his own, I assume."

"I don't tell George what to do."

"But I'll bet he told you what he was planning and you didn't object."

"I don't remember."

"I thought so. You want to use this office while I'm—suspended? I can lock up anything personal and the place is yours."

"Yes, I think I will. You know, to show continuity, to demonstrate that the ship of state sails on."

"Fine."

"I assume, though, that you'll stay in the mansion—at least until your status gets resolved?"

"Christ Almighty, you want me to move out of Gracie Mansion? Are you serious?"

"I was just asking."

"Well, to use the favorite expression from the limited vocabulary of our esteemed governor, fuck you."

"No offense, man. No offense intended."

· · ·

With Governor Foote's press conference about to happen, Eldon and Gullighy drafted a statement denouncing the governor's action. The mayor did not want to meet the press just yet, so he left City Hall to head home to Gracie—assuming Putter Payne had not already taken it over.

· · ·

Both *The Times* and *The Post-News* described Governor Foote's indignant voice as she had read out her letter to Eldon to a loud, crowded press conference. But their editorial page reactions were, predictably, quite different. *The Times*'s editorial began:

As of yesterday afternoon, this city had one Banana Republic too many. The proliferation of trendy clothing stores with that name was joined by a different type of banana republic—situated in the office of Governor Randilynn Foote. Her strange actions in suspending Mayor Eldon Hoagland and threatening to remove him from office are nothing short of incredible. No such course of conduct has ever been followed in this state before. And for good reason. Suspension and removal are the ultimate means of dealing with a corrupt or criminal or massively incompetent public official.

Mayor Hoagland certainly has not covered himself with glory in recent weeks. But his conduct, however misguided and inept, does not rise to the standards of misfeasance or malfeasance that surely were meant to govern the governor's nearly unfettered removal power.

Governor Foote's bizarre maneuver can only be seen as political—rapping the city as a means of shoring up her image upstate, and in the process targeting perhaps the only politician in the state with the ability to stand up to her.

Her actions are worthy of a banana republic where democracy is ill understood. They have no place in New York, city or state.

The Post-News took a different tack:

A breath of fresh air swept through New York City yesterday, wiping away memories of last week's traffic-jam gas fumes, as well as the dubious odors emanating from City Hall. It came in the form of Governor Randilynn Foote's announcement of her courageous decision to suspend Mayor Eldon Hoagland and initiate procedures to remove him from office.

That the governor has the power to do this is undisputed. That use of this power is unusual goes without saying. But what is important is that our governor had the guts to do what she did—to suspend a mayor who has become a subject of ridicule around the world, and one incapable of leading our city any longer.

Eldon Hoagland stepped in it when he became embroiled in that disgraceful dog incident in August. Now our governor has given him a push, which surely will lead to his departure from City Hall. None too soon.

Eldon read the morning papers at a leisurely pace, even though *The Post-News*'s editorial made his blood boil; there was, after all, no pressure to get to the office.

Midmorning, he received a call from Noel Miller, who asked if he could come by the mansion. Eldon readily agreed, assuming that Miller wanted to talk about legal strategy in the battle with Governor Foote.

"How do you size up the legal situation?" he asked his corporation counsel, once they were seated in the mansion parlor.

"It's not great, Eldon. There's not much hope of challenging the suspension; the governor appears to have the absolute right to do it. Then, when she brings formal charges, you'll have the right to be heard—by her. She's the judge and jury, all by herself. Maybe a court would find that she's being arbitrary and, if she is, that her removal power may be limited. But it is less than clear. I assume, though, that you'll fight her, to the extent you can."

"Damn right."

Miller was nervous, his left leg jiggling ever so slightly. Then it became apparent why.

"I'm glad to hear you're going to fight. I wouldn't have expected anything less from you. But there is one thing. I may as well be up-front about it. I'm afraid that as the corporation counsel I can't be your gladiator in this one. Eldon, old friend, I've been thinking about my situation almost nonstop since Randilynn's announcement. Fact is, I was up most of the night pondering it. And I've come to the reluctant conclusion that I must remain neutral. That my first loyalty is to the city itself. I can neither defend you nor assist the governor in her ouster efforts. There's no real legal learning on the subject, but this is the position I'm afraid I have to take to maintain the integrity and objectivity of my office."

"I'm disappointed, to put it mildly. We've known each other for years, we went through that election campaign together, and I thought you were my ally. And friend."

"I'm both those things, Eldon. But I have to call this one as I see it. What you need is a high-powered attorney to formulate and execute a real battle plan."

"How on earth do I get a private lawyer?"

"I have some suggestions for you."

"More to the point, how do I pay one?"

"That's a problem, I'll admit. If you prevail, it seems to me clear that the city would pick up the bill."

"And if I don't, I pay?"

"That would appear to be the case."

By now Eldon was eager to get rid of his visitor, to see him out before he himself exploded in a mixture of contempt and anger. "Well, you've certainly put another straw on this poor old camel's back, Noel. I'd like to say I respect your decision, but in all honesty I don't."

Once Miller had gone—he all but ran for the outer door—Eldon slumped in his chair, very discouraged. He had been responsible for Miller's public career, a nice capstone to a lifetime of successful, if mostly anonymous, private practice. So what was his reward? Having his appointee back away when he was most needed, obviously more eager to protect his own reputation than to march side by side with Eldon. It was particularly galling, since Miller had become a rich man; he was not at all dependent on his city job and could well have risked criticism for acting on Eldon's behalf, even if forced to resign for doing so.

Then there was the matter of money. A first-rate lawyer would be expensive, probably inordinately so. The only resources to pay such a person were the pension he had accrued during his years of teaching, a small farm he and Edna had purchased in Minnesota and Edna's modest savings and 401(k) accounts. Would it be wise, or even fair to Edna, to dissipate these assets to pay for his defense?

He would have to ponder that. After lunch and a nap. He might even have a Bloody Mary—unheard of on a weekday when he was performing his duties as mayor. He must try to enjoy as much as he could the enforced vacation Randy Randy had imposed upon him.

.   .   .

Eldon was awakened from his nap by a call from Jack Gullighy, the only one he received during the afternoon. Gullighy, who remained at City Hall but without access to the acting mayor's office, filled his boss in on developments.

Despite the suspension, the ALAers were loudly heralding their next demonstration. Gullighy reported that police intelligence, confirmed on the ALA Web site, reported that a planeload of sympathizers from England—protestors against genetically modified food—were expected for the event.

"They tell me the Brit crowd makes your ALA friends look like pussycats, if I may be permitted that term. True fanatics," Gullighy said. "A conservative Buddhist group from California also promises to show up. To show their concern for all forms of life."

"Plants, too?"

"I suppose so."

"How's Putter doing?"

"Haven't talked to him. But I was told, if you can believe it, that he showed up this morning with a golf bag."

"Hope he doesn't damage the furniture."

"I'm also told George Hayes has been with him most of the day."

"No surprise there."

Eldon told Gullighy about his visit from Noel Miller.

"That's what I like," Gullighy said. "Courage in the face of adversity. What are you going to do, Eldon?"

"I don't know. I'm going to talk everything over with Edna tonight. Call you tomorrow. And Jack?"

"Yes?"

"You'll stick with me until this is over, won't you? Not pull a Miller?"

"Boss, you can count on me. We'll go down together," he said, then added quickly, "Or triumph together."

"Yes."

. . .

Not being interrupted, Eldon spent the rest of the afternoon reading, and thinking about what he read: *The Federalist Papers*, particularly James Madison's essay on the dangers of factions in No. 10. It was the first serious study he had done in months and the tonic effect was good. But by dinnertime he felt like a subject under house arrest.

"What are we having for dinner?" he asked Edna.

"Julio is doing his special chicken fricassee. To cheer you up."

"Thanks, but no thanks. Let's go to Massimo's."

Massimo's was a tiny Italian joint near the mansion, narrow and probably once a shoe store before it's latest incarnation. The food was good, the staff genial and the dour owner usually not in evidence. Eldon and Edna often sneaked off there when Julio's food had become intolerable. The staff treated them like mere mortals, leaving them to themselves at a back table.

The place attracted a mixed crowd of the young and the old, mostly neighborhood types on cook's night out or, like the Hoaglands, escaping for a brief respite from home.

Eldon had noticed before the polyglot composition of the staff at this "Italian" spot—a genuine thirtyish Italian as the maitre d', but a Korean cashier, a girl behind the wine-and-beer bar who was Brazilian, a carrot-topped pizza maker who couldn't possibly have been Italian (probably Irish), a variegated wait staff and busboys Eldon referred to (almost correctly) as "Incas," plus a teenage black delivery boy for the place's considerable take-out business.

Eldon recalled fondly the night their waiter, Mickey, had suggested that they have the lasagna Bolognese. "The regular chef is off," he explained, "and his substitute on Tuesday is a lasagna *expert*. Always have the lasagna on Tuesday."

"Is he from Bologna?" Eldon had asked.

"Oh, no. He's Chinese!"

As they started drinking their bottle of middle-range Chianti, Eldon looked about, saw the restaurant's miniature United Nations once again, and smiled—a rare smile in his first day of suspension.

"You know, Edna, this place is amazing. A half dozen nationalities, three and a half different colors, all with the rather nice objective of efficiently serving up some decent food. It's a miniature New York City—or what New York City should be."

"That's true, dear. We're lucky to have it."

"I only wish *my* little restaurant were humming along in the same way. These people can pay attention to what they're doing. They don't have *The Post-News* and half the world's dog owners looking over their shoulder."

It being Tuesday, Edna ordered the "Chinese lasagna."

"Oh, he's not here tonight, Dr. Hoagland. He's off this week."

"You don't mean you actually have an Italian chef?" Eldon asked.

Mickey (himself an Asian) laughed. "No, nothing that simple. The substitute's from the owner's place downtown. He's Jamaican."

287

"All right, then the Jamaican lasagna."

Eldon decided to have the same. He then told his wife about Noel Miller's visit, and his concern about "objectivity" and "integrity" in the corporation counsel's job.

"As governor of Judea, you mean? You think he's ever heard of Pontius Pilate?"

They dissected their former friend some more before focusing on the troublesome question of hiring a lawyer.

"It could bankrupt us, Edna. Take away every bit of security we've got. Such as it is."

"Maybe you could raise a defense fund."

"That's so sleazy. And probably put me in the debt of people I'd rather not owe for the rest of my term, if not the rest of my life. Besides, I'm not sure I have a whole helluva lot of steadfast friends at the moment, if Miller's any example. My telephone wasn't exactly ringing off the hook today with expressions of support."

"It's your unlisted number."

"I'm afraid the result would have been the same if I had an eight hundred number that was on a billboard in Times Square."

"Jamaican lasagna!" Mickey announced.

The food was good sustenance. They ate without conversing, until Eldon asked his wife, speaking rapidly, "What should we do? It seems to me Randy Randy has me cornered. I can fight, pawning our retirement in the process, or I can resign.

"Randilynn is my judge and jury, and we know how she's going to come out. I can contest the dog charge—at best I committed a misdemeanor, something about 'overdriving, torturing and injuring animals' if I recall correctly what the cowardly Miller told me. Not exactly high crimes and misdemeanors, is it? Then there was the massive traffic tie-up—no crime there, and the voters can always punish me for that. If I were foolish enough to run again. And the bigamous marriage, in which I was a totally innocent party. But can I trust Sue Brandberg to tell the truth—that I didn't know? Or is she still on the warpath about that damnable dog of hers? Ready to say anything to get even?

"And what if I have a high-priced, scorched-earth defense and prevail? Can I govern after that? Can I get people to listen to an inebriated dog killer when I talk about serious issues? I don't know the answers, do you? You should. You're the one who told me to leave the comfort of Minnesota for Columbia, when there was no guarantee I'd get tenure here in New York. Who told me I could be an effective department chairman, able to handle that bunch of politically correct kindergartners. Then had the guts to tell me to step down when they overwhelmed me. Who, after some persuading, encouraged me to run for mayor—'Less talk and more action,' you said, without ever complaining what the change did to both your personal and professional life. So, Edna, what do I do now?"

"Eldon, dear, let me say two things. First, you're in a maelstrom you did not create—well, maybe you did a little bit, but you understand how unfair circumstances have been. How you respond is up to you. That brings me to my second point, which is, whatever you decide, I'm with you. We haven't been married for forty-one years for nothing. If you want to fight, I'll be right there beside you. For richer or poorer, in sickness and in health, et cetera, et cetera. But if you want out, that's fine with me, too. Your mind is full of ideas about things to write—which will never happen while you're cutting ribbons or jollying people up at ethnic dinners. I'm with you whatever you decide."

Edna's impassioned speech had deterred Mickey the waiter, who now approached with an offer.

"You've finished your bottle of wine. Have another glass on the house. We're all friends here and we'd like to cheer you up, Mr. Mayor. Be our guest."

"Mickey, you're great. The answer is yes. And when are you going to run for mayor?"

"No way, sir. This restaurant is complicated enough for me."

Edna and Eldon drank from their refilled glasses. He didn't say much but was touched by Mickey's unsolicited concern. And his wife's reconfirmation of 41 years of loving support.

"You know, Eldon, what our plans have always been. To retire back to Minnesota, with you taking a teaching job if one's available and me starting a modest practice, if there's any demand for it. Would it be so bad to carry out our plans a few years early? I wouldn't mind. You can still smoke there without being thought of as Typhoid Mary. Which reminds me, I need a cigarette. Let's go."

They paid the check and left, shaking hands with the supportive staff as they made their way out. Polanski and Leiter, the new bodyguards, joined them outside—no one had seen fit to terminate the suspended mayor's security arrangements.

"It's an incredible night for this late in October. Let's walk home."

"No, Eldon. You might run into another peeing dog. And besides, why not enjoy our elegant Chevrolet while we can?"

. . .

Eldon slept badly, weighing his options as he tossed and turned. By 5 a.m. he had made up his mind. He would resign. He would not give Randilynn Foote the satisfaction of prolonging his public agony. And he would do it right away, before the next ALA demonstration. He woke Edna and told her his decision.

"I love you," she told him.

By seven o'clock he had awakened Gullighy. The press secretary was exhausted, having listened until very late to a new date's tale of her unpleasant divorce, before bedding her by way of solace. But ever the good soldier, he agreed with Eldon to arrange a press conference that very afternoon at Gracie.

Eldon worked on his statement through the morning, ignoring the newspapers altogether. He read it aloud to Edna and Gullighy, both of whom pronounced it brilliant. At one o'clock, even as the TV trucks were setting up outside, he called Randilynn Foote to tell her of the announcement he was about to make. Her own behavior may have been incredible, but it was not going to deter him from what in normal circumstances would have been common courtesy between two elected officials. The conversation was brief and cool, without so much as "You're doing the right thing" crossing the governor's lips.

He also called Putter, on what had been his own private line until two days before.

"As of midnight tonight you'll be the mayor of the City of New York," he told him. "I wish you luck, Artie, all the luck in the world. Don't forget we ran together in the last campaign. I backed you then, and whatever our differences, I'll support you any way I can now."

"Thank you for that. I'm sorry things turned out this way. But you can't fight the power, not when Randy Randy's got it all. You had no choice but to step off the train. But I sure hope I can call on you for advice, that you'll help me get it all together. I'm going to try my damnedest, Eldon, I really am. Going to try to be the best mayor I can—twenty-four/seven/three-sixty-five. I promise you that."

"We should sit down and talk, whenever it's convenient."

"Yes, we should. Maybe tomorrow or the next day."

"I'd appreciate it if you could come up to Gracie. I think I've seen the last of City Hall."

"Sure thing. What exactly are you going to do now, do you know?"

"Go back to Minnesota. Settle down on that little farm we've got back there. Maybe write some, maybe teach some."

"God be with you, Eldon. Is there anything I can do for you now?"

"Well, yes, there are two things. We didn't keep our apartment, so I'd like a week or so to move out of here, to pack up our stuff. And remember those two bodyguards of mine—Fasco and Braddock? I'd consider it a personal favor if you'd reinstate them to their jobs. They're first-rate, loyal guys and will serve you well. The animal righters will probably give you some static, but I'd really appreciate it."

"Done and done. I won't sweat what a few crazies have to say."

"Give me a call when you want to come up."

"Sure will. Peace, Eldon."

Unlike his tormenter, Eldon was not about to hold a petty grievance against Putter, for his complicity in connection with the Wambli rally. And, he was satisfied, he was entirely sincere when he wished his successor well in his new job.

.   .   .

Eldon read his remarks through one more time before stepping out on to the Gracie Mansion porch on the dot of two o'clock, Edna and Jack Gullighy flanking him. He faced an astounding array of electronic gear and what one veteran observer judged to be the largest attendance at a mayoral press conference ever. He put on his glasses and slowly adjusted them. He began to read from the sheets in his hand:

"After giving the matter careful thought, and talking it over with my wife, I have decided to resign my position as mayor of the City of New York, effective as of midnight tonight. Artemis Payne will thereupon become the new mayor. I talked to him on the telephone earlier this afternoon and wished him well. I repeat those good wishes now.

"I am resigning not out of any sense of guilt or wrongdoing, but rather because a group of single-issue agitators seems determined to make this city ungovernable as long as I am mayor. And because the governor of this state has seen fit to exercise powers never before employed to make my future as mayor untenable.

"For the past weeks, this city, and city government, have been distracted from serious business by a personal mishap of mine involving the death of a dog and unsupportable and totally false allegations about my conduct in office.

"If I were being tried for these offenses in a court of law, or even the court of public opinion, I am confident I would be exonerated. But instead I face a 'trial'—if I can abuse that word—in which a partisan governor would be both judge and jury. The city does not need the confusion and bitterness such a 'trial' would entail. Hence my resignation.

"I am proud of my administration and those who worked with me to achieve the goals we set forth in the campaign two years ago. But now I must move on, lest my continued presence on the public scene divert attention from pressing forward with the programs we have proposed. It is my earnest hope that the initiatives we have started can come to fulfillment, once the petty complications of recent weeks are forgotten.

293

"The Founding Fathers of this country, particularly James Madison, were concerned about the effect of 'factions' on our political life. Today we have our own modern-day version of factions—groups of people whose political interest and awareness are focused on one issue only. I submit to you that single-issue politics is the greatest detriment to effective government that we face today: people unwilling to compromise, people pursuing their selfish goals to the exclusion of others. And I can think of no more vivid example than the members of the Animal Liberation Army.

"So my parting words to the people of this city are these: Beware of single-issue politics and the divisiveness and civil gridlock it fosters. We all must try to compromise our differences, to recognize that others may have viewpoints or interests at variance with our own. Let us recognize that we must always seek common ground to enable us all, of whatever faction, to live in peace and freedom."

TWENTY-EIGHT

Eldon had one piece of luck shortly after his resignation. The cover subject on both *Time* and *Newsweek* the Monday after he left office, his plight caught the attention of Henry Bartlett, the president of the newly established Elmwood College in Bagley, Minnesota. Bartlett and he had been colleagues years before at the University of Minnesota.

Elmwood had recently received gifts endowing a chair in political science in honor of that perennial Gopher State politician, Harold Stassen. Sympathetic to Eldon's plight, and with an opportunity to attract a talented, if at least temporarily infamous, figure to the new campus, Bartlett offered him the professorship.

It was an opportunity almost too good to be true. The Elmwood campus was very near where Eldon had grown up, and also within easy distance of the Hoagland farm. Once Eldon consented, the trustees of Elmwood quickly confirmed his appointment.

The Hoaglands stayed on at Gracie Mansion until the movers came in mid-November. They did so despite the daily call to Eldon from Artemis Payne, ostensibly to inquire about the former mayor's well-being but really to determine when exactly he planned to vacate the mayor's house.

Eldon and Edna were not deluged with invitations in the days before their departure. They spent most of their evenings packing boxes, Eldon trying valiantly to cull his formidable library of books, most of which had remained in the Gracie Mansion basement for want of shelf space during his time as mayor.

Before leaving, the Hoaglands entertained at a buffet dinner for his City Hall staff. It was a wearing occasion; everyone tried to be jolly and upbeat, but there was a pall over the event that no amount of high spirits could lift. Jack Gullighy tried his best to change the tone of the party, but even he could not do it. He also announced to Eldon that night that he was going west to help the computer billionaire in his Colorado Senate race; it was time to make some real money again.

. . .

Eldon also had a farewell evening with Leaky. Carol Swansea was discreetly absent, though she had left behind a warmable supper, with the admonition that the two overgrown undergraduates should eat it. Leaky augmented the meal with a fine bottle of Grands-Echézeaux 1990, noting that the former mayor "deserved nothing less."

After dinner they settled down to an evening with the scotch bottle. The ears of Governor Foote and various editors should have been burning as the two angry and slightly inebriated pals inveighed against them. Then Leaky asked his old friend if he had any regrets.

"Of course I have regrets! I left the comforts of Columbia because I had a *program*—*goals* for the city. All on the scrap heap now, unless Putter Payne chooses to carry them forward, which he's under no obligation to do. And of course my name will be linked forever to that damned dog. Nobody will give me credit for anything else. Remember that congressman a few years ago who jumped in the fountain with a stripper—Fannie Fox, right? Mention his name today and that's the only thing that anybody recalls, even though he was one of the most powerful men in Washington."

"At least Wambli wasn't a stripper."

"Yes, I suppose I should be grateful," Eldon said, taking a long, reflective sip of his drink.

"Actually, I don't think I'll mind being back in Minnesota. This city has become like the Balkans—every little enclave has its own agenda, which it pursues without regard to the rights or opinions or feelings of anyone else. That's true whether you're talking about animals, abortion, dirty artworks, race, the police—you name it. You accept my views, without compromise or accommodation—or else. Factions, factions, factions. Enough to send you to Dewar's, Dewar's, Dewar's." He reached for the bottle and poured a hefty refill.

"Agreed. But let me ask you a question, Eldon. One that's been bothering me. What motivates those animal righters? We went to Alabama, for Christ's sake. Civil rights. Trying to help other human beings. Those animal rights kids don't seem to care about people at all."

"Needless to say, I've been thinking about that. My take is that helping other humans has become too complicated. People one helps aren't always grateful. They turn on you. Or they don't live up to expectations. Animals are always grateful. They don't talk back. No drawbacks or disappointments. So the righters have the feeling of doing good and they get kicks doing it—trashing evil corporations, upsetting the medical establishment, terrorizing rich ladies in fur coats and so on. Great fun, and all psychic benefits and no burdens.

"Or, Leaky, look at Edna. You think it was easy for her to give up patients in favor of teas at the mansion? Or more to the point, you think it's been easy for her, dealing with every conceivable skin disorder at the AIDS clinic where she's been working? Christ, Leaky, she wakes up at night after nightmares about the ravaged bodies she's seen up there. How many of those self-indulgent brats could have dealt with what she's been seeing every day?"

"Maybe you can change things back in Minnesota."

"A little, perhaps. I hope so. But right now it's one more drink and then I have to go. No bodyguards to get me back to Gracie, you know."

"You'll make it."

As Leaky opened his apartment door, Eldon turned and embraced him.

"Milford, you've been a great friend. My best friend."

"That goes for me too, Eldon. But what's this 'Milford' business?"

"Look, I'm so paranoid I'm afraid that someone from *The Surveyor* or *The Post-News* will hear me out in the hall. If I called you Leaky, they'd broadcast that nickname all over New York."

"That's all right. After all these years I'm used to it."

"No 'Going Back' tonight, I think," Eldon said.

"No. Save that for next time, when I come out to Bagley."

"Maybe we could do 'Shoot the Rabbit.' Remember it? Bea Lillie?"

"Sure. . . . Let's go."

They sang exuberantly:

Shoot the rabbit,
Shoot the rabbit,
Old folks, young folks all get the habit . . .

"I forget the rest."

"So do I. But imagine, *imagine* shooting poor little rabbits.

Tut, tut, fucking tut," Eldon said unsteadily. "But thanks again, Milford—Leaky—for lifting my spirits. Good food, good wine, good scotch."

"What do you suppose Randy Randy drinks?"

"Who cares?"

. . .

The governor herself was also taking her licks in other quarters. Except for *The Post-News,* which did everything but compare her to Joan of Arc, press and public opinion alike were critical of her arbitrary and drastic decision to force Eldon out. Her approval rating dropped significantly and reporters and commentators began speculating if she could win reelection when her first term was up.

. . .

Scoop Rice was not among those doing the speculating. Despite his minor-celebrity status with the reporters he hung out with at Elaine's, he decided that journalism, at least the kind practiced by Justin Boyd, was not for him. A Harvard friend was starting a newsmagazine on the Internet. He had managed to arrange substantial financing for the venture, so when he asked Scoop to join the effort, the erstwhile investigative reporter was willing. He was to be a correspondent at large, covering whatever he wished. He wasn't certain exactly what his focus would be, but it would not be the minor personal foibles of those in public office. Perhaps the peccadilloes of members of the Fourth Estate would occupy his attention. And he would do it without resorting to the shoddy tricks he had learned from Justin Boyd.

Scoop requested a final audience with his editor.

"I was about to call you," Boyd told him when he came into the editor's office. "I've got a new story idea for you."

"Justin, I—"

"Fits you perfectly. Add to your reputation as a mayor-eater."

"I don't think—"

"Wait, wait, let me finish. I just heard that our new mayor, Mr. Payne, is known around City Hall as 'Putter.' Did you know that?"

"I'd heard it."

"Apparently he spent a lot of time as the public advocate playing golf. And now that he's not responsible to anybody, he'll probably play even more—come spring, of course. I want you to find out where he plays, get people on the record—caddies, bartenders, club pros—about the time he spends on the links. Then we'll watch him carefully when the good weather starts and reveal the results to the public. Interested?"

"Justin, I came in here to resign."

"*Resign?* My dear fellow, you're my star reporter!"

"Maybe so. But a friend of mine is starting an Internet news-magazine and wants me to come along with him." (And I won't have to trick vulnerable Albanian wives or carry suitcases full of mice to get my stories, he thought but did not say.)

"To do what?"

"Correspondent at large is the title that's been suggested."

"Covering what?"

"I'm not sure, but I think maybe covering the press."

"Oh, for heaven's sake. What's there to write about?"

"Well, for starters, I thought maybe a study of the delight certain editors get in kicking public figures in—how do you say it?—in the achers. Surely as eggs is eggs, that would be an interesting topic."

The terminal interview did not last long.

(Several months later, Boyd himself was kicked in the achers when Ethan Meyner, tiring of *The Surveyor's* seemingly intractable deficits, folded the paper. A return to London would have been impossible; he couldn't go home again. He thought of becoming the new Lord Bryce, writing discerningly about the American colony, but no publisher trusted him to do the task properly. In the end, after spending the proceeds from the generous termination settlement Meyner had awarded him and from the sale of the Bentley, he took a job in desperation as the Morton Zuckerman Professor of Communications at the newly founded journalism school at Thurmond University in Spartanburg, South Carolina. Not what he had always longed for, but neither was being the Harold Stassen Professor of Political Science at Elmwood.)

．　．　．

The Hoaglands settled into their new, quiet life. Edna started up a dermatology practice and expressed herself amazed at the number of skin disorders among the local citizenry. "I think there must be something dreadful in the air out here," she told her husband.

Both were grateful that there were no more inedible dinners from an incompetent chef it would have been politically incorrect to fire; no more press coverage of their daily lives; no more blown-up effigies of Wambli; no more poison darts from *The Post-News.*

Eldon did ask the proprietor of the country store near his farm to order a second daily copy of *The New York Times* (another Gotham expat being the regular buyer of the first one). It was thus he learned that Artemis Payne—who never called, either to chat or for advice, once Eldon had left New York—had appointed Sue Nation Brandberg as his commissioner of cultural affairs and, for that matter, was "dating" her as well. (*The Times* was not quite that explicit, but when the shots in the Sunday *Times* by its society photographer showed the mayor and Sue together week after week, Eldon—and more especially Edna—drew their own conclusions. They did not know that the new mayor was quite capable of delivering an Americanized version of OOOH! SHPIRT! that the widow Brandberg found most pleasing.)

. . .

On New Year's Eve, just before the start of the spring semester at Elmwood, the Hoaglands had a party. Some old friends, going all the way back to high school, were there, as were President Bartlett and his wife.

There was much curiosity about what Eldon would be teaching. He told his guests what he had already agreed with Bartlett: a lecture course, Current Issues in Municipal Government, and an upperclass seminar, Postmodern Political Journalism. The titles were the college catalogue writer's; Eldon himself for shorthand called the lecture course Factions and the journalism seminar Faction, using the *Columbia Journalism Review* term.

One of his listeners at the New Year's party said he did not quite understand the "Factions/Faction" nomenclature.

"I do," Eldon said quietly.

ABOUT THE AUTHOR

James Duffy, a retired lawyer, has written seven mystery novels—all starring amateur detective Reuben Frost—under the pseudonym Haughton Murphy. He resides in New York City.